JERNIGAN'S WAR

KEN GALLENDER

KEN GALLENDER
JERNIGAN'S WAR

www.jerniganswar.com

Special thanks goes to Betty Dunaway Gallender whose devotion and collaboration help make this and subsequent books possible.

Special mention goes to Billie Emrick Gallender who was born in 1930 and raised in the depths of the Great Depression. It was Billie who instilled the fear of being unprepared, having been raised in abject poverty in the Louisiana Delta. She lived in fear that America would return to the desperation that existed in her youth. She also envisioned and feared what we are beginning to witness in America and the world.

ISBN: 1482634457
ISBN 13: 9781482634457

Library of Congress Control Number: 2013903995
CreateSpace Independent Publishing Platform
North Charleston, South Carolina

BIOGRAPHY

Ken Gallender has always been able to spin a yarn. As all good southerners do, Ken likes to "visit" with people putting them at their ease with his warm personality and subtle wit. Ken lives in Gulfport, MS, with his wife, dog, two grand dogs and three grand cats. He is an avid outdoorsman having spent countless days on his Grandfather's farm in the Louisiana Delta, walking turn rows, hunting and fishing. His great love for his family and country has guided his entire life. Ken's motto has always been "Family Comes First, Take Care of Family." His greatest fear is having his country descend into chaos at the hands of witless voters and corrupt politicians willing to take advantage of them.

CHAPTER 1

1ˢᵀ BATTLE

Dix Jernigan woke with his face in the leaves and dirt, a terrible pain radiated from the back of his head. His mouth was dry and gritty from lying in the dirt and his right knee was aching. He could hear voices coming from inside his house and the sounds of chairs being thrown around. The sounds grew louder and then quiet again as though someone was fiddling with the volume control. He soon realized that the change in volume was in time with the throbbing pain in his head. He looked around as he crawled on his hands and knees over to his Jeep and pulled up on the wheel and fender to get to his feet. He ran his fingers over the back of his head, feeling that his hair was sticky and wet from fresh blood. His fingers slipped into the gash and he felt the bone of his skull deep in its recesses.

Dix wiped the blood off his hands onto his pants, eased the back door of the Jeep open, and unzipped the bugout bag that was on the floor board behind the seat. He pulled out an army 1911 .45 and paused as he let his head clear a moment. A piece of pipe with blood and hair encrusted on the threaded end lay up against the wall in front of the Jeep where it had been discarded. Dix pulled back the hammer on the .45 hearing it click into the cocked position. It was at that moment his son drove up and stopped behind the Jeep. Before Dix could warn him, a large dirty man with dread locks walked out of the back door with a shotgun. It was the shotgun that Dix kept in his den. The large man was concentrating on Jake, Dix's son, and didn't see Dix level the .45 across the seat of the Jeep. Dix shot through the open window on the driver's door. The .45 slug tore though the man's left arm just below the shoulder shattering the bone in his upper arm and continuing on into his chest cavity where it turned his heart and lungs to jelly before exiting and lodging in his right arm. He hit the wall hard as the momentum of the bullet was absorbed by his body. The shotgun bounced harmlessly on the floor of the carport.

Dix walked around the front of the Jeep as his son came up with his pistol drawn. Dix whispered, "Get your rifle, there are more of them in the house, run to the south yard and set up a position on the opposite side. Your mother's in the house, I'm going in. They'll probably try heading out through one of the back windows. Kill them; don't shoot through the house unless you can hit one through a window. No matter what happens, kill them."

Dix gave Jake time to get into position then eased up to the door so that he could peer inside the house. The walls wouldn't stop a bullet; but Dix was counting on the fact that most thugs couldn't hit the broad side of a barn and wouldn't realize that the walls in the house wouldn't stop a bullet. He figured they would be hyped up on an adrenaline rush or on drugs. If these were ex military guys, he would have been dead already.

Dix eased through the back door and into the kitchen holding his pistol at eye level. He glanced into the breakfast area and living room and found them empty. He heard his wife gasp in the den as he eased his way around until he could see into the room. She was sitting in his chair with a busted lip and a cut over her right eye. A wiry, unkempt man with a cap on backwards held a gun to her head as he knelt behind the chair. His pistol was a revolver, and Dix immediately noticed that it wasn't cocked. Dix's wife, Mattie, sat very still with her eyes closed. This was a scenario that they had practiced and discussed at great length. Dix took careful aim at the man's head. The man said, "Drop your gun or I'll.........................." He never finished his sentence. The .45 slug took the right quadrant of his head off. Dix touched his wife's shoulder and asked in a whisper, "Are there any more?" She nodded, "One more in the back." As he turned his attention to the rear of the house, he heard Jake's AR-15 open up. The three loud reports were spaced about a second apart. Jake was shooting as he'd had been trained, every shot was accurate and deliberate. Dix knew there would be three holes in the bad guy. One final shot told him that Jake had finished off the last of the intruders.

As he looked through the house for more intruders and damage, Dix thought back to the events of the last three days. He had not seen this one coming. He should have been more alert. The two outside dogs had died three days earlier; Dix guessed they'd been poisoned. The dead men had evidently wanted them out of the way.

Before cleaning up the bodies, he walked back through the house and found that the little inside dogs had been kicked into the media room. Other than being kicked and terrified they were ok. Dix called outside to Jake, "Drag him behind the house, out of sight." The adrenaline was starting to wear off and he was in tremendous pain. He grabbed a bottle of aspirin and chunked four in his mouth, chewing the bitter pills as he dragged the body from the den out onto the rear patio. He walked around the back of the house, cranked the four-wheeler and hooked it to his large garden trailer. He and Jake loaded the three bodies and drove them back into the wooded portion of the property. On the bodies they found two pistols, one was a Ruger twenty two, and the other was a Smith and Wesson .357 magnum. There was some cash on the bodies, which Dix took. They could always use more cash; their toilet paper was running low. The only other things of value besides some jewelry in their pockets were their weapons and leather belts. These idiots were amateurs; either scavenging the area, staying in one of the neighboring abandoned houses, or possibly living out of a car. He and Jake pulled them into some thick bushes and left the bodies to rot. Animals and bugs would make short work of the corpses.

By the time Dix had hosed off and put away the four-wheeler and trailer, Jake had the blood cleaned up in the house and Mattie was sitting with an ice pack on her face. Dix examined Mattie's face carefully, "The last thing I remember was stooping over to pick up a screwdriver I dropped by the dog food bowl. They must have knocked me in the head with the pipe when I was stooped to move the bowl. How long was I out?" Mattie thought about it, "Not long. The first one you shot was going out to finish you off when Jake drove up." "Alright," Dix told them, "From this moment on, everyone will be armed 24 hours a day."

This was the third time their home had been attacked. Prior to this, the dogs had warned them, and they were able to confront the bad guys before they got to the house.

Dix retrieved his glasses from the ground on the other side of the Jeep, went back into the kitchen, mixed himself a strong drink and took a Loritab. Jake and Mattie shaved the back of his head, filled the gash with antibiotic cream, and stitched the wound closed with sterilized cotton thread. Dix got up and loaded pistols in shoulder holsters for Mattie and himself. Jake was already in the habit of wearing his because he and his friends were still making foraging and trading runs around the community.

Jake gathered up the spent hulls and threw them in the spent hulls' bucket for reloading or trading. The family motto was "waste nothing." "We need to get some more yard dogs," Dix remarked to Jake. "It's already covered, Dad. Daniel's Catahoula Cur dog just had pups. I put our name on two already." The Catahoula Cur is a very old breed from the area around Catahoula Lake in Louisiana. They trace their ancestry back to a cross between the Spanish war dogs and the local Indian dogs.

CHAPTER 2

DESPERATION

The electricity had been intermittent for the last few days and finally quit for good. The cable TV was out and the local station was down. The only news they could get was on the shortwave. It was bad everywhere. A week ago they'd heard reports of Chinese troops being deployed to the West Coast. That particular short wave station had stopped coming through soon after that report.

Most of the homes in the area had been abandoned as people left to look for food in the country. The food storage that Dix had insisted on, was keeping them alive. His mother was a product of the Great Depression, getting ready for bad times and survival had been ingrained in the Jernigan family for generations. The garden was starting to produce reliably, mostly greens since it was winter and too early to plant peas, corn and potatoes. The goats and chickens were providing meat and eggs.

They were on guard 24 hours a day. Starving people were everywhere. It was hard turning people away, but it was now dog eat dog. Fewer and fewer were showing up or stopping. Those that showed up now were getting meaner and leaner.

The government had declared martial law when the economy collapsed two months earlier. It was obvious to most people who studied such matters, that the governments of North America and the European Union had planned this. They continued to spend, print and borrow money until the economies collapsed. They then declared martial law and suspended elections. They and their backers in the banking world used this as an opportunity to seize property and assets. The one problem they didn't anticipate was the fact that the U.S. military refused to fire on its citizens. It was one thing to pass out food and provide humanitarian aid. It was yet another to round up citizens and put them in former FEMA camps that were now being used as concentration camps. A door to door attempt to confiscate guns, ammo and precious metals turned into a blood bath. It created a backlash against law enforcement and government employees. This led to a complete breakdown of all civil authority.

Riots started about three days after the food stamps could no longer buy food. There was no food to buy, credit cards quit working and cash was worthless. The cities burned as people began to starve. There was a mass exodus into the countryside, populations of farm animals and game disappeared. Groups of people banded together, roads were blocked and every traveler was robbed, most were killed. Other people were banding together in tribal fashion where they could defend themselves and their scant food supplies. Those without guns and ammo quickly fell victim to roaming hoards.

Although Dix and his family lived in a densely populated area, they were able to fend off the mobs. The dogs were aggressive in barking, alerting the family who soon became skilled at waving people off by shooting around their feet. Two young couples who were friends with Jake had moved in with the family. Dix now had three young men under thirty to help guard the property and work. One had combat military experience which came in handy. Unfortunately, all were out scavenging and trading when this incursion occurred.

CHAPTER 3

PORTER'S JOURNEY

Porter Jones sat on the hillside looking down upon the city. He had two gallons of water in milk jugs slung across his shoulders. They were tied together with an old belt through the jug handles. He had three cans of beans, 4 cans of Vienna sausage, and a sack of Hershey silver bells that were starting to melt. He had an old Remington semi automatic .22 rifle, 250 bullets, a hunting knife, and a dirty Boy Scout back pack filled with everything else he owned. He was thirteen years old and his life was turned upside down. The tears streaming from his eyes cut trails though the dirt on his face as he looked down on the city below. His parents lay dead along with his little brother. Four strangers had come to the house pretending to beg; when his father tried to turn them away they shot him. Porter ran to his room and got the .22 rifle his grandfather had given him. It was an old rifle that originally belonged to his great grandfather. He only knew his great grandfather from some old videos that were taken at Christmas when his dad was a small child.

His dad refused to let him keep the gun loaded. He hid in the closet and loaded the rifle with shaking hands. He could hear gun shots and his mother screaming. His little brother cried out but he was powerless to help so he kept loading. The gun held 11 bullets in a tubular magazine in the stock. He spilled bullets on the floor of the closet as he accidentally overloaded the magazine and had to stop and take a couple of bullets out. When the short Hispanic man kicked open the door the last thing he expected was a boy with a small rifle to shoot him in the chest. The man stumbled backward and discharged the pistol he was holding. The bullet missed Porter and went into the wall behind him just over his head. The Hispanic man collapsed on the floor with a small .22 bullet resting in his heart and two more in his lungs. Porter went into adrenaline overload and ran into the front of the house where the other men were busy ransacking the house. He emptied his rifle on the remaining three men. The three men ran from the house trailing blood and cursing. One collapsed in the front yard, another in the road.

Porter fished around in his pocket and reloaded his rifle. He stood shaking when he found his parents and little brother dead in the living room. His little brother lay across his mother's body. Dropping to the floor, he sat for hours with his gun across his lap. Overcome with grief he sat in disbelief. The sun went down and he sat in the dark. Sometime in the night he fell asleep and didn't wake up until morning. When he woke, he dragged his family out into the back yard where he dug a large shallow grave. He covered them with a blanket before filling the grave with the sandy soil and capping it with the biggest rocks he could find so that animals would have trouble getting to them. He could hear gunfire and see smoke above the houses across the street. Their home backed up to the mountains to the east of Los Angeles. He realized that his only escape was up into the mountains behind his home.

Porter gathered up the remaining food and the last two gallons of water in the house. The water and electricity had been out for weeks. He checked the bodies of the dead men; the one in his bedroom had a .38 pistol that was empty. He put it in his back pack with his other belongings. There was some jewelry in his pockets and a pocket knife. Porter took those too. Sometime during the night someone had gone through the pockets of the dead man in the front yard and the one in the road.

Porter took the blanket off his bunk bed and slit a hole in the middle so he could pull it over his head. He needed the blanket because his heaviest jacket would not keep him warm in the mountains. He put the food in a big canvas bag that his mother used for shopping; she tried to do her part in saving the environment. In his back pack he put his parents' rings and on his arm he had his father's watch. He took the latest family picture and put it in a plastic bag in a zipper pouch on the inside of the pack. His parents weren't big on camping, fishing or hunting. His mother tried her best to make them vegetarians, so he had to retrieve the Vienna sausage hidden in his dad's golf bag. He put on his newest tennis shoes and packed a couple of pants, shirts, and all the socks and underwear he could stuff in. The final space he used for his toothbrush and tooth paste, his sleeping bag he tied to the top.

The only reason he had been allowed to keep the little .22 was because his grandfather practically coerced his mother into letting him have it. His grandfather had made a lot of money in a couple of business deals before he retired. He made Porter's parents an offer they couldn't refuse. He told them that he would pay off their home mortgage and in exchange they would have to let Porter have the .22, be a member of the NRA, be a member of the boy scouts, and join a shooting club. After all it was just an antique .22 and being small his mother thought it looked almost harmless.

His grandparents had divorced while his dad was just a boy. Porter's grandmother had forbid his dad hunting with his grandfather and pushed him into more urban interests. As a result, his dad knew a great deal about golf and tennis and next to nothing about hunting, fishing and camping. His Grandmother had been dead for several years and couldn't object now to him learning to camp and shoot.

Porter had spent two weeks at his Grandfather's home in the country when his folks went on a second honeymoon the previous summer. His Grandfather paid for the honeymoon under the condition that Porter and his little brother come to visit for those two weeks. Other than speaking with his grandfather on the telephone every month or so, he had never had any contact with him. He spent those two weeks, fishing and camping. As far as Porter was concerned that was the best two weeks of his life. The home was located in the heart of Louisiana out in the middle of nowhere. Porter figured that was the place he needed to go. He couldn't stay in Los Angeles as there was no water, no food and millions of starving people. Porter looked in his Geography book and studied the route he would have to take to get to Louisiana. He found a road atlas in the glove box of his Dad's truck. He tore out the maps of California, Arizona, New Mexico, Texas and Louisiana, folded them up and put them in his pack. For now all he had to concentrate on was going east.

CHAPTER 4

DECISION TIME

Porter looked out the front door and saw a gang walking down the sidewalk. He hung back from the window and decided to head up into the hills behind the house. He went out the back door and up the mountain. It was not so steep as to prevent him from making his way up through the brush. From this vantage point he could look across the neighborhood and city.

So there he sat with his water and his rifle resting across his lap thinking about his situation. He could see buildings on fire and hear sporadic gunfire as the world he had known came unwound. He was dusty from taking a tumble and rolling down the hill earlier. Luckily he and his rifle were ok. He wiped the tears and dirt off his face onto his shirt sleeve. He had no idea how he was going to make it across the desert and into Texas and then Louisiana. Porter thought to himself, "I've got to eat, drink, sleep and evade thieves and killers. I can do this!"

He climbed the mountain until he came to a road. He stopped when he heard voices coming and retreated to the safety of the scrub brush on the side. He felt a sense of relief when a police cruiser pulled up beside a family that had walked into view. This feeling of relief was short lived when the policemen stopped, killed the family and started rooting through their pockets and their belongings. After relieving the family of their meager belongings, they got back into the cruiser and proceeded down the mountain and out of sight. Porter was so shaken that he had forgotten that he was armed and could have done something. Porter walked up to the dead family as they lay in the road. Flies were already buzzing the bloody bullet holes. He could hear another car coming and rather than wait he moved on across the road and down into the valley on the other side of the road. The sight of the vacant, open eyes would haunt him for the rest of his life. But what could he have done? He didn't know.

It took Porter the rest of the afternoon to make his way to the floor of the valley. He was terribly thirsty but resisted the urge to drink from his jugs, having no way of knowing when he would find water again. Porter recalled the tumble he had taken earlier in the day. He quickly realized that there was no one to take him to the doctor or the emergency room, a small injury could kill a person. The valley floor was narrow at this point and there were no homes here. Lucking up on a large rattle snake, he quickly dispatched with it with a rock. With his knife he skinned the snake and speared it on a stick. He built a fire using his Boy Scout magnesium fire starter. He found water in a rock depression so he drank from one of his jugs of clean water. The snake made a good meal. He took the skin and laid it out on a stick so that the smoke from the small fire could dry and cure it. He had no idea what to do with it, but it was pretty and if worse came to worse he could eat it. Porter could hear gunfire on the mountain top in front of him; so he decided to spend the night where he was, nice and secluded. He no longer feared the night. When he first joined the Boy Scouts he was afraid of camping at night. Even with the rest of the guys in the troop around him, Porter was terrified of the night. Now there was nothing in the dark more terrifying than what had happened to him in the last 24 hours. He drank from the half empty water jug and fell asleep in front of the fire.

CHAPTER 5

RESCUE

D ix's daughter, Maggie, and her husband, Bill, lived in New Orleans; but, Dix had lost contact with them over a month earlier. Dix's son in law was a physician and worked in the emergency room of one of the hospitals. They were staying put because the authorities were providing food and lodging at the hospital and physicians were in short supply. Rumors out of the city and reports over the shortwave indicated that New Orleans was basically a road warrior scenario.

Dix decided to make a trip into the city to see if he could find and retrieve Maggie and Bill. He called the family together for a meeting. Jake's friends, Aaron and Tracy Jones were the first to come in. They were a young couple that Jake met since moving to the Gulf Coast. Tracy was pregnant; but, Dix hoped he would not be called upon to deliver the baby. The other couple arrived with a fresh baked loaf of bread. They were not married but had been living together for more than a year. Craig Wilson was formally a corporal in the marines and had two tours of duty in Iraq under his belt. Tonya Gant was just a college girl who wasn't in college any longer. Craig had the skills to kill and Jake had been learning hand to hand combat from him. They all set around while the hot bread was sliced up and slathered with canned butter. The canned butter came from New Zealand where it was shipped to areas without refrigeration. Dix had bought several cases along with other provisions that he had been accumulating. Everyone was in agreement about trying to rescue Maggie and Bill. Jake and Aaron volunteered to go but Dix nixed the idea over everyone's objections. Dix argued that this was a one man trip. Their survival depended on numbers and they were at an absolute minimum as it was. Dix would go alone.

Since traveling by road or air was out of the question, Dix needed to find another way to get in and out of the city. He knew where a friend kept his catamaran sail boat stored. His friend had bugged out two months ago in his motor home to his retreat in Idaho. There was no way to know if he made it. It would have been a miracle if he even made it across the Mississippi River. Using the catamaran, Dix figured that he could head out through Back Bay, into the gulf and up the Mississippi River to the city. He estimated it would take two days to get to the city, one or two days there, and two days back.

Their supply of fuel was getting very low. Dix had enough diesel fuel to bugout in the motor home; but, he would have to sacrifice some for the catamaran's diesel engine. The boat house was about three miles from his house. Dix waited until after two in the morning before he and Jake headed to the boat house. They pulled out of the drive with the headlights off and drove slow and quiet. As usual they were armed to the teeth. When they arrived at the boat house they found that it had been looted like every other abandoned structure in the country. Fortunately the catamaran was still there. Dix went on board and found that although the cabin had been ransacked, nothing had been destroyed. The batteries were missing from the engine compartment; but, the engine was intact. The fuel tanks were empty; but, Dix expected that.

They spent the next day accumulating what they needed to get the boat running. In addition to the batteries and fuel, Dix loaded a case of MRE's, bottled water and an AR 15 with six- 30 round magazines in addition to the one in the rifle. He added a Browning high power 9 mm with two thirteen round magazines, a boat anchor, batteries from his fishing boat and four five gallon cans of diesel. He also took a bugout bag with medicine, and enough supplies for him to live for a week should he have to abandon the boat and try to walk home.

After a prolonged argument with Mattie, about going alone, they loaded up the gear and headed out. It was around 2:00 am again and they quietly made their way back to the catamaran and loaded the gear onto the boat. Jake waited until Dix got it cranked and the doors open on the boat house. After Dix motored into the bay they conducted a radio check. Dix waited in the middle of the bay until Jake radioed back that he was safe at home.

Dix kicked the diesel engine into little more than a fast idle and headed for the open bay and then out into the Gulf of Mexico. In the dark of the early morning there was no noise or movement. He turned on the GPS when he reached the open gulf. The sun was coming up and he could see for miles; but the wind was cold blowing off the water. With the help of one of the winches, he raised the mast and unfurled the sail, killed the motor and headed almost due south.

Dix had spent two weekends on the boat with his friend last summer so he knew the basic lay out and operation of the vessel. The boat had a shallow draft so sticking to the channel was not an issue. He navigated by the GPS until it was too dark to see ahead, finally setting anchor in about eighty feet of water. The wind had pushed the seas to about five feet which made for a miserable night. The small cabin was cozy and the bunk was comfortable but the constant motion kept him from sleeping.

The next morning Dix cranked the engine and let it run until the batteries were fully charged. He opened an MRE and ate the crackers and jelly along with a bottle of water. After another six hours of sailing, he was at the mouth of the river.

His sailing skills were not up to the task of sailing up the river against the current. He tried it for a while but the turns in the river plus the debris floating down the river made it impossible. He cranked the little Yanmar diesel and motored up the river trying to stay in the middle of the stream when possible. It had been some months since the corps of engineers had cleared the channel. There were a number of sunken vessels aground and in various states of decay. There were also dead bodies flowing downstream. At least one body floated by about every thirty minutes. He kept a wary eye out as he made his way towards the city.

At mid afternoon a large aluminum boat carrying several men approached from the rear. Dix popped off a couple of rounds over their heads with his rifle. Instead of backing off, they shot back. Dix kicked the engine out of gear and opened up with his rifle. They were still under power. In the time it took for them to stop their boat in order to aim, he had emptied a magazine. They were shooting back from about two hundred yards, and, for the most part, missing him and the boat. An occasional round hit the boat; but, they were having trouble maintaining accurate fire. Dix, on the other hand, put every round into the passenger compartment of their boat. Their boat pulled into a position that was parallel to his in the water about 150 yards downstream. Dix concentrated his fire on the engine. His EOtech holographic site was precise and well sighted. The cowling on their outboard was coming apart. He was certain that several of the full metal jacket bullets had torn through it and the aluminum engine block. The engine was smoking and soon stalled. He turned his attention back to the passenger compartment. The shooting had stopped by the time he emptied the second magazine. Both boats were drifting downstream in the current. Their boat seemed empty; there was no sign of life, only the burning engine. Smoke was starting to billow from the back of the boat in front of the engine. Dix replaced the empty magazine and turned his attention back to the catamaran kicking it into gear. In less than two minutes he had disabled their boat and probably killed one or more of them. He kept an eye on them as he turned the next bend in the river. The catamaran was running fine, and there were only a couple of bullet holes in the cabin.

Dix moved back to the helm inside the cabin as he neared the city. There was a string of partially submerged barges sitting near the bank of the river; he pulled the cat up among them so that it was hidden from the river as well as the shore. Someone would have to be on top of the barges looking down in order to see where it was anchored. After lowering the mast to further hide it from view, he finished his MRE while waiting for dark.

Dix changed into a life vest and a pair of swimming trunks. He placed his bugout bag containing his clothes and gear into a large garbage bag and then put that bag inside another garbage bag. He then sealed the bag with duct tape to keep out the water. He swam around to the end of the barge and stayed next to it until he reached the shore. The barge shielded him from the main current of the river. The water was very cold and Dix was blue and shaking by the time he reached shore. He wasted no time drying off and getting dressed. He shook the water off the garbage bag, folded it and put it in his bag. His boots felt good on his cold feet. He built a small fire from dry drift wood to warm himself. After he was warm, he killed the fire and attached a green LED lamp on the bill of his cap. He used it just until he reached a level above the high water line on the levee where it was somewhat clear of debris.

Dix carefully made his way to the top of the levee where he could look out across the city. There were many small fires burning in the city. There were no lights; but there was occasional gunfire and commotion. There was no vehicular traffic that he could hear.

He sat for a long time to get his bearings and consult his GPS. The satellites were still working. He determined that he was on the levee behind Audubon Park, an area that Maggie had called The Fly. In happier times, college students and families used to spend free time on this part of the levee. There had been a baseball field and a dog park. All of that had been razed. His daughter lived in an upstairs apartment on Broadway only about three miles from there. He marked this spot in his GPS and made note of his location on a notepad in his shirt pocket. He then turned off the GPS to conserve the battery. He carried a map of the city he had printed off some months earlier before the internet went dead.

Dix casually and methodically made his way down the levee and through the park, heading towards St. Charles Avenue. He wanted it to appear to anyone watching that he was just a drifter out scavenging for food. His AR15 was slung so that it hung out of view behind him. He could deploy it with one motion. His shoulder holster held his Browning 9mm. He carried two knives, a folding pocket knife and a large hunting knife. A multi tool was also in his pack.

Anytime he saw someone, he froze next to the nearest tree or vehicle, knowing that it is almost impossible for humans to see something motionless at night. Most of the night vision equipment in public circulation was no longer working because they all require batteries. Police and military would still have functioning equipment, but most others would be dead.

The smell of dead bodies hung in the air. There was a bonfire in the middle of the road ahead. He eased up to where he could observe without being seen, careful not to silhouette himself against the fire. He could see a bunch of people around it; but, they seemed to be minding their own business for now. Dix elected to block around it rather than go near the fire. When he was a little closer he realized that there was a body on the fire or rather over it. They were either cooking or cremating someone. He didn't want to find out which.

Dix arrived at his daughter's building from the rear. It was a narrow quiet street. He estimated the time to be around 10:00 pm. When he reached the back entrance, two small dogs were barking from under the house. He briefly switched on the light and was both glad and sad. Maggie's two dogs, Bernie and Hereaux, were living under the old house. They were unkempt and starving. He knew his daughter was not home; these fellows would not be out there if she was. He broke out an MRE and a bottle of water and fed them. He took off their collars with the noisy dog tags; he didn't want to attract any attention as he made his way carefully around to the front door. He didn't need the spare key to the door, it had been broken open. He once again flipped on the green LED light and unholstered his pistol.

Dix slowly made his way up the stairs with the little schnauzers hot on his trail. It was quickly apparent that the place had been ransacked. No one was home, and there was no food. He barricaded the door at the top of the stair so that he could take his time going through the apartment. Using a pair of scissors and some flea spray he found, he tended to the dogs, trimming off all their matted hair and killing the fleas. The gas was still on so Dix lit the burners on the stove for heat and pulled out a candle lantern from his bag, turning off his head lamp to conserve its batteries. The water was out so he drained water from the hot water heater and filled his bottles. He put out a dish for the schnauzers. They found their crates and sacked out. He found their heart worm medicine and flea preventative, gave it to them and left them alone. It was after midnight and he was very tired. He thought about leaving them and continuing on but he hadn't slept in a couple of days. Here he was secure, fed and warm. Now was not the time to move on, he needed rest. He blew out the candle and fell asleep on the couch. Other than the dogs hearing something and barking in the middle of the night, all was quiet.

CHAPTER 6

ESCAPE

It was mid-morning when he finally woke. His neck was sore from the stitched up wound near the base of his skull. He broke out another MRE and split it with the dogs. There was nothing else in the apartment that he could use at the moment. He took some more water from the hot water heater and bathed and shaved. He washed the pups in the water in the tub before he pulled the plug. He found the dog's leashes and decided to do something unexpected. He put the bugout bag across his shoulder and made sure his weapons were hidden under his clothes. He put the dogs on their leashes and proceeded to take them for a walk. He wanted to brazenly walk the streets as though he owned them. He held the dogs with his left hand and had his right hand through the slit in his coat next to the pocket. The safety was off and he was holding the pistol grip of his rifle. In one motion he could deploy it and fire. He checked his map and began the three mile walk to the hospital.

The first half mile was uneventful. He came to a barricaded street with several young unkempt men hanging around. He was certain they had been employed as drug running gang members before the collapse. One of them walked out with a semi-automatic pistol held sideways, "Dude, I don't know what you are doing here but this is your ...."

Dix didn't give him time to finish. In one motion he dropped the leashes he was holding in his left hand, swung the rifle up and starting shooting as he brought it up to eye level. The first shot hit the gang banger just above his knee, the second entered just below his navel and the third hit him in the throat. With both eyes open Dix fired on the next nearest person as soon as the holographic circle covered his body. He didn't wait to see if his mark was true but instead concentrated on the third thug who almost had his gun up. He fired three shots before the gang banger dropped to the ground. He turned back to the second one but didn't have to fire again.

Dix called back the pups and proceeded out of the area. All the shooting was sure to arouse their friends and anyone else in the area. He took time to pick up their guns and ammo which he stuffed into his bag of gear. He then ducked between some houses and replaced the partially emptied magazine in his rifle with a fresh one.

Dix realized that he had been very lucky so far. It was probably a reckless move to brazenly walk down the sidewalk with dogs on leashes. But the last thing the gang bangers expected was a silly old man out walking his dogs.

He stopped for a moment in another garden and checked the GPS. He was one mile away from the hospital. If the hospital was still under control of the police and authorities the next problem would be getting past their security perimeter. There was no way on earth they would let him come in armed. He proceeded down the road until he was within sight of another barricade. This one was in front of the hospital. He decided to get within yelling range of the men manning it. He circled around until he was within earshot of the sentries and yelled, "You at the barricade, I need your help."

A young man yelled back, "You're out of luck; we don't leave our cover for any reason. If you want to approach you better be near naked and unarmed or we shoot first."

Dix assured him, "I have no intention of approaching. I'm looking for Maggie Schoffield and her husband Dr. William Schoffield. I'm Maggie's father. The last word I got was they were sheltered and working here."

The guard answered, "They're here, but as I said, no one gets in or out of here armed."

"Get my daughter. I'll wait here."

While he waited, he broke out some water for him and the dogs and opened his 4th MRE. He was keenly aware of his surroundings but there was no movement or sound from any direction. He split his MRE's with the pups; the food was really pepping them up. He heard Maggie yell out, "How do I know it's you, Daddy?"

"I've got Hereaux and Bernie, they'll vouch for me."

Maggie and Bill came running out with Bill carrying his shotgun. They escorted Dix back to the hospital. With tears running down her face Maggie wanted to know, "What about Mama and Jake?"

Dix reassured her, "When I left them they were just fine, we've had to start killing people to stay alive. Are you ready to evacuate?"

"Oh yes! We ran out of hospital food yesterday, there are some MRE's left and the guards still have ammo but half of them slipped out last night."

Dix nodded, "Can you gather up some medical supplies, Bill?"

"I've already got a pack put together, and I cleaned out the vending machines."

"How's your ammo holding out?"

Bill frowned, "We're down to just what's in our guns." Dix opened his pack and pulled out the pistols and ammo he took from the gang bangers. All three were Glock nine millimeters with extra magazines. He handed one each to Maggie and Bill, "Stick these behind your belts." "How long has the electricity been off? I'm surprised that the city isn't flooded with the pumps off."

Maggie filled him in, "The Corp of Engineers had several of the pumps under guard and the emergency generators running. But, they abandoned the city three days ago."

"What about transportation, Maggie? Where are your vehicles?"

"My Forrester and Bill's truck are in the parking garage. They've both been stripped."

"Then are there any police or military vehicles?"

"There are a couple of Humvee's but I don't think they'll let us use them."

"We'll see about that," Dix said, "Who's in charge now?"

"There is a scared Army Sergeant, who has lost touch with his command, and lost most of his men."

"Take me to him," Dix said as he walked deeper into the hospital.

They walked down a long hall to the lobby where the Sergeant had a command post set up. Sand bags lined the glass walls and created a funnel where any foot traffic was channeled just one way in and out. From the look of the dark circles under his eyes he hadn't had any sleep and he had the weight of the world on his shoulders. Dix looked at him, "Son, it looks like you've caught hell! Where do you stand?"

The young Sergeant grimaced, "We've discharged or buried all the patients, I've been out of touch with my commanders for two weeks, my men are deserting, and we will be overrun at any time, because they think we have food."

"What do your men want to do?"

"They want to get home to their families while they still have a little food and ammo."

Dix told him what he had learned from the short wave: that they were looking at a total societal collapse. What was happening in New Orleans was the same thing that had been happening all over the world.

"Where's your home, son?"

Pulling out a picture, the sergeant showed it to Dix, "My wife and kids are at my Dad's ranch in West Texas."

"Then to get home you're going to have to cross the river and travel cross country. If you can get us back to the Fly, I have a boat with a diesel engine. I can take you upriver as far as Natchez, but I am going to need some more fuel."

"Will a hundred gallons do it?"

"Sure, but we're going to need a Humvee to get back to the boat."

"I have two men who'll want to go with me, and two of my guys still have family in the city and want to make a run with them down into Cajun country."

Dix told the sergeant, "Round everyone up and let's hit the road. Can I load up a couple of empty magazines of .223/5.56?"

"Help yourself, there are some ammo cans behind the desk." Dix reloaded his magazines while the others were getting saddled up.

The plan was set, both humvees were loaded with guns, MRE's, ammo, and fuel cans. The two humvees headed out together and when they reached the levee, they waved off the one heading south and continued up and over the levee and down to the barges on the other side. Dix stripped off his gear and fished out his life vest and ran upstream. He yelled back, "Start unloading the fuel. Two men need to get on top of the levee and stand guard."

The catamaran was right where he left it, and undisturbed. He cranked the engine, hauled in the anchor and backed it out into the current. He bumped it into forward gear and nosed it up on the bank where they were waiting with the fuel. They emptied five of the cans of diesel into the fuel tanks. They then siphoned the remaining fuel in the hummer into the empty cans and relieved the Humvee of its battery. The two men standing guard on the levee started shooting just as they loaded the last cans of ammo and fuel. They ran down the levee and jumped on the boat just as Dix backed it out into the current, kicked it wide open, and maneuvered over to the far side of the river. They watched from the boat as attackers ran down to the hummer. The soldiers laid down suppressing fire forcing the men to take refuge behind the Humvee. They were soon out of range of the attackers so they ceased firing and got busy reloading their empty rifle magazines from the ammo cans on board.

The river at New Orleans is almost a mile wide. The catamaran seemed small in the huge river but its engine ran flawlessly as it made its way up the river. Dix cut the throttle back to conserve fuel. The pups made themselves at home. Hereaux found an empty compartment to sack out in, while Bernie was all over the deck looking at everything. As they approached the first of several bridges they were careful to watch for snipers. There were people on the bridges, but they passed under without incident. Once a boat started out from shore, but they backed off when one of the soldiers put a bullet through the bow. They ran the boat until dark and tied up to some willows in a cut off of the river. The sarge gave his orders, "We'll sleep in shifts; I want two people awake at all times, no lights, no noise." They cracked open a case of MRE's and each had a meal. Dix once again split his with the pups. His pot belly was getting smaller. He knew that it would come in handy one day.

The next morning Dix fired up the engine and headed back upstream. The GPS showed their slow progress. It took them three days to reach Natchez, MS. Dix dropped the soldiers off on the Vidalia, Louisiana, side of the river. He told them to travel to Wildsville, LA, to the home of his uncle, Jack Watts. "You will have to tell him that I sent you, he has a house and barn, you may luck up and even get a meal, good luck guys, I'll see you when this is over." Dix handed each of the men a box of .22 bullets and a handful of loose pre 1964 silver dimes. "This is the only currency people will consider. The dimes are worth about $50.00 each in the recent currency so don't let someone get them for near nothing."

Dix wasted no time in turning the catamaran downstream. He kept the throttle a little above idle and let the current carry them. It should only take them half the time it took fighting the current upstream. Two more nights and one short gunfight later, they were back in the gulf and under sail. He still had over half the fuel, ten cans of 5.56/.223 ammo and two cans of 9mm ammo. They spent one last night anchored about two miles from Ship Island. Bill pulled Dix's stitches from his head wound and declared him healed. The next morning they pulled up the anchor and sailed over to the entrance of the bay. They lowered the mast, cranked the little diesel and motored through the bay into the canal leading to Gulfport Lake. He radioed the house and Jake answered, "We thought we had lost you! We've had to fight off attackers two days in a row." "Was anyone hurt?"

Jake laughed, "Just the bad guys."

"We'll do it the same way I left, bring your truck. I've got Maggie, Bill and the pups."

When Jake arrived around 2 am, Dix cranked the little diesel and idled over to the ramp where they unloaded everything. "We'll put it back in the boat house where we found it." He ran the catamaran over to the house and backed it in. The fuel tank was almost empty so he didn't bother to try and drain it. Dix took out the batteries and his lowrance and closed the doors. They were home in no time, none the worse for wear.

CHAPTER 7

THE ENEMY APPROACHES

The next morning Porter awoke to the sounds of birds. He finished the gallon of water he had drunk from the night before. Porter refilled the empty gallon jug from the rock depression full of water. Helicopters could be heard overhead and large booms echoed up the valley. He started the ascent of the next mountain. The mountain he climbed up was higher than the one behind his home. When he reached the top and looked back over the valley he no longer saw a bustling thriving city. He saw columns of smoke. A heavy haze hung over the valley like a fog. Helicopters were coming in over the mountain and disappearing in the direction of the port. He could hear heavy jet engines somewhere out of sight but high in the sky. Explosions could be seen in the distance. Further down the ridge of the mountain a rocket came out of the trees and disappeared into the sky. A trail of smoke was all that remained as is screamed out of view. A faint boom echoed across the mountain from far away in the sky. Moments later the entire ridge of the mountain below him exploded as high explosive shells riddled the mountain top. Porter ran. The mountain was afire and he took refuge in a concrete and metal building at the base of a radio tower. Porter was scared now, how was he going to survive this mess he found himself in?

It only took a couple of hours for the fire to consume the entire area and burn itself out. Porter carefully left the building where he had waited out the burning. He walked down the road, otherwise the hot coals from the burned woods and brush would have melted his tennis shoes. He came to an area of absolute carnage. There were dozens of Chinese troops dead and blown apart in what once had been a roadside park. He silently walked among them. The sight of the torn and mutilated bodies was not something he would soon forget. He found backpacks, food, guns, ammo and miscellaneous equipment, some only partially damaged. He thought quickly and starting dragging what he found down a hill into a ravine. He found a spot where he was hidden and sheltered behind some large rocks. He made four trips with equipment down into his hideout. He was heading up for his fifth trip when he heard movement ahead. He stopped at the edge of the clearing. A group of men had arrived and were busy looting what remained. He waited long enough to make sure they were not aware of his looting and the path he took down into the ravine.

When he got back to his hideout, he placed his .22 rifle where he could get his hands on it in an instant. He emptied the packs and spread out the contents. He took the best looking of the AK47's and gathered up ten loaded 30 round magazines. He had taken a pistol and shoulder holster off one of the men who appeared to be an officer. He adjusted the holster to fit his small frame. Porter thought it was a nine millimeter and it had three 7 round magazines, one in the pistol the other two in pouches on the right side of the rig. He practiced with the unloaded gun until he mastered its operation. He then loaded it and placed it into the holster where he could get his hands on it. He put a large knife that was sheathed on his belt. He put a small stone knife sharpener in his pocket along with his pocket knife. He chose the cleanest of the backpacks and adjusted it to fit. It was larger than the Boy Scout pack that he had been using.

Porter took a large musty smelling coat suitable for cold weather and spread it out in the sun on one of the rocks. He hoped the exposure to the sun would make it smell better. He had a good supply of food, most of it in the form of sweet cookie tasting cakes in vacuumed sealed pouches.

There was no way he could carry everything. He rinsed out two of the canteens and filled them with the last clean jug of water he had. He sat the other gallon jug in the sun to let the ultraviolet light kill any pathogens suspended in it. This was a trick he learned while earning a Boy Scout badge. He decided to load the pack with his possessions from home. He was able to strap three of the AK47 magazine pouches to a vest he found. Each magazine pouch held two magazines. The other four he stowed in a pocket on the back of the pack. He couldn't bear to part with the .22 rifle. Fortunately it could be taken down into two pieces. He placed these down either side of the pack so that all he had to do was open the top and pull them out. He put his .22 bullets in a pocket on the inside of the pack. In the middle he folded his extra clothes, toiletries, and his family picture. Finally he topped it off with his beans and sausage.

He discarded all the other gear including the snake skin. He could barely walk with the pack, rifle, canteens and ammo. It was just too heavy so he unpacked it once again and decided to eat all the can goods. The sweet cookies were much lighter and weren't packed in heavy steel cans. The rest of that day and the next he spent resting and eating the extra food that he had found. He figured that it was better to consume the extra food than leave it. He had once read a story about an Indian who had escaped on horseback. While heading back to his home the horse became lame. The Indian killed the horse and stayed with it; cooked and consumed it over the following weeks. He continued on only after the entire horse had been eaten.

Porter practiced walking with the full load including his blanket tied in a bundle over the top of his pack. He continued walking around with the pack and finally had the load diminished and the pack adjusted to fit. His mother's jewelry and that from the man he killed he kept in his left front pants pocket.

The morning of the third day he put on the vest and pack. He had never taken off the pistol or the shoulder holster. He put the rifle sling over his shoulder and neck and had the rifle hanging in front of him. It was loaded and after having played with it for several days, he knew how to use it. A couple of the men back at the NRA shooting range had them and had let him shoot them a couple of times. This rifle was different, it had a third setting on the safety that he assumed would let it fire on full auto. He had resisted the urge to shoot it because he didn't want anyone to know he was hiding in the ravine. His mother's canvas shopping bag was stuffed between the pack and his back for added padding. He had drank all of the water from the milk jugs and still had his two full canteens. He discarded the milk jugs because he simply had no where to put them. He left all the other gear included the empty .38 pistol scattered around the campsite. He was afraid that the time would come when he would have to discard his .22 rifle.

After a long climb up out of the ravine he was having second thoughts about the load he had chosen to carry. The scene at the top of the ridge was a very different scene than he remembered. The bodies were bloated and covered with flies. Birds and wild dogs were picking at the bodies, all the extra gear was now gone. Porter quickly put the scene behind him as he headed down the highway. This road led to another that would take him east over and out of the mountains. He trudged down the road under the burden of his pack. The weather was mild and only once did he see anyone. He left the road each time he heard traffic coming and stayed out of sight.

It was late in the afternoon when a group of men came out of a side road several hundred yards down the road. Porter had stopped in the shade to rest. No one would notice a lone figure sitting on the side of the road in the shade of a small tree. He waited until they had disappeared down the road before he proceeded. When he reached the side road he turned and walked up it. The road was really a driveway to a home. He slowly made his way up the driveway until he came within view of a house on the hill. The home appeared vacant, the windows were busted out and the door was open. A skeleton was scattered in the front yard. He wondered if the skeleton belonged to a bad guy or an innocent victim. He didn't go into the home, but concentrated on the large garage in the rear.

The garage was an older building, possible a remnant of an old farm or ranch building. The side door was open; he paused before going in to see if he could hear anything. There was no sound so he stepped inside. Light filtered through the windows on the sides. The dust danced through the rays of the strong afternoon sun. The building appeared to be ransacked as the boxes that once stored tools and hardware were dumped in the floor and were laying empty on top. He noticed one spot that was clear next to the wall. And when he looked closer he saw the trail left on the dusty floor from a wheel that made an arc from the wall out into the room. He also saw a set of footprints that was left in the dust leading away from the hidden door. Chills ran up his neck when he realized that he had stumbled upon someone's hideaway. He quickly started backing towards the entrance when a booming voice from it proclaimed, "Congratulations boy, you are the first person to spot my hideaway." Porter almost wilted; but, bucked up and turned around. The big man was laughing, "I'm not going to kill you, what's your name kid?"

"Porter Jones, Sir, everyone just calls me Porter."

"My name's John Johnson, son; but, all my friends call me Big John, are you hungry?"

"No sir, I've been eating Chinese rations; so I'm not hungry yet."

Big John looked at him shrewdly, "What are you looking for?"

Porter shrugged, "Nothing in particular, I was hoping I could find a bicycle or something, I'm heading to Louisiana to my Grandfather's house and at the rate I'm going I'll never make it."

"I might can fix you up with something you can use, meanwhile why don't you help me skin a goat I've got strung up out back, you stand guard and I'll skin the goat." They walked around back to where Big John had a large old Billy goat hanging by his rear legs. Big John pointed to a gap in the bushes where Porter could sit unobserved. "Make yourself comfortable in there, is that AK47 loaded with one in the barrel?" Porter nodded yes as he hid in the bushes. Big John leaned his big shotgun up against the tree and said, "It's a good idea to shoot first, if anyone walks up male or female and they're pointing a weapon at me or you, just aim and shoot and don't stop until they are down." He helped Porter adjust the sling so that it was easy to get to his shoulder to shoot. Big John made short work of the old goat and had him skinned and quartered in no time flat. He rolled up the skin and threw the quarters into a large garden cart. They took the entrails and bones and buried them under the mulch pile. They cut the horns off the skull before chunking it into the woods. The horns would make knife or tool handles.

The hidden door in the garage led down to a 1950's era bomb shelter. Big John's dad had built the shelter, Big John had inherited the property after his parents died and moved back to the home where he had grown up. It was quite spacious and even had an escape tunnel that let out into a ravine down the hill where they chunked the goat head. That night they cut the goat into small strips and dropped them into a barrel of salty liquid laced with flavorings. They cooked some in a skillet and along with some onions it made a hearty supper. Porter slept on a fold out army cot that night and enjoyed his first shower in weeks. He let the water accumulate in the tub where he washed out his clothes. Not wanting to wear out his welcome, he thanked Big John for the food and bath and offered him a handful of .22 bullets as payment. Big John refused, "You don't owe me anything for the grub and bath. You're the first company I've had since all this went down. I don't have any family and you are welcome to stay a while. I've got plenty of food for now and I can't stand guard 24 hours a day. Besides, you're going to need transportation and it's going to take a few days to put it together.

The next morning, Porter asked Big John, "Why don't you come with me, I'm sure my grandfather wouldn't mind?"

"Porter, that's mighty kind of you to offer, but we've got one little problem. The only thing keeping me alive is a pace maker that has a battery that's almost used up. It was supposed to have been replaced 6 months ago, but under this new health care system they set up I was put on a waiting list. The bottom fell out before my name was called. I figure sometime in the next three to twelve months it will go dead and me along with it. This is as good a place as any to ride it out. I grew up here, my folks are buried just up the road and I'm pushing 75. No, this is where I'm making my stand." Porter didn't know what to say. He just looked at the ground "I'm sorry Big John." After a few awkward moments Big John clapped him on the back, "Let's look into that transportation I was talking about."

Out back in the brush Big John had a large camouflage tarp over a pile of stuff he had hidden from the barn. He pulled out a funny looking motorcycle with two tractor tires. "I bought this thing last year with the idea of exploring all the trails around here but my heart started sputtering on me so I just never got around to using it. I only made one camping run on it. I even have a trailer to pull behind it with camping gear. You can run it almost all day on a couple of gallons of gas and it will go up to about 35 miles an hour. I had the tires filled with foam so it and the trailer will never get flats. It is called a Rokon Trail Blazer. Both wheels have internal storage for gas and both are full along with the gas tank. You have about ten days of gas, and with the extra ten gallons I have back at the barn that will give you another five. That should get you close to Louisiana. It will at least get you across the desert. Once you get across the desert you can trade it for a horse or a mule if you can't find any more gas. This all terrain bike will climb a 60 degree incline which is almost steeper than you can walk up. It will also float so you can float it across a river or lake if necessary. After we practice with it a little this afternoon, we'll look over the maps and my atlas and figure out the best route for you to take." The rest of the afternoon was spent teaching Porter how to operate and maintain the motorcycle.

The next morning they loaded up the trailer with the supplies and tools Porter would need to make the journey. In addition to Porter's pack and gear, Big John gave him a tool kit with everything he could possibly need to work on the motorcycle. He included an extra spark plug, fuel filters, air filters, and several quarts of motor oil. He gave him a bag of the pickled goat, extra water in a five gallon jug, a tarp, a length of rope, several LED flashlights, and a roll of duct tape.

They set up targets and with ammo that Big John had stored, Porter learned how to shoot the AK47. He found that the rifle was very inaccurate on full auto; but, he was very proficient firing it in its semi automatic configuration. He also had a shovel, machete, and an old axe. The final item Big John gave him was a bolt cutter. Big John told Porter, "As you remember when we were studying the map, I recommend that you take as many back roads and trails as you can find. It will take you a lot longer, but until you start crossing the desert you will be in constant danger of attack. Use these bolt cutters to cut through fences or to open locked gates. If you run across a deer or any game it might be a good idea to make a kill. That food in the backpack and jar isn't going to last you very long. You saw how I gutted the goat and skinned him. Just clean any animal the same way. Take that motorcycle and pull your kill out of sight up a trail where you can take your time."

Big John stood in the door and watched as Porter drove away. He almost turned the bike over when he looked back to wave. Big John chuckled and wondered if he had done the right thing sending the boy on his way. He had lied when he told Porter that the pacemaker would last another few months. He was already having trouble breathing and when he glanced at his fingernails he noticed they were a deeper purple than normal. Big John walked down into his shelter and locked the door. He poured himself a glass of wine and opened up a favorite old book. He peacefully fell asleep in his chair where he would spend eternity.

CHAPTER 8

SAVING THE GIRL

According to the shortwave it was a total "Road Warrior" scenario in America. Untold millions were dying from starvation, murder, and disease. The smell of death was everywhere. Mankind, the most dangerous animal on the planet, was on the hunt and on the move.

Night time was now the most dangerous time at the house. People were starting to use the cover of darkness to encroach on them. With no lights, and no yard dogs, the lights had to stay out in order to preserve their night vision. The mattresses were no longer on beds but on the floor. The walls in the bedrooms and wherever else they could be barricaded were piled high with sandbags, bricks, and anything else they could find that was heavy and relatively bullet proof. Most of the window panes had been shot out and had been replaced with clear plastic.

The next night Jake and Dix made another run. The advantage of driving at night was that it would be hard for someone to spot and shoot at them. This time they made a thirty mile run up to Jake's old girlfriend's home in the country. Jake knew that her family had a secure location, but had not heard from them in two weeks. Once again they left after midnight and again both were armed with AR-15's and Browning High Power automatics. They carried what had become a standard battle pack. This included six 30 round mags for each of the AR-15's and two extra 9mm mags for the Brownings. Each had a folding knife in his pocket and a Kbar on his belt. They had just enough gas to make the round trip, and 6 MRE's for food. They took an old 4X4 Ford pickup so they could haul back supplies if they found any.

About half way to their destination the truck came to the top of a large hill. Down below they spotted a barricade on the highway. It was illuminated by an open fire with some men around it. The night was cold so the men probably had the fire for warmth. "We've got two options, we can try and find a way around, or we can do something unexpected."

Jake shook his head, "We don't have the fuel to go around."

"Ok son, you get up on that hill about 200 yards from them. Take your radio but walk slowly and carefully because they may have someone up there. When you're in position radio me and I'll slowly drive up and see if they'll let me pass. If they let me through, I'll stop about a half mile up the road and you can work your way to me. If they decide to take me, I'll turn on the headlights which will be your signal to kill everyone you see. I'll be firing from the truck and then from the ditch on the left. We'll have to talk by radio when the shooting stops or slows down. Hopefully they won't expect anything this late at night."

Jake disappeared into the darkness and called back over the radio after about 30 minutes. "There are five of them that I can see around the fire. It's a good thing its cold or they might be scattered around."

Dix pulled the truck up to the barricade and rolled down his window. Gunfire blew out the front glass. "It was a good thing I leaned out the driver's window to get a better look" he mused, as the bullet missed him and also shattered the back glass. He flipped on the lights and rolled out the door onto the ground. He couldn't see what was going on but he heard gunfire and yelling. He rolled into the ditch, shouldered his rifle, and was able to finish off one of the attackers trying to get up. He called on the radio and Jake answered, "Are you hit?"

"No, Dix replied, "did you get them all? I finished off one that was getting up."

"They're all taken care of; I double tapped all of them from up here after I had them all down."

"Meet me as planned. We've probably woke up the entire country, so hurry. I've got the barricade open and I want to get away from the light."

Dix killed the lights and drove slowly down the road. He knocked the shattered glass out of his window and waited for Jake. Jake soon showed up and they proceeded on their way. Jake reloaded the empty magazines from an ammo can stored in the truck, while they drove in silence. The temperature was in the low 40's and the wind was cold as hell. The heater in the truck was on high, but did little to protect them as the wind rushed through the truck. It had begun to rain in a fine, chilling mist.

Dix slowed the truck as they made their way to the driveway leading up to the small farm. The drive was barricaded, so they parked the truck on the shoulder and geared up. They could expect to be confronted, but by whom they didn't know. They decided to wait until dawn so that they would be recognized. Under the cover of their oil coats and hats they remained out of sight but where they could see their truck. The rest of the night was quiet, cold, and miserable. The dawn came and all was quiet. Dix noted that the woods and trees were noticeably quiet, no squirrels and few birds. The country around them was unusually quiet; no sounds of traffic, airplanes or anything. They made their way up the driveway until they were within sight of the house. The house was dark. There was no smoke from the chimney, no dogs, nothing. Jake called out, "Anyone home?" There was no answer. This time he shouted, "Its Jake! Heather, are you in there?" Again they were answered by silence.

"We're going to have to go in,"Dix said. There's no need for both of us getting shot. You cover me from the wood pile on the side."

"Dad, you can't keep taking all the chances."

Aggravated, Dix answered, "If I rescue Heather, and you're dead, what the hell am I going to do with her? I am expendable, I'm getting old, and my job is to keep this family together as long as I can. You'll understand if you live long enough."

Jake started to argue but Dix stopped him, "This is not up for debate, son, I can't shoot as good as you, I'm slow, and I don't look like a threat. A gray haired middle age man walking up isn't as threatening as a young buck. Besides, I'm in charge until I go down."

As soon as Jake was in place, Dix hid his rifle under his coat. He reached through the flap in the pocket of his coat and put his hand on the pistol grip of the rifle. The safety was off. He reached the house without incident. He banged on the door with his left hand, keeping his right hand tight on the grip of the rifle. Again there was no answer so he tried the lock. It was broken and the door swung open. He pulled out his radio and called Jake, "Stay put I'm going in." The light was dim in the house so he flipped on the green LED light on the brim of his hat. He found the badly decayed body of a man in the front room. Animals had obviously been at work on him. He found another body in the kitchen, again in the same state of decay. They had no weapons.

Dix called Jake and told him, "I'm coming down. There's nothing but two dead men in the house."

Jake radioed back, "I'm coming up."

"Not yet," Dix replied, "let's get the truck up the hill and out of sight. We can't take a chance on losing it because it's at least a day's walk back home." They moved the barricade, pulled the truck up around the house, and re-barricaded the driveway. They went into the house and Jake identified Heather's father from the boots he was wearing, a pair of broken glasses, and steel plate on his skull. It was an injury from an explosion in Vietnam. Jake said, "I can't identify the one in the kitchen. We've got to go to their bugout position."

"How far away is it?"

"It's about a quarter of a mile down through the woods on the back of the property. They have an old hay barn that they fortified and stocked."

They made their way down to the woods and onto a light zigzagging trail. Jake raised his hand upward in a fist, "Stop! They probably have a booby trap set somewhere along here. Her dad was using some of the traps he had come across in Vietnam." He scrutinized the ground along the path "Look, there's one now." A hole with bloody metal spikes lay open ahead. Jake took a long stick and probed the ground as he went. He found three more traps without disturbing them. About halfway down the hill they heard gunfire just out of sight ahead. Jake said, "It sounds like it's coming from the area of the barn."

They heard a man yell out, "We know you're in there! Y'all come on out so we can visit. We promise not to hurt you." They were answered by gunfire.

Jake and Dix spread out and slowly crept down through the woods until they were overlooking the barn, the fenced in yard around it, and the fields beyond. A small amount of smoke was coming from a stove pipe sticking out of the back wall. On the far side, directly across from the big double doors in the front, a man with a lever action rifle was crouched behind a pile of stacked wood. Another was crouched behind an old abandoned tractor. They would wave their hats every so often to distract the people in the barn while two others were sneaking around the side. Jake whispered, "I'll take the two sneaking around, you take the two in the front." Dix whispered back, "I'll wait until you shoot before I open up. It'll take a second for them to realize they are being hit."

Jake disappeared further down the side of the ridge. Dix took aim at the farthest one. Dix aimed the red dot on the man's chest so that the bullet would travel diagonally through his chest cavity. Jake began to shoot and a half heart beat later, Dix put his first round through the man behind the tractor. Not waiting to see the effect, he turned his attention to the man at the wood pile. The man was moving, so Dix fired as the holographic circle and dot covered his torso. He kept squeezing off rounds until the man was down. He then turned back to the one at the tractor who was trying to crawl away. A second round through his chest caused him to collapse on the ground. Looking back at the other man who showed no movement, Dix popped him through the head just as a precaution.

Jake came back up, "All clear from my end."

"Same here," Dix reported. "I assume you didn't recognize any of those guys."

"I've never seen them before in my life. I just hope it was Heather and her mother we rescued."

Jake called out, "Heather, are you in there?"

"Jake is that you?"

"Yes! Is it clear for me to come in?"

"Yes, but hurry, I need help!"

Dix looked at Jake, "I'll stay here. We've made a lot of noise and will have attracted a lot of attention. Call back if you need help. Otherwise I'll stand watch up here until you need me."

Jake bolted down the hill and into the barn. He found Heather cradling her mother as he came in. "Is she hit?" Heather looked up at him,

"No, it's her heart. We ran out her medicine last week when the house was overrun. We've been hiding out here, Dad's dead, and we were afraid to try and bury him. She collapsed when they started shooting at us. I fired back and when I looked back she was clutching her chest."

Jake gently reached for her, "Let's get her warmed up and see if we can make her more comfortable."

At that moment she opened her eyes "I told you Jake would come." She sighed and again closed her eyes. They moved her to a pallet next to the stove. Her breathing was labored and she clutched Heather's arm. Heather broke down in sobs. There was nothing Jake could say that would take away the feeling of grief that overwhelmed her. They could only watch as her mother's breaths grew weaker and then ended. It was though a candle had burned down to its last spark and faded away.

Dix made his way around to each of the dead men and picked up their guns, ammo, knives, belts, and looked at the contents of their pockets. There were gold wedding bands, some gold dental crowns, old silver coins, and diamond engagement rings. He pulled off their belts and stuffed all the small stuff into a large canvas bag that one of them had. After carefully packing away anything of value or anything they could use, he left them to rot. When he got to the barn, all the while looking around, Jake and Heather were coming out. They told him what happened. Dix said, "Let's get the truck and load up everything we can haul and head home." He turned to Heather, "Can we bury your folks here on the farm?"

"Oh yes, they loved this place. This is where Dad was raised."

"I think we need to consider this as a bugout location. I want to hide the guns and ammo off these guys and some MRE's and gear here in case we have to make a run for it." He stopped and looked around, pleased with his plan. "Who is the dead man in the kitchen?"

"That was one Dad killed before they killed him," Heather explained. "Dad sent us out the back after he shot the one in the kitchen. He told us not to come back for him."

"What happened to your Uncle Bob and his son, John, Heather?"

"They went up to Granny's old house trailer to get some tools they had stashed behind her shed; they never came back. Two days later we were ambushed. I'm sure they must be dead or they would have come back."

Heather's dad had an old backhoe in the barn that still ran. Dix cranked the diesel engine and dug the graves in the orchard. He dug three graves, one each for Heather's parents, and one for the supplies they buried. Her dad had made some cache pipes out of six inch PVC pipe with screw end caps; Dix filled these with supplies, guns, ammo and MRE's. He buried them about a foot deep. He and Jake gathered the remains of her dad and rolled them up in a rug that was in the living room. They wrapped her mother in a rug from their bedroom. They gently placed them in the graves. After a short prayer and lot of tears, they were covered. "We'll get proper stones for them one day when all this is over."

They loaded everything in the truck and put the last ten gallons of gas that was stored in the barn into the pickup's fuel tank. "How far is Granny's old house trailer?"

Jake pointed, "It's about a half mile up the road north of here." They put the barricade back up and headed up the road, all the while keeping a sharp eye in both directions. They pulled into Granny's driveway. It was broad daylight but they didn't see anyone outside. They found Heather's Uncle Bob and his son, John, dead in the yard between the house trailer and the tool shed.

"Let's see what we can find to wrap them in and get them out of the weather, Jake." In the shed was an old tarp that had seen better days. They placed them on the tarp, rolled them up in it and carried them into the tool shed. The old shed had a dirt floor, so they dug a crude grave with a shovel from the shed and covered them up.

They looked behind the shed and found where her uncle had cached some freeze dried food and ammo. Dix had outfitted Heather with a holster and revolver from one of the dead men and she had her SKS that her dad had taught her to shoot with. They stayed parked out of sight behind the house trailer in the woods, taking turns sleeping as they waited for night. From where they were they could see the truck and trailer. Dix figured that anyone coming up would be interested in the truck and its contents and wouldn't notice them until it was too late.

As dusk enveloped them, the light rain turned to snow. The temperature was falling and a rare event was taking place. It was snowing in south Mississippi, something that only happens every ten years or so. They climbed into the truck, Dix pulled it into four wheel drive and they proceeded slowly down the road. The wind coming through the windshield was punishing as they made their way south. Dix turned to Heather, "What happened to your Dad's old Bronco?"

"Dad parked it behind the pump house when we ran out of gas."

"Do you mean it's still running?"

"Oh, yes, it was running great; it's just out of gas."

Dix turned around and went back to the farm. "I think we need to swap into something with a windshield."

They found the Bronco under a tarp behind the pump house. Heather's dad had restored it with a newly rebuilt 351 Cleveland V-8. It had a four inch lift and a roll bar. It also had a receiver hitch and a Warn winch. Dix had been envious of Heather's dad the first time he saw it. There was an ATV trailer attached, so they quickly transferred their cargo and fuel. They left a small amount of fuel in the pickup so they could retrieve it later. They cranked up the old Bronco and headed down the road. It ran great. Dix smiled, "How much do you want for her?"

Heather smiled back at him, "It's yours. Dad would have wanted you to have it."

The moonlight reflecting off the snow gave them plenty of light with which to see. They stopped the Bronco about a half mile from where they had the firefight on the road. In the light they could see the barricade beside the roadway. There was no fire and no bodies. Dix said, "We have several choices, we can go though there at about 80 miles an hour, we can sit here and wait a couple of hours to see if anyone shows, or we can do it like before. If we do it like we did before, I suggest that you and Heather work your way through the woods and we do it the same way. I think if anyone saw the way it happened last time they will be ready this time and I don't want you two to get hurt."

"How about me and Heather work our way all the way around to where we originally stopped, Dad. I'll set up a firing position and radio for you to come barreling through wide-ass open."

Dix nodded, "Sounds like a plan; but, I want both of you armed and geared out with complete bugout packs. If I'm taken out and lose the Bronco you can at least walk on in."

It took them almost two hours to walk around and get set up. Heather was back up for Jake who would fire if there were any signs of hostility. Dix cranked the Bronco and rolled down the windows. He had his rifle on its sling over his head so if he left the vehicle it would be with him. He punched it and sped through the open barricade. He never turned on his lights, using the light from the moon and snow to guide him. He was through the barricade and on top of the hill before he stopped just long enough for Jake and Heather to jump in. "I guess we killed all the bad guys last night." Jake commented, "Six months ago we wouldn't be able to sleep at night if we killed someone. But after a few weeks of seeing what people can and will do, it almost seems routine."

Dix agreed, "Our job is to stay alive until there is some semblance of order. Then our job will be to restore the constitution and then hunt down and punish the politicians and their backers. But before then, I'm afraid we'll be fighting foreign troops." It only seemed logical that there would be some communist countries that would not lose control of their populations. The prospect of fighting UN troops was a sobering fear.

They made it home without incident. Jake radioed the house and told them they would be arriving in the Bronco and not to shoot. William radioed back, "We've got a sniper in the house next door. We've been taking fire from him all day. Someone is upstairs and we don't want to waste ammo shooting blind."

Dix radioed back, "Get a couple of the 22's and start peppering the hell out of the windows in the house. Lower the barricade on the south side of the property. Jake and Heather will come on in. They are going to drop me off on May's road. I'll get to the house on the north side while you keep them occupied. I'll set it on fire and shoot them as they come out."

They stopped up the road just long enough for Dix to fill up a beer bottle with gasoline. Once he heard the gunfire from the house he ran up to a window on the north side of the building and punched a pane out with his rifle barrel. He poured in the bottle of gas, lit the empty bottle, tossed it in and soon had a good fire going. He ran back into the darkness and waited. With all the windows shot out on the south side the fire had plenty of air. It was soon blazing out of control; two men with rifles came out of a window on the second floor and attempted to get off the roof. Dix hit them both, knocking them off the roof. He heard the deep boom of heavy rifle shots from the south side where he and the boys were waiting. After it was obvious that no one else would be coming out, Dix radioed that he was coming in. The fire was too hot to get the weapons off the two he killed so he continued on to the house.

Dix walked into the house, and in the candle light he hugged his wife. "Make Heather comfortable. I think we're going to have a daughter-in-law soon."

CHAPTER 9

MORE MOUTHS TO FEED

Porter motored down the road then turned up a gravel road that headed up into the mountains. The GPS given to him by Big John had told him where to turn. The bike ran strong and smooth as he wormed his way up the road. His destination was a trail that led east down out of this range of mountains, across the next valley and up into the second of the three ranges of mountains that lay between Los Angeles and the desert southeast. Porter's destination today was a campsite that Big John had used the year before. He drove down a trail and came to a small clear stream. A ring of rocks was ready for its next fire. The temperature was hovering around 40 degrees and the musty Chinese coat felt good. He walked back up to the top of the trail and carefully brushed out the tractor tread tracks with a pine limb.

That evening he sat by a small fire. Snow flurries were drifting by and he wished he was at home with his family. He mourned quietly as he rolled out his sleeping bag and lay under the tarp that was hung over a rope suspended from two trees. He slept with his rifle next to him. He used his mother's canvas bag filled with pine straw as a pillow. Under it he placed his Chinese pistol. He nibbled on his last Chinese cookie before dozing off.

The next morning he awoke to find the ground covered with snow. Large rocks lay behind him the fire was in front. Three large dogs were looking at him from across the fire. They were trying to get to the goat meat on his trailer. Porter pulled out his pistol and started shooting; the dogs took off trailing blood and yelping. He had just learned a valuable lesson. He remembered from his boy scout lessons that he should hang food out of the reach of predators while camping. He had almost lost his only food before he could make a kill. He replaced the empty magazine in his pistol and wished he hadn't wasted all the ammo. One or two shots would have been plenty to get the dogs on their way or possibly just throwing rocks. He considered trailing the wounded dogs. He had read that the Chinese eat dogs, maybe he could also; but, he wasn't starving yet and the thought of eating a dog was repulsive.

The snow was coming down steadily and it was cold. He considered staying put but decided that it was probably better to travel during the bad weather. The bad guys were probably holed up next to a fire someplace. He put his ball cap away and pulled on a stocking cap. He put socks on his hands after he cut some finger holes. He packed up his gear and ate a handful of the salty goat meat. He drank from the stream and hoped that he wouldn't catch a bug. "Maybe the dirty living will bolster my immune system," Porter thought to himself, "so I could eat and drink from less than desirable sources, if things get really bad." He consulted his map and the GPS. The map book and chart Big John gave him helped him plan his trip. He headed down the mountain trail on the Rokon, its engine was running strong and smooth. The wind was cold on his fingers so he ran it less than wide open. He was glad that it was snowing; his trail would be covered up in a matter of minutes. The little motorcycle easily tracked up the trail as he wormed his way east. The warmth from the engine radiated on his legs and made the travel bearable.

He stopped for a rest break and pulled out his .22 and reassembled it. Several times he had spotted birds, rabbits and squirrels but couldn't shoot because the AK47 would have vaporized them if he shot them. He twisted the AK47 around behind his back and held the 22 with his left hand. It wasn't long before he had two fat rabbits gutted and tied to his back rack. He finished the day without incident and took a trail up the mountain. He set up a camp out of the wind and out of sight of the road and trail. He built a small hot fire using pine cones and dead pine. He topped this off with some oak limbs. Once it had settled down to coals he suspended the rabbits over the fire to let them cook. He fashioned mittens from the rabbit skins with the hair on the inside. He used some twine to sew up the slack. He decided that the next rabbit he killed he would skin prior to gutting so that he wouldn't have to deal with a damaged pelt. The rabbits were delicious and he went to sleep feeling full and satisfied. His bag of goat meat was suspended in a tree away from the camp but within range of his AK47.

The night was cold but he was comfortable in his sleeping bag next to the fire. Nothing bothered his food suspended in the tree. Once again, he dined on goat meat for breakfast as he packed up his gear. According to his GPS he would be heading into the Joshua Tree National Park. After traveling most of the day he made his way down out of the mountains and left the snow behind him. He was heading into the desert country. The mountains had done their job of squeezing the moisture from the air. The humidity was lower and the temperature was rising.

He was coming into the park from a gravel road coming down off the mountain. He came to a gate on the outskirts of the park. There was no one in sight so he stopped and using his bolt cutters, cut through the lock on the gate and proceeded on into the park. He didn't know if there would be any park rangers still around or if they had gone renegade like the police in the mountains behind his home. He didn't run wide open, the gravel road was uneven enough to warrant caution. He also didn't want to run into any surprises such as road blocks. He kept mental notes of side roads and trails in case he needed to double back.

About 10 miles down the road he came upon a little girl standing by the road crying. She appeared to about five or six so he stopped to check on her. She sobbed and pointed, "Bad men hit my sister." Porter looked in the direction she pointed, "How many bad men are there?"

"Three, they drug her into the woods; but, she told me to run." Porter told her, "Stay here and don't leave this motorcycle no matter what you hear." He picked up the AK47, flipped off the safety and headed up the trail at a fast walk. He came to a camp where three men were standing over a young woman. They were having a heated argument over who would get to go first. They were stripping off their clothes, while the young lady was naked on the ground trying to cover herself with her hands. Porter raised the rifle and made seven shots before they all went down. He walked to them and shot each one through the head before turning his attention to the girl. As he replaced the magazine in his rifle with a full one, he asked her if she was ok. She was about his age with blond hair and was sobbing and couldn't speak. She crawled around and found her jeans and shirt. Porter looked around, "Are there any more?"

She shook her head, "These are the only ones I've seen; there could be others. I've got to find my little sister."

"She's ok. She is just up by the road with my bike."

After she got dressed he led her back to the Rokon and her sister. "Come on, we've got to get out of sight." He put the little girl behind him on the rack behind the seat. He let the girl sit on the trailer. He turned back and went back a couple of miles to where he remembered a trail. He motored down the trail until he was a half a mile or so off the gravel road. Stopping, he opened up the 5 gallon jug of water and let them use a small amount to clean up. He handed the older girl the 9mm, showed her the safety and told her, "If you need to shoot something, flip off the safety and pull the trigger. Flip it back on when you're finished, I'll be back in a bit." Porter turned to leave. Scared, she jerked around, "Where you going?"

"I'm heading back to their camp to scavenge what I can." He hastily unloaded the trailer and the rack on the back of the Rokon. He replaced the partially empty magazine in his magazine pouch with a full one from his back pack. In his mind, it was important to maintain his magazine pouch and rifle with fully loaded magazines, in case he ran into trouble.

Porter ran flat out down to the camp where he had killed the three men about 15 minutes earlier. He tried not to look at the dead bodies as he quickly gathered up their food, guns and packs. They had an old pickup with several cans of gas in the back. He went through their pockets and didn't find anything of real value. He ended up with a trailer full of canned goods and three duffel bags of belongings. He also had three long guns, pistols and several boxes of bullets. His final find was two five gallon jugs of water.

He was fully loaded when he got back to the girls. The sun was going down and he put the Rokon sideways on the trail so he could use it for cover if they had company. He looked at them and introduced himself, "I'm Porter Jones from Los Angeles. What are your names?" The little one held out her hand, "I'm Ally, this is my sister Sandy and we're from Palm Springs." Sandy added, "Our last name is Bailey. Our parents were killed last week when we ran off the road at a road block. The men who caused it gave us a jug of water and a box of crackers and told us to beat it. We've been walking for days. We started eating lizards and have been finding water faucets in the park. Most of them were working."

Porter built a small fire after building a wall of rocks to hide the flame from sight. "I cleaned out their campsite, I only left the clothes they were wearing, they were too bloody to use anyway." He unloaded everything from the trailer. He pulled out the skillet, scrubbed it out with sand and pebbles, then wiped it clean with his dampened shirt tail. He set it over the fire, dumped in the remaining goat and on top of that two cans of pork and beans. He cleaned off some forks in the sand and ran them through the flames of the fire. He let the girls eat from the skillet first. After they were full he finished off the rest and they washed it all down with water. He cleaned the big skillet again and poured in some water to heat. He opened his stash from Big John and found a wash cloth, towel and a bar of soap and told the girls to get washed up for bed. He gave them tee shirts to sleep in and rolled out his sleeping bag for them between the Rokon and the fire.

He climbed up to a rise so that he could see the camp as well as the gravel road. He saw no activity of any kind. The sky was clear and he could see more stars than he ever knew existed. He resisted the urge to go through the rest of the gear he had secured from the bad guys because he didn't want to waste the batteries in his flashlights. He stayed on guard well into the evening pondering his dilemma. He was doing good to feed himself, now he had two more mouths to feed. Stopping to rescue the girls could have been a mistake. Just as he was about to head back into camp he saw headlights coming from way down the road in the direction of the bad men's camp. The lights slowed and turned down the road where the dead men lay. A few minutes later the lights came out of the road followed by the lights from the truck where he found the gas. Both vehicles disappeared back down the road. They didn't even take time to bury their comrades. The cold finally drove him back to the fire which he topped off with some heavy brush he found on the trail. The girls were sleeping together in the sleeping bag. Other than an abundance of freckles, they were both pretty.

The next morning he awoke by the fire. He was stiff from having slept on the bare ground. He had been warm on the fire side and frozen on the back side. He would have to figure a better sleeping arrangement for the next night. They ate Vienna sausage for breakfast and he finally took the opportunity to look in the duffels and cardboard boxes of supplies he swiped from the bad guys. He dumped them out on the tarp and started going through the pile. There was no way he could carry everything so he had to decide what was worth carrying and what they would have to abandon. The first thing he sorted out was the guns and ammo. Two of the men had rifles, the third a shotgun. One of the rifles was a 30-30 deer rifle with a cheap scope and a box of ammo. Another of the rifles was a Chinese SKS with a can of ammo on stripper clips. The stripper clips made reloading the SKS rifle quick and easy. This was good news because it used the same ammo as his AK47. It was also a good size for Sandy because it had a short butt stock which would make it easier for her to shoot. The shotgun owned by the third man was a 12 gauge Remington pump. It had a bandoleer with buckshot, birdshot and a couple of deer slugs. There were two pistols, a Beretta 9mm with a shoulder holster and four 15 round magazines. The other was an old Smith and Wesson revolver. It looked like an old pistol a policeman or security guard would have carried. There were also 100 rounds of 9mm ammo in two boxes.

He reloaded the empty clip for the Chinese pistol and adjusted the shoulder holster to fit Sandy. Her hands were small but the Chinese pistol was a good fit. The Beretta was a little big for his grip but he figured he would quickly grow accustomed to it.

After climbing up to his observation point from the night before he could see no activity in any direction. There was no sound, no smoke and no dust on the gravel road. He took the chance and taught Sandy gun safety and to shoot their weapons cache including the weapons he chose to carry. Ally wanted a weapon also, so Porter gave her a ball peen hammer that had a raw hide loop on the handle so it could be hung from a nail in its prior life. Now it fit Ally's wrist. Porter told her, "You can break a noggin, a toe, or a shin bone." Ally grinned at the prospect. He also had a large hunting knife to go on Sandy's belt.

He took inventory of their food next. They now had at least two weeks worth of beans, Chef Boyardee and other assorted canned goods. He stuffed all the food into one of the empty duffel bags. He found a surprise in the third bag. In 20 opaque plastic containers with tight fitting green lids he found one ounce coins. There were 20 gold coins in ten of them and 20 silver coins in the remaining containers. This represented a small fortune. He put these into the bottom of the ammo can.

They went through the clothes and discarded the dirty ones. They shortened the legs of a couple of pants for Sandy and shortened two belts for Sandy and Ally. They found warm shirts and jackets and rolled up the sleeves. Ally had to make do with Sandy's blue jeans with the legs cut short. They saved their own dirty clothes for later use.

The rest of the cardboard box contents held some metal camping plates, knives, forks, spoons, can opener, and some large cooking utensils. All of these were put in the skillet and lashed together with some cord. There were also some bars of soap, paper towels, two fifths of tequila, and a dish brush. He discarded a large axe and shovel. He elected to keep a machete.

He and Sandy spent the rest of the afternoon going over the map and by her best recollection they retraced her and Ally's trek across the park. Porter determined that he had driven down from somewhere near Eureka Peak and were now on the edge of Covington Flat. Their goal was to reach Pinto Basin Road, travel southeast to Black Eagle Mine Road, and from there out of the park. Porter decided to make this run at night, the bad guys would probably be asleep or sitting around a fire and they could travel undisturbed.

Porter and the girls split a large can of ravioli, cleaned up their utensils and carefully packed all the gear. Ally would ride lying down in the trailer so she could sleep. Sandy would ride behind him sitting on the canvas bag of pine straw as a cushion. He hung the gas cans on ropes so they hung across the front and rear racks with one tied to the front rack. The water was put in the trailer along with the packs and duffels. They created a depression in the gear on the trailer so Ally would ride secure nestled down in the trailer. Sandy wore the SKS across her back and Porter had the AK47 and his magazine pouch over the Chinese coat. Ally was in the sleeping bag and Sandy had on one of the jackets with the sleeves rolled up. According to his dad's watch it was about 10 pm and it was a bright moonlit night. Porter had grown accustomed to seeing at night since he started trying to save his flashlight batteries in the past week. The loaded Rokon and trailer looked like something you would see in a third world country.

Porter couldn't run the bike wide open because of the load. He estimated his speed at about 15 miles an hour. He just barely had the bike in second gear. Although the going was slow, he didn't have to use the headlight to see the road. The Rokon was fairly quiet at this speed and the going was smooth. Once they came upon a camp near the road. They could see the campfire with men sitting around it. They didn't stop and the men didn't seem to notice so they continued on into the night. They reached the edge of the park just as the sun was coming up. Porter found a trail and headed up the road that ended at an old mining site. There were some old abandoned buildings and equipment. Porter hopped off the bike and went through and around all the buildings to make sure they were vacant. There was no indication of any recent activity or occupation. He pulled the Rokon and girls behind the largest building out of sight. They split a can of beans for breakfast. Not wanting to be trapped in a building, Porter strung a tarp from the eave over to the Rokon so they could rest in the shade until they could resume their trip again in the evening. Even though she slept in the trailer Ally was still tired. It was much warmer today so she and Sandy slept on top of the sleeping bag. Porter slept sitting up leaning against the wooden building. Other than some gnats and ants he slept undisturbed.

He was waken by a very nasty Hispanic man holding a machete to his throat. Porter bolted awake and almost cut his own throat when he jumped at the touch of the cold steel. It was at that moment that a ball peen hammer came down squarely on the big toe that was exposed in his dirty sandal by a little girl with blond curly hair. The man cursed, jumped, and turned as Sandy, who had walked behind another building for a bathroom break, shot him with the SKS. He went down and before Porter could shoot, she shot the man through the head while he was on the ground. Porter hopped up and quickly made a run around the location. He proclaimed, "You girls are awesome; I was a dead man for sure!" He followed the man's tracks in the sand and found that they wormed their way off and back to a camp out of sight. Other than a few more cans of food, there wasn't anything they could use. The man appeared to be infected with scabies and lice so Porter elected to abandon the camp site and move behind another building rather than drag him off. He cleaned off Ally's hammer and again complimented and praised her on her quick thinking. Ally beamed! Sandy hugged his neck, "Thank you for saving us, you could have just given us some food and left us again."

"If I had I would probably be dead right now."

Sandy said thoughtfully, "From now on one of us needs to stand guard while the others sleep, we're completely on our own and we're going to have to take care of each other to make it. Do you think your grandfather will mind if we show up with you?"

"I'm sure he wouldn't mind, if he does, we'll just find a place to hide and live until things return to normal. We've got a lot of desert to cross in the next few weeks, I figure the best thing for us is to keep moving unless we can find a place to stay and rest." Porter reminded her, "Don't let Ally get near that dead man, whatever critters that are on him will be crawling off looking for a new home. We can't afford to waste any water for washing until we get to a river or pond somewhere."

Porter topped off the gas and checked the oil in the Rokon. He checked the air filter and it appeared ok. Once again they waited until dark and their eyes adjusted to the dark. Ally rode leaning back in the trailer with her back to the bike. She wanted to watch the road from behind to keep an eye out for bad guys. After being a hero she was anxious to help guard. Once again they ran in second gear because of the load.

The next week they repeated the process of sleeping during the day and running at night. They came to a secluded spot on a river in Texas. Porter was uncertain of their exact location. He estimated that they were making about 200 miles a day. They took several days to rest, bathe, and heal from the long travel. They were encountering a lot more people as they left the desert. So far all were friendly and for the most part ignored them. They still took turns standing guard as this had become a way of life. They washed all their clothes and let them dry. There weren't any fish to speak of but Porter was able to kill some squirrels and birds with the .22 rifle. They crossed the river and traveled on for another week and were well into Texas when they came to another river. Unfortunately, the GPS had given out a week earlier. They camped on the river to hunt, rest and clean up. On the third day a yearling bull showed up on the river early one morning. Porter shot him through the head dropping him in his tracks. He and Sandy skinned him on the ground and carefully cut all the meat from the bones as well as cutting up the heart. Porter remembered how Big John had carefully removed the meat and put it in the skin. They washed the meat in the river. Porter took some barbed wire fence and made a rack over the fire. He could move it back and forth as needed as he smoked and dried the strips of meat. Sandy cooked steaks in the skillet, he washed the hide in the river, and stretched it between two small trees where he could scrape all the extra fat and meat scraps from the hide. He had never tanned a hide but figured it would make a good ground cloth if nothing else. They gorged themselves on the meat over the next two days. It felt good to eat without the worry of running out of food hanging over their heads. They wound up with a month or more supply of smoked jerky. Other than needing some salt it was delicious. They boiled river water in the skillet and refilled 2 of the 5 gallon jugs. The fuel tank on the Rokon was full and there was one jug of gas left. He had not had to open the fuel tanks in the wheels. So as of now, they had about a week of fuel remaining. He kept the empty fuel tanks and used the empty five gallon water jug from Big John to store much of the jerky. It had a two inch opening so they could easily get the pieces of jerky out as needed. They used the tequila as mouth wash and all of them shared his toothbrush, Porter figured they were family so it didn't matter. He felt like an old married man without the marital relations. He couldn't help but think about the relations since they took turns standing guard during baths in the river.

CHAPTER 10

DIX GETS EVEN

The fighting intensified over the next few weeks. Everyone stayed put as desperation gripped the city. The short wave indicated that things were desperate over much of the world. There was no word coming from the communist countries. It was assumed that they had better control of their populations.

The Europeans woke up and had to fight their Muslim population who took the collapse as a message from Allah to start their final holy war. The Muslims killed most of their leaders in the oil producing nations but they were repelled by the people of Europe, ending the Muslim foothold in Europe. A nuclear bomb went off in Tel Aviv.

The gloves came off after Tel Aviv disappeared. The Israeli's took out the remaining Arab capitals, several thousand Mosques, and Mecca. They expelled the majority of their Muslim population and killed the rest. Then they too went silent as their government collapsed and their population went into survival mode.

Back in Mississippi, all hell had broken loose. The family was hit by a group numbering around 40 that came at them from the south. Dix was out in his work shop when they came. The house came under tremendous fire. They pulled up with guns, trucks, and motorcycles and just attacked. They were probably former military, as they were using overwhelming firepower. Dix had his AR disassembled and was cleaning it when bullets came streaming through the wall. One bullet splintered the workbench and sent his rifle parts across the room. A splinter stuck in his forehead and left a stream of blood down his face when he yanked it out. He couldn't know what was going on in the house.

He grabbed an axe, chopped through the back wall and dove through the jagged metal of the building. Other than a deep gash on his arm, he was ok. Dix pulled out his 9mm and ran into the brush behind the burnt out house next door. He circled around to the woods on the back of their place where he had a bugout location. When he got there he opened the hidden tool box pulling out his grandfather's Springfield 30-06. It was a WWI era rifle Dix had outfitted with a scope. He cycled the action and put a round in the barrel. This was a rifle capable of making 1000 yard shots.

Dix strapped on a bandoleer and picked up an ammo can of cartridges. He positioned himself back in the edge of the woods behind a pile of concrete from an old slab that he had broken up after Hurricane Katrina. Their small farm was at one time a country home but over the years the city and neighborhoods had built up around it. It still had outbuildings and was sitting on 10 acres of land. Dix had wanted to relocate to a remote location out West or in the Ozarks, but there was no work, so he decided to ride it out on the farm. Dix figured that if they could survive the initial few months, there would be enough people dead from starvation that the scenario unfolding before him would not take place.

Lying over the pile of concrete he sighted on the first man he saw and pulled the trigger. He never felt the kick and didn't look to see if the shot connected but concentrated on the next target, and then the one after that. Five shots, five kills, and he stopped to reload. They had not located him so his secret was safe. His family was still fighting so they did not know he was shooting from his position behind the house. Once again he spotted a man on his belly in the ditch. The only shot Dix had was the man's left foot and ankle. The 150 grain bullet pretty much took his foot off at the ankle. The next shot he had was a nasty looking gal hanging back behind the cars. He hit her through the chest and she disappeared behind the car. He realized that he'd been spotted as bullets began cutting through the bushes around him. He spotted the shooter in the ditch on the other side of the road. A round through his head ended the threat. He searched a few moments for another target.

Shooting was still coming from the house, so he crept around behind the neighbor's house and into the woods beyond. He worked his way around to where he was directly south of his house, which placed the bad guys between him and the house. He was hidden in a fence row and had a good view of the field of battle. He was now in a target rich environment. He thumbed several more rounds into the magazine topping it off and started laying them out one after another. He lost count of shots and kills.

After no less than half a dozen hits they turned their attention on him. He lay on the ground behind a large oak and reloaded. The old tree was being chewed up. He knew what they would do, they would concentrate fire on his location to keep him down while others would circle around and hit from the side. He crawled on his belly straight away from the tree until he crossed a driveway and got behind an abandoned truck. By lying down and looking under the truck he could see four of them coming from the east side of the old yard, spread out, they knew what they were doing.

Dix waited until two of them were lined up and pulled the trigger. A 150 grain 30-06 bullet travels at around 2600 feet per second. One human body will not stop it. From the angle he shot, the bullet traveled though the pelvic girdle of the first man, and up at an angle catching the second man in the throat. Dix couldn't cycle the bolt action fast enough so he used his 9mm to cut the legs out from under the other two. He emptied the clip and reloaded. Once they were down he riddled them with the 9mm. He slapped in his last magazine and decided to make a move.

He didn't wait, but ran east across the road and behind the houses on that side of the street. They had long since been burned to keep people out, but the remaining brick walls gave him cover. The shooting had stopped at his home. He could still see men shouting and running. He once again set up, this time in the rubble of a house that was across the street but at an angle to his house. From this spot he could see his house through the scope and the strangers in the house. The front door was broken down. There were several bodies in the front yard. Clearly Jake and the boys had done some good. Through his scope Dix could see a man peering from around the back of the house. It was not one of his people. Dix placed a round though the corner of the house and dropped him. Three more broke across the yard running fast to the south. Dix dropped one and reloaded. He kept his eye on the road where he figured they would cross. In all probability they would cross where he did. He aimed and waited. He saw the first one look around the back of the old truck that he had hidden behind. Dix put a round through his head and cycled the action. He fired through the bed of the pickup and saw a spray of blood above the back. He turned back to the house and reloaded. He refilled the bandoleer out of the ammo can he was still dragging. Then filled his pockets and left the can. He moved back behind the house and went into another yard behind that one. He didn't want to show himself between the houses.

He knew in his heart what had taken place in his home. Now his sole purpose for living was to kill the bastards. He made his way around to the north side of the house. He was about 400 yards down the road where he found a ladder that allowed him to climb on top of a house where he could get a good view of his home and yard. Looking through the scope he sat quietly and observed. He wanted them to relax and start moving. His position was not protected; he only had stealth on his side. After about thirty minutes they started peeking out. He waited until he could see four or five before he started the execution. The first one was under his carport looking out from between the Camellia bushes. The second one was in the boat shed. Dix figured that he would have to patch the boat if he ever used it again. The other three dove for cover, but they didn't know where the shots were coming from and they hid in the wrong places. Dix reloaded and slung the rifle. He climbed off the roof and crossed to the house next door. The fighting would be in close, he wished he had a shotgun or his AR.

Suddenly engines fired up and the running vehicles from his home came roaring out of the driveway. He didn't fire, fearing that his family and friends may be the ones trying to escape. He made it into the row of azaleas on the north side of the house and crawled under. A half a dozen men could be seen running toward the vehicles they had abandoned on the road and across the street. Dix could see one had long red hair, another had an afro. He cut both of them down and lost sight of the others. The sun was lower in the sky and in the long shadows he was having trouble finding targets, all he could do was try to disable the vehicles. He put rounds through the engine compartments. None of them stopped but he could hear one engine knocking real loud.

They were gone as quickly as they come. They didn't wait around to gather their wounded if there were any. Dix reloaded his rifle and ran into the carport. The back door was busted all to pieces. Cartridge casings were everywhere. Dix found what he feared. Everyone was dead, along with a half dozen of the raiders. Even the Schnauzers were dead. The house had been ransacked and the loose weapons and food were gone. Dix collapsed on the floor and shook. He puked and then sat back up. A rage built up within him that he didn't think he could possibly contain.

They had stolen all the vehicles including the Bronco. Dix went back across the road and retrieved the ammo can that still had several hundred rounds of 30-06 ammo. He opened the gun safe they had failed to breech and pulled out several full magazines for his Browning 9mm pistol. He had work to do, and the longer he waited, the chance of him catching up with and killing the raiders lessened. A quick trip around the property found a lot of dead and three wounded. He finished one off and left the others enjoying their agony, they would not survive their wounds. The Catahoula puppies that Jake had gotten for security were still alive in their pen. Dix let them out. Even if he didn't make it, they'd have plenty to eat, thanks to the bodies of the raiders he'd killed.

He ran out back and found the Yamaha four-wheeler still intact. The fuel tank was full and his last five gallon can of fuel was still under the shop in the back. The electricity was out and his generator had taken fire. He would be unable to put his AR back together tonight because he would never find all the pieces in the dark. He put together a bugout bag from the supplies he managed to find.

The weather was still cool so he put on a leather coat and cranked the four-wheeler. He pulled out of the driveway and headed south in the direction the raiders were running. He came to the first main intersection and stopped. He continued when he spotted the car with the damaged engine on the side of the road straight ahead about four hundred yards in the direction he had been riding. He killed the engine and took rest aim across the seat with his rifle. Through the scope he could see three raiders. He placed the crosshairs on top of the first one's head and squeezed the trigger. The bullet hit him between the shoulders and Dix found the next one in the scope. This one was trying to get something out of the car. Dix caught him in the mid section rolling him onto the road. The other was trying to hide behind the car. Shooting through the rear glass, the bullet traveled straight though the car and out the front windshield. Both windshields exploded and the raider staggered out holding his eyes. Dix cranked the four-wheeler and roared up, knocking him over. The nasty S.O.B. was pinned under the four-wheeler. Dix walked around and put the blade of his Kbar under the man's ear and let the razor sharp blade make a gentle incision. "You've got a decision to make, do I slowly start removing pieces or do you tell me where you guys have set up shop?"

After losing an ear the bastard spilled his guts, they were a bunch of ex-military and had taken over the airport because it was the only place with a generator and a supply of fuel. They would send out scouts looking for signs of people with food and supplies. They would overwhelm the small groups and lay up until the stolen supplies were used up. Dix asked the raider, "How many are left?" "I don't know man, we lost a lot today. We didn't realize we were attacking another army."

"You weren't. You attacked me." With that answer, Dix slit his throat.

Those idiots didn't realize that Dix's hobby was shooting and collecting firearms. He had been adding to and refining his collection for the last few years. His irrational fear of fighting for his life was coming true and his skills honed over of years of hunting, fishing, and shooting were at his disposal.

Dix rounded up their weapons and strapped them to the four wheeler rack. He found Jake's AR with the Eotech sight. He also found a dozen of his Magpul 30 round mags still loaded. The one in Jake's gun was empty. He didn't find Jake's Browning 9mm. Dix put the AR sling over his shoulder and shortened the stock so it hung behind on his back. He put the bag with the dozen mags over his shoulder so it hung to his left. He ran the four-wheeler flat out until he reached the airport. He lightened his load by leaving six of the full AR magazines with the four-wheeler, hidden in a ditch. Proceeding on foot, Dix carried his Springfield and the full bandoleer around the outskirts of the airport fence. The landing lights were no longer on, so unless they had night vision scopes, he was ok. He had to assume since they were ex-military they might have night vision scopes or cameras.

He found an open gap in the chain link fence. It looked like a tracked vehicle had opened it up. He made his way down the side of the runway until he came to a point where he could see the terminal and the control tower. The tower was dark but there were lights on in the terminal. Crossing to the tower Dix found the door unlocked. It was pitch-black dark and there were no sounds from inside. He slipped in and let the door close behind him. He would be a sitting duck if he was cornered in here, but the tower would give him a commanding view of the airport. He waited for an hour to make sure that he was alone in the building. Then flipped on his green LED cap light and proceeded up the stairs. Half way up he switched it off and finished the assent in the dark. Once he was in the actual tower, his eyes adjusted to the near darkness. Several monitors were still powered but all the glass was blown out of the tower windows. He could see the terminal and the activity inside.

Dix could easily make kills from here, but it wouldn't take them long to realize he was firing from the tower. He decided to take ten shots from the tower and then head into the terminal and kill until he was killed himself. He located his targets throughout the facility. His first shot hit a raider unloading a truck, the second was one sitting in the passenger area eating. He purposely aimed at raiders who were facing his direction. The 30-06 belched fire like a dragon. After nine shots and 4 hits he put the tenth round through the generator's radiator. He reloaded his rife and made an 11th shot through the second generator's radiator for good measure. He reloaded on the way down. Bullets were hitting the tower as he ran out the door into the darkness.

He took the luxury of stopping to catch his breath. The generators soon fell silent. He pulled the AR around and put the Springfield in its place. His eyes were usually accustomed to the darkness, but the only bad part about shooting was that the muzzle blast blinded him. He slowly made his way toward the terminal. If they had night vision he would be under fire right now. They were as blind as he was. He silently approached the rear of the terminal. A light switched on and someone shouted, "Kill the light! You want to get shot?"

The light went out. The voice had come from 20 yards away. Dix sat for about 20 minutes, tried to keep from breathing. As he grew more accustomed to the darkness he could make out four of them sitting and looking out into the night. If he could see them, then they could see him, especially if he moved or opened fire.

He eased the gun sling off his shoulder and then the magazine pouch, the Springfield, and finally his leather coat. He took his Kbar and cut one of the sleeves off his leather coat. He inserted the barrel of the AR into the sleeve and folded the excess under. He then cut the shirt sleeve off his shirt and cut a couple of strips from it. He tied the coat sleeve in place over the end of the rifle. He eased the AR up and put the Eotech sight on the first raider. In quick succession he killed all four. The coat sleeve had muffled the flash and a little of the sound.

He had killed eight, which was wildly more successful than he could have imagined. He moved back into the darkness and sat in the shadow of an abandoned fire truck. The moon was bright and he could see into the night. He was freezing cold but the adrenaline was still coursing through his veins. He thought of his wife and family lying dead at the house; he had absolutely nothing to live for but the desire to kill every single man in this facility.

He removed the magazine in the AR and replaced it with a full one. He loaded back up and proceeded slowly back to the spot where he just killed the four raiders waiting in ambush. He knew this would be the last place they would suspect him to be. Several raiders were busy milling around and picking up guns and checking their comrades. Dix emptied a magazine into them and replaced it. He walked though the dead and dying and into the building, shooting another that was running for the door.

Dix bolted up the stairs into a shadowy spot behind a column. Emergency battery powered lights had come on inside the terminal when the generators died. From where he waited in the shadows he could see the entire length of the terminal. He sat quietly and waited. He lost track of time as he sat with his back against the wall. It was warmer here and his mind wandered while he waited. The Springfield dug into his back and his arm was aching, he remembered that it had a gash. He knew it was full of dirt and that infection was likely, but he hadn't planned on living this long.

He saw several raiders working their way through the terminal. One would move while the other two stayed behind cover. Dix waited until they were half way down in case others were backing them up. He heard a noise off to his left in the area of the escalators leading up to the second level. A rifle bumping the metal side broke the silence. They weren't sure where he was hiding and that was enough for Dix.

He took aim at the one bringing up the rear who kept his head out a little too far when he was covering the lead. Dix waited until the one coming down the escalator had almost reached the bottom.

He shot the one he was aiming at through the head and turned and dropped the one on the escalator. He killed the one nearest to him down the corridor but was hit by the middle raider who got off a shot. Dix's last shot killed the raider who shot him. The bullet had hit his leg halfway between his knee and ankle; blood was gushing from the wound. Dix stuffed a handkerchief in the hole from the front and the cuff of his old shirtsleeve in the exit hole on the back. He then secured them in place with the remaining sleeve of his shirt. He got to his feet and tested the injured leg. It was definitely weak but there was absolutely no pain. His toes felt funny, so there was probably nerve damage. Dix was not upset that he was injured; he was upset that his wound might interrupt his plans to kill every single one of the S.O.B.'s.

He was still dribbling a little blood but it was coagulating, so the worst was over. Other than being a little light headed he felt pretty good. In fact he felt almost euphoric. He had gone quite awhile without eating or drinking and he had lost a lot of blood. He shot the emergency lights that were nearest him and found some jugs of water and food cached against the wall. He drank his fill and found some canned fruit. He popped the top and drank the juice before eating the contents. A package of crackers topped it off. He drank some more fruit juice and soon felt better. He found it odd that his arm hurt worse than his leg. He found a quiet place behind a counter and hid. He didn't realize that he had fallen asleep until he woke up in the middle of a dream where he was trying to revive Mattie. A horrible void filled him when he came fully awake.

The sun was just coming up and he could hear voices. One of them shouted, "I want them found! They can't hide forever."

The voice was coming from a wiry little man with a greasy mullet. He had on a biker outfit, and you could see the tattoos on his neck. He didn't see Dix sitting next to the counter in a shadow. Dix shot him in the gut with the AR, knocking him to the ground. He kept shooting with great prejudice until the one giving the orders and the four with him quit moving.

Dix replaced the empty magazine in the AR and limped down the corridor. There was a lot of activity outside. He could hear a truck cranking up and saw three men through the window throwing gear into a pickup. Dix opened up with the AR through the large plate glass window. Its glass shattered and fell as he emptied the magazine on his targets. He killed one trying to jump in the back. The other two took off and he concentrated his fire until the magazine was empty. The truck was almost to the opening in the airport fence where Dix had come through last night. He dropped the AR and reached for the Springfield, putting it to his shoulder and started shooting. The 150 grain bullets were not deterred by the cab of the pickup. They passed though the cab, through the occupants and out the front. The truck veered to the side and hit the fence. It rolled to a stop. The passenger door opened and Dix put his last round through the man trying to get out. He reloaded and waited to make sure that no one else was coming. After a long while, he got up and began to look around.

He spent the next three hours limping and looking around the airport. He found a medic's bag and was able to clean his arm and leg and put a pressure bandage on the leg. He found the Bronco and proceeded through the door it was parked beside. A stringy haired woman tried to shoot him from the side of the door. Dix knocked her arm aside just as the gun went off. With his ears ringing he snatched the pistol from her hand and backhanded her in one motion. She fell back and Dix got a closer look. She had a bullet burn that went down her face and through her ear and was wearing his wife's favorite scarf. He shot her in the chest with the Browning 9mm that he realized had belonged to Jake. He let her lay suffering while he kicked the door open into a hallway. A half dozen or so other trashy looking women tried to run. He emptied the AR though the cloud of cigarette smoke, sweat and cheap perfume. He knew they were with the raiders, and killing them was like killing rats as far as he was concerned. Human vermin is what they were. He took the scarf, taken off the dead woman, and gently folded it, he would place it with Mattie when he got home.

He loaded up the Bronco with everything he thought he could use. A trailer he found nearby helped him carry all the extra gear, canned goods, and MRE's. He loaded up their cans of gasoline and found a 55 gallon drum that he filled with six quarts of motor oil and topped off with jet fuel. Jet fuel is very clean kerosene. When you mix motor oil at the rate of about one quart per 11 gallons, you have the equivalent of diesel fuel. This would fill up the catamaran when he needed it. He found their cache of valuables and helped himself to a bag of gold and silver coins. He reloaded all his magazines from their cache of ammo and headed back to the four- wheeler. He loaded the four-wheeler in the back of the trailer that was hitched to the Bronco. He wasn't worried about hiding in the night because it didn't matter if anyone tried to stop or kill him; he had nothing to lose. He couldn't explain or understand why he took the time to gear up. He had a deep primordial fear and hate that was resonating from the very bowels of his soul.

He was half way home and the nightmare was not over. Two young guys with their pants down below their buttocks had the road blocked with a garden tractor and trailer. Dix stopped the Bronco and limped out. He looked at the young idiots, "What do you want?"

The nearest one said, "Give us your truck," while holding a pistol sideways like they saw on TV. Dix just limped on around behind the Bronco and grabbed the AR off the rack on the four-wheeler.

They looked in disbelief when he came back around and started shooting. It never occurred to them that a little grayed haired crippled man could take his time and shoot them. Dix had forgotten that he was wearing his Browning 9mm. He cranked the lawn tractor and pulled the trailer out of the road. He could see movement in the trees next to the stop, but he ignored it.

He made it home and proceeded with the grim task of laying his family to rest. It took him two days to dig the graves and bury the dead. He put the scarf on Mattie and kissed her goodbye. He covered her and the kids with blankets. He put Heather and Jake together on one side of Mattie, and Maggie and Bill on the other. He placed the little schnauzers with them as well; after all they were family too. He covered them all with a deep layer of soil. The work was slow and agonizing, not only was he in extreme pain but the mental anguish was exhausting. He placed them all around Gretchen Oak in the back yard. Gretchen Oak was planted over the grave of Gretchen, a treasured family pet.

Dix was working and living like a zombie. He ate, drank, slept, and healed. No one bothered him or the property. He moved from the house out into the motor home on the back of the property. The smell of decay was overwhelming around the house. All the decaying bodies still laying about the yard and road kept strangers away, and the puppies he'd saved were learning to bark at any suspicious noise.

After about two weeks Dix was walking a little better. The wound was still open and draining; but, he kept it full of antibiotic cream. After a month he was able to travel. Every day he thought about suicide but he realized that Ben and Frank, the little Catahoula pups, wouldn't make it without him. He had started living for them. They were his family now. He had plenty of food after cleaning out the raider's supplies. The little Catahoulas were barking at every sound; but, at least he could sleep with them on guard.

CHAPTER 11

A NEW FAMILY

Porter just turned 14, according to his dad's watch it was November 15. Sandy was 13 and a half and Ally was 5 and a half. Christmas was coming soon and there was a little girl expecting Santa. They crossed what he thought was the Pecos River at a wide, very shallow spot. They were in Texas, but he was uncertain of exactly where. At the top of the bank they came to a gate in the fence. It wasn't locked so they went through and closed it behind themselves. The trail they were following led up behind an ancient barn. They ran down the cow trail for about an hour. In the distance they could see a ranch house on a hill far away. The trail led straight to the house on the hill. Smoke was coming from the chimney. They slowly motored their way up the trail. When they were within sight of the porch they could see a man leaning against the post smoking a pipe. There were chickens all over the yard and dogs barking and running in their direction. Porter looked around and saw no one else anywhere. The man wasn't aiming a gun at them so he proceeded to within 100 feet of the porch before stopping. The man said, "It didn't take you guys very long to eat my little bull, are you hungry again so soon?"

Porter bristled, "He wasn't wearing a collar!"

The man laughed, "Come in, we haven't had any decent company in months."

"I'm sorry I killed your bull, I can try and pay you for him."

"That was the fourth time the little bastard jumped the fence, he's been a pain in my behind ever since he was born." Over the man's shoulder Porter saw a lady walk to the door wiping her hands, "I bet you guys could use a good meal."

"Mam," Sandy spoke up, "We don't understand; everyone we've come across up to now has either tried to kill us or has run from us."

The lady smiled, "We've watched you for days; we've also had to kill a bunch of bad guys. You wouldn't have driven up here in broad daylight if you had evil intentions." She opened the door and to let several small dogs out. They had a couple of Australian Shepherds who came bounding up barking. A very pregnant little rat terrier and a small furry brown mongrel came running out of the screen door. All were barking and very interested in the rolled up cow hide. The man introduced himself, "I'm Charley Cross and this is my wife Bonnie, we've got three sons out hunting and standing guard, they spotted you about the time ya'll set up camp on the other side of the river." Porter introduced himself and the girls and told them their story. "You guys can stick around awhile, we've got plenty of food and you can help the boys hunt."

The boys had three wives and several small kids running around. The house was large with a full basement. Bonnie introduced them around to the other ladies and the grandkids. Charlie helped Porter stow the gear in a metal building by the house. Porter couldn't help but notice that Mr. Charlie wore a pistol and carried an AR15 type rifle hung behind him. It was a .308 caliber and had a scope, Charlie bragged he could shoot and hit with it about as far as he could see.

"We are about 15 miles off the nearest highway. I've got sensors on the road about 5 miles from here, we patrol the property daily and two of my boys are in hidden lookout spots that allows them to cover most of the ranch at all times." Charlie continued, "My youngest son, Steve, is on his way to relieve his older brother Sam. Sam will ride across the North side of the ranch and then south along the river to relieve my other son John on the southern side. John will then circle back around and make it back here before dark. We are always in radio contact, when they spot someone, they call me and I ride out to see what's going on. That's how we spotted you guys. Steve spotted ya'll when you first set up camp across the river. I had just come through the gate when I heard you shoot the yearling. I try to keep the cattle away from the roads and river, but that little bull has been a horse's butt ever since he was born. I was planning on eating him this spring anyway."

"I'll be glad to pay you for him, I'm sorry; but, we were just running out of food."

"Don't you worry about that, I'll let you pay for him, we can use a good hand around here to help stand guard and hunt; meanwhile you need to eat some biscuits and gravy. Bonnie and the girls just about have lunch ready."

Although Porter was reluctant at first, he ate like he was a starving man and noticed that Sandy and Ally weren't holding back either. Bonnie and the three daughters in law made a big fuss over Sandy and Ally and had them in fresh clothes that fit better. A generator came to life and they rewashed all their clothes and had the girls washed and primped in no time. With fresh clothes, brushed hair and ribbons they looked very pretty. Charlie took Porter down to the basement where all the men shared a bathroom. He gave porter a razor and told him, "Get in that shower and give yourself a deep scrub and shave. Wash your hair and I'll give you a haircut out back. You'll find some of my son's clothes that they've outgrown in that cedar chest in the corner. Hang your guns on that nail where you can get your hands on them in a hurry. I know how it feels to be out of reach of my weapons. I expect you sleep with your pistol in your hand." Porter grinned, "How did you know?"

"I know because I sleep with my hand on mine." He reached over and flipped a switch that silenced the generator.

Charlie took Porter out back, set him in a chair, and put a towel around his neck. With Ally pointing out mistakes, Porter sat for a haircut, his face was still stinging from the shave. John came riding up on a big mule and greeted them with a wave. "I see he finally convinced someone to let him give them a haircut. He flunked out of barber school 30 years ago, but they let him keep his scissors."

That evening was the first time in weeks they had slept under a roof. The girls slept upstairs on a spare bed, Porter slept on a cot with a mattress by the wood stove. Charlie cautioned Porter, "We try not to run any lights at night. Someone can see light from a long way at night around here. That little glass window in the stove will light this room enough for you to see. Just take care that you don't fall down the stairs if you go down to the bathroom in the basement. You can use your flashlight once you're downstairs." "If the dogs start barking," Charlie warned, "John and I will come running. You get dressed, grab your coat, and take position behind all the firewood on the porch. Just make sure you don't shoot me or one of my boys. If you hear gunshots look for the flash; don't shoot back unless I say so. If someone comes walking up we have lights that will be triggered. Don't hesitate to kill them. If they are sneaking up here at night they are up to no good. Don't worry that you might kill somebody in error. If they are on foot at night in this country they are not lost. And by the way you need to keep some wood burning in the heater or the house will get real cold. So, before you get in bed, bring in 8 or 10 arm loads and stack it next to the heater."

That night he slept like a baby. Other than getting up to add wood to the fire, he slept the whole night. Sandy woke him up the next morning by tickling his ear with a broom straw. He woke up and found Sandy grinning at him. What happened next he couldn't explain. One minute they were grinning at each other, the next they were experiencing their first kiss. In fact it was Porter's first time to ever kiss a girl. He had thought about it a lot; but, had pretty much considered it an impossibility until sometime in the distant future. They smiled at one another and hugged. They soon heard steps on the stairs as Ally and the other three kids came barreling down the stairs. The sun was just peeking through the window. Everyone gets up early when they go to bed at dark. The house was soon alive, the wives of the three sons were named Holly, Cheryl, and Lynn and they, along with Bonnie, soon had the wood stove in the kitchen hot and breakfast cooking. Charlie asked Porter, "How strong is your arm?"

"I don't know, why?"

"Follow me, son." He took Porter out to another building where they had a wheat mill set up. In the room were stacks of five gallon buckets that reached the ceiling. Charlie pointed to them, "There is enough wheat in this room to feed our family and you guys for 10 years. We have two other buildings with corn, beans, and other staples. Come spring we will have a huge garden. We will can everything we don't eat immediately."

Porter nodded, "What about water? I know you have a generator for electricity; but, won't you run out of fuel for it before ten years?"

"We have four windmill driven water pumps on the ranch along with solar cells and batteries here on these buildings and on the house. We only run the generator to use the washing machine and to top off the batteries. It runs off of propane; we have four 500 gallon tanks that should last us until this crisis is over."

"Sounds like you've got everything covered to survive in style!"

"Well, you've seen the chickens and cattle. We've also got eight horses, two stallions, five mares and a gelding. We also have five mules. We ran a hunting guide service out of here before the bottom fell out. We try not to run our vehicles, gasoline is the one thing we are short of. We save it for emergency travel only, our trucks and cars are in storage. I've got 500 gallons of diesel for the tractor. We crank it only when we need to pull something the mules can't handle and to run the hay cutter and bailing machine."

Charlie grinned, "So now you start earning your keep. You start turning that flour mill and I'll feed in the wheat." In no time they had an empty five gallon bucket full of fresh ground flour. They sealed everything back up and made sure the door to the room was closed tight. "You have to be ever mindful of rats and mice. Our three old cats do a good job of catching them; but, you can never be too careful."

When they got back, breakfast was ready and once again they ate like starving men. There were scrambled eggs, chicken fried venison, onions and potatoes and hot biscuits with cream and syrup. While Charlie and Porter ground the wheat, John had milked the cow out back. Porter, Sandy and Ally had never drunk fresh milk and tasted real cream. Porter's mother would have never let it in the house. It had only been a few weeks but it seemed like a lifetime ago that he had been home with his family.

CHAPTER 12

THE VOYAGE NORTH

Dix had not heard from his sister and her family for several months. He had two options to go check on them. He could go by boat or by vehicle. He had enough fuel in the bronco and in the four-wheeler to make the drive; but, the more he thought about it, the more he realized that he would have trouble traveling by road. If his experiences here at home were any indication of what he could expect, he would be fighting a 170 mile battle.

If the catamaran was still running, he could make a return trip up the Mississippi and then up the Big Black to her home north of Jackson, MS. He still had the diesel left over from his trip to get Maggie and Bill out of the city as well as the extra 55 gallons in the trailer. He had ten five gallon cans of gasoline from the raiders and he had the tanks on the fishing boat that were still full. He had to make a run to check on the Catamaran.

He didn't wait until night because he was no longer trying to avoid a confrontation. He had killed so many people that the prospect of killing or getting killed didn't really matter anymore. In a perverted sort of way he hoped he could kill some more bad guys. He was halfway down the road when he came to the spot where the gang bangers had blocked the road before. Once again it was blocked with the same lawn tractor and trailer. When they realized it was Dix, they quickly cleared the road and beat it. He got to the boat house and found the Catamaran exactly as he had left it.

On the way back home, they cleared the road for him again. At least he'd made it clear to a few believers that he meant business.

Dix put all his food as well as the extra rifles, ammo, and magazines into his boat. He used the winch on the four-wheeler to pull it up off the ground from a tree limb. He backed the boat and trailer under the four-wheeler and let the winch unspool until the four wheeler rested in the boat. He took the large dump trailer he used behind the four-wheeler and up ended it into the boat. Its body was heavy plastic so the weight was no problem. He also restocked his bugout location in the woods behind the house. He filled the box with a rifle, ammo, and food. It saved him once; it may very well save him again.

Dix removed all the family photos and hard drives from the computers and put them in a six inch PVC pipe. He dropped in several boxes of baking soda that he had dried in the gas grill. These would absorb any moisture inside the tubes. He sealed them up and buried them under Gretchen Oak.

Dix replaced the Eotech sight on Jake's rifle with a Trijicon sight from a rifle he confiscated from the raiders. He sighted it in behind his house. This sight did not require batteries. The goats and chickens had disappeared during all the fighting, so the only chore left was to make a large sign and attached it to the wall of the carport. It said, "I will be coming back, if I catch you here, I'll kill you..............KEEP OUT OR YOU'LL BE JOINING

ALL THE SKELTONS LYING AROUND HERE." Dix knew in his heart that the odds of him ever coming home were remote; but, he also knew the idea of having a home to come back to was something he needed.

He took his tools back to the catamaran, installed a gun rack and loaded all the supplies in the catamaran. He filled the water tanks and filled the boat with everything he could stuff in, including his water filters. He launched his fishing boat, pulled the battery out of the Bronco and drained the fuel tank. He used the Bronco battery in the catamaran and cranked it up. He motored over to the launch where he tied the bow line from the fishing boat to the back of the catamaran. The fishing boat had all his fishing gear, crab nets and throw nets.

Other than sunk and derelict vessels, the canal looked as though it did on every fishing trip he had made over the years. He thought of all the times he and Jake had made this run. Profound sorrow almost overwhelmed him. He kept telling himself that now his duty was to save his sister if possible; and if not, to take care of his elderly uncles if he could get to them.

Ben and Frank were all over the boat. They were practically fearless. Dix named them after the two dogs his dad had when he was a boy. They too were Catahoula Cur dogs and started the long tradition of having them in the Jernigan family. He passed a couple of boats with people fishing. They made no hostile moves and neither did he. Maybe there were some normal people that hadn't been killed. He wondered if they had been through anything like him. Dix thought, "They must be out of food or they wouldn't be trying to fish."

He motored out of the bay and out from under the bridge. It was a little hazy or he would have been able to see the ships at anchor on the horizon. He put up the mast and sail and made his way out into the open Gulf. Once again he sailed out around the end of Ship Island.

He couldn't help but wonder it Maggie and Bill would have survived if he had left them in the city. Did he carry them to their deaths? That thought would haunt him to the end of his days. He found himself talking to his wife, Mattie, as if she was with him. He found that if he made conversation with his family members as though they were alive and with him it was somehow more bearable.

A storm was building up from the Southwest. The wind was whipping up the waves so Dix dropped the sails and motored around to the Northeast side of the island. He dropped anchor and added another bow line to the fishing boat and tied it to the back of the catamaran. Other than cold wind and blinding rain the island broke the twenty foot waves. The cabin was warm and dry. He, Ben, and Frank rode it out. Dix and the dogs split a can of soup over a pot of rice he cooked on the stove. Except for Ben pooping in the cabin, the night was uneventful.

The next morning the weather broke and it was warming up. Dix motored back around the island, put the sail back up, and headed south to the mouth of the river. A helicopter slowly flew from the south and passed directly overhead. It made a long slow circle obviously observing Dix and the catamaran. It turned and resumed its flight north. Dix recognized the red flag with yellow stars painted near the tail, it was the flag of Red China. They were wasting no time moving in. Dix was certain their motives were not search and rescue. He continued on, as there was nothing he could do one way or the other. His first job was to try and rescue his sister. He knew that he had been much better prepared than she and her family.

He reached the mouth of the river, where a sandbar had a dozen or so human bodies washed up and bloated on its edge. He kept the motor revved up just high enough to make good headway. Dix had no desire to hit something in the river and disable or sink the catamaran.

As before, there were sunk and semi-submerged barges, boats and tugs. A large sailboat was aground on the west bank. It was riddled with bullets. A nagging feeling kept eating at Dix as he thought about the Chinese helicopter. He eased the catamaran into a side channel created to park barges. The banks were overgrown with willows and were covered in debris. He turned around and shoved the fishing boat behind the catamaran so if he had to make a run, he would be headed in the right direction. In an emergency he would not have time to turn the boats around. He broke out the soup and rice and he and the boys finished it up. He kept them out on the deck so he wouldn't have dog poop in the cabin again.

Dix dug around in his ammo cans and found what he was looking for. Several years ago he had ended up with ten rounds of 30-06 armor piercing bullets from some horse trading. He replaced ten of the hunting rounds in the bandoleer with the armor piercing rounds. Dix had learned long ago that God had given him a gut feeling. His gut feeling had told him that staying on the Mississippi Gulf Coast would be suicide in the event of a collapse. He didn't listen then; but, he was listening now.

It was late afternoon so Dix decided to spend the night where he was, somewhat hidden and out of the current. He was sitting on the deck watching the stars and thinking. He thought about breaking out a bottle of bourbon but the last thing he needed was to start drinking. He would be passing past the Port of New Orleans and the city in the morning, he needed to stay sharp.

The feeling was coming back into his wounded leg and although it was almost healed it took episodes of aching. He suspected that a bone had been clipped as what he thought was a fragment worked its way out of the wound the week before. When it wasn't hurting it was itching; but, at least his toes were no longer numb.

He dozed in the darkness and as usual his dreams were occupied by attempts to save various members of the family. He awoke when he thought his father was calling his name. It was not his father, but Frank with a low growl in his throat. Dix touched him and he quieted; but, Dix could hear what was bothering him. A low rumble from a big diesel engine was coming up the river. A spot light was aimed up the river. Although the pups were still very young, they were very alert, maybe they sensed the stress he felt. They were growing into superb animals and would be an invaluable part of his life or what was left of it. Dix felt like he was on a train out of control and didn't know when it would be derailed again.

He sat quietly with the Springfield across his lap and watched as the vessel slowly plodded its way up stream. The big light never swung his way so he did nothing. He had no way of knowing what or who was in it. It was only after it passed that he had an idea. He could follow it hidden in the dark and no one would hear him as he motored behind it. He could follow it unnoticed all night and with a little luck maybe even past the city.

Releasing the lines and cranking the engine on the catamaran Dix powered into the wake behind the vessel as it slowly made its way up the river. He hung back a couple of hundred yards just out of the wake of the ship. It was not huge as ships go, but it was typical of ships that operated around the Port of New Orleans. The ship slowed as it approached its docking point. Dix slowly went around it in the dark. Its search light was lighting the bank and docks and threw just enough reflected light to see the way into the night. It wasn't until he passed and looked back did he see the helicopters on its deck and the Red Chinese flag on the funnel.

Dix motored on slowly into the night until he was well beyond the city. A bright moon reflected off the water allowing him to see well enough to navigate. The sun was starting to rise when he found a break in the trees indicating the mouth of a bayou in which to take shelter. He turned into the opening and motored up into the bayou until it opened into a lake that at one time was the channel of the river. The Mississippi River has moved and meandered and changed its path countless times over the millennia. This was just one residual vestige of one of the countless meanderings of the old river. In fact locals referred to these lakes as Old River.

Dix turned the catamaran facing out and dropped anchor. There were no camps or human activity on this section so he felt safe for the time being. He fired up the propane stove and boiled a pot of grits. Putting oil in a skillet, Dix fried some Vienna sausages and made some pancakes from biscuit mix. He ate all he could hold and the pups finished what was left. He followed it up with a pot of coffee. It had been weeks since he had allowed himself the luxury of drinking coffee. He had been saving the coffee for trading. He still had the bag of gold and silver that he took from the raiders.

Dix had about 75 gallons of diesel for the catamaran left after topping off the twenty gallon tank; which was way more than enough to make it past Port Gibson, MS, where the Big Black River joined the Mississippi River. If the fishing boat turned out to be too large to navigate the Big Black River, Dix's back up plan was to travel up the Yazoo River, but the Yazoo would take him to Yazoo City, north of Jackson, MS. This area had a tremendous amount of people on welfare and food stamps. The "Road

Warrior" scenario would have occurred and would probably still be in full swing.

He spent the rest of the day listening to the short wave. From what he could understand, the new world order crowd invited the UN to come in and restore order; but, it seemed that the new world order was dominated by the Red Chinese. They were dividing the country up into two sections divided by the Mississippi River. They were rounding up people and putting them in camps, a lot of the very young and the old were simply being executed. Militia groups were forming up and resisting. Our recently elected Socialist President was appealing for calm as he and his fellow Socialists facilitated the takeover. Dix thought, "First, I have to kill sorry dog Americans, now I've got to take on the communists." He thought about the big Red Chinese ship docked in New Orleans. The last thing they would suspect is a lone wolf punching a hole in the bottom. Dix looked around and thought about what he had on hand that could sink a ship. He had his fishing boat that he could use to travel fast and light. He had rifles and ammo and ten armor piercing bullets. He wondered how many men could be aboard a vessel that size. He guessed a dozen or so could run it, so he quickly figured twenty four men assuming two shifts. He had personally killed that many or more in the last few weeks. If he could disable the engine, and cut the lines it might even run aground and block the river. If it sank cross-ways of the river it would block the river possibly for months. He had a battery powered electric drill with three charged batteries and a five gallon jug of gasoline. He pondered; what if he drilled a hole through the side where he could peep through and see the engine. He could take the 30-06 with the armor piercing bullets and put a few rounds through the engine. Then empty the gasoline through the hole and light it through the hole. It would mean one hell of a fire in the bowels of the ship. That's what Dix decided to do.

He waited until dark and fired up his fishing boat. He ran it down the river until he was along side of the ship. He sidled up to the ship and left the engine in gear with the steering wheel turned just enough to keep the boat wanting to push the ship. Once he was satisfied that the boat was somewhat stable he pulled out his drill and drilled a one inch hole through the side of the ship above the rail of his boat. He looked through the hole and saw the huge engine directly across from him. He knew it would be there because he had lined up his boat with the smoke stacks which led down to the engines. He took the can of gasoline and a siphon hose and drained it through the hole. He let the fumes spread for a few minutes, he then took a match, lit it and punched it through the hole. The gas ignited and the flame puffed out of the hole singeing the hair on his fingers and arm. He put the muzzle of the Springfield through the hole and shot into the block of the big engine, firing three shots for good measure. The sound was muffled as the muzzle was inside the vessel. Dix steered around the upriver side and waited until the fire sirens started screaming. He cut the bow line so that the front of the ship slowly started moving away from the dock and out into the river. The rear line now had slack and the ship almost imperceptivity started moving backwards.

Dix replaced the two armor piercing rounds in the Springfield with a full magazine of 150 grain hunting rounds. By this time all hell was breaking loose on the ship. Black smoke was billowing from the hold and the generator quit running, it may have been oxygen starved from the fire. As a result the bilge pumps quit working. He started putting 30-06 rounds into the bridge where he saw people walking around on it. He then refocused his fire into the engine compartments of the helicopters. Jet turbines don't hold up well to 150 grain pieces of lead cutting though them. The huge vessel had built up momentum and soon the slack in the rear ropes was taken up. It was then that the rear rope had reached its limit and broke with a crack. The big ship was officially a runaway.

It was dark when Dix pulled out into the current allowing his boat to drift with the current. He was desperately trying to think of a way to sink the ship since it was now drifting without power and there wasn't a tug in sight to save it. By now the fire was an inferno; he took his time and shot every one he could see on deck. He reloaded four times before they figured out where he was. He finally fired up his boat and disappeared into the night. He idled the boat's engine and watched as the fire soon got completely out of control, apparently there was aviation fuel below deck. Shortly thereafter a tremendous explosion rocked the vessel. The shock wave hit Dix and almost knocked him out of the boat. It never occurred to him that the boat contained munitions. He thought to himself, "the next time you light one up, RUN." The bottom was blown out of the ship and it sank across the channel blocking all access to the port from the South. He chuckled to himself, fired up the boat and headed back to the catamaran. He hated to have used up five gallons of gas, but that was absolutely spectacular!

The sun was coming up when he got back to the catamaran. The pups were glad to see him as he swung around behind the catamaran and tied the fishing boat off to it. He climbed on board the catamaran, fired up the engine and headed back out into the main river. He traveled all day without incident and found another cut off the main river and anchored up for the night. He opened a big can of beans and cooked some more rice. He and the dogs finished off the meal and sacked out for the night. As he lay in his bunk he couldn't help ponder on his life and how everything about him changed. Fifteen years earlier his problems were house notes and school tuition; and it seemed that the weight of the world was on his shoulders. 12 years ago his previous worries were overshadowed by the failing health of his parents and in-laws, and the weight of the world was still on his shoulders. 10 years ago he lost a job and shortly thereafter a hurricane hit, once again the world was on his shoulders. Last year, the candidate fielded by the Communist Party in the United States, was elected President and the economy collapsed shortly thereafter. In the present his entire family was murdered, he had eagerly taken countless lives and relished it. He had sunk a ship and blocked one of the largest river systems in the world to navigation. Now he was laying alone in a bunk, in an old boat, in the middle of nowhere, trying to stay alive with no hope of any type of future and as usual, the weight of the world was resting on his shoulders. His goal for tomorrow was to get as far north as he could and attempt to go up the Big Black River.

CHAPTER 13

HOME ON THE RANGE

"I don't want to wear out my welcome, it's probably time that I hit the road," Porter told Charlie after a week of resting up.

Sandy and Ally hopped up, "Don't you mean we hit the road?"

Bonnie piped up, "Nonsense, we'll let you know when you've worn out your welcome."

"Besides," Charlie said, "You haven't paid for that yearling yet. I figure it will take you at least until next spring before you work off that debt. Winter is fixing to come on with a vengeance and that is no time to be traveling. And there is something you ought to know," Charlie told him solemnly, "War has broken out, the Chinese have landed at Houston and New Orleans, you couldn't make it to Louisiana if your life depended on it right now. From what I hear on the short wave, patriots are forming a resistance and our military at Fort Hood are mobilizing."

Porter piped up, "My grandfather might need me, I need to try and get to him."

"From what you've told me, your grandfather wanted you to be a man, that's why you saved those two girls. You can't help your grandfather by running headlong into a battlefield. From what I can tell those two girls aren't staying here without you; like it or not, you've got a family that you are responsible for. This country is full of mean, desperate people. We Texans have taken care of a lot of them but the country is still full of them. Stay here until spring. Your grandfather is holed up somewhere, you said yourself he was armed and had dogs and a farm. You and I both know that you and he are cut from the same mold, look how good you've survived, and he is a lot more savvy and experienced than you."

Porter remembered, "He said he was an airborne ranger in Vietnam, I know he had an M-16 like your rifle, but it shot 5.56 ammo."

"I tell you what Porter, I'll get on my ham short wave radio tonight and see if we can reach someone near him that can get a message to him. I assure you if he was an airborne ranger, the people attacking him are in more danger than he is. You're looking at a former ranger from Vietnam, the only Jones I knew was a guy they called Coony."

"That's him, they called him Coony because he was a Cajun from south Louisiana."

Charlie grinned from ear to ear, "It's a small world, he saved my life, I promise you son, you don't have to worry about him. He was the only man I know who could shoot a quarter out of the air with an M16 shot from the waist. He was my Sergeant for two years and went on dozens of drops into the jungle with me and lived to talk about it. It's settled, if you will stay here until spring, I'll personally go with you to find him. You are part of this family, welcome son."

John told Porter, "You have no idea the respect my dad has for your grandfather, this will be the first fall and winter in my lifetime that your grandfather hasn't come out here to hunt with us. Come on, I'm getting ready to relieve my brother on the North stand, it will take me most of the day to get there so I've got to go. I want you to help me catch my mule so I can show you how to saddle her up. I also want to introduce you to your mule or the gelding, I recommend the mules; they're a lot more reliable and durable, but that's up to you."

They used a bucket with a little crushed corn in it to entice the animals over to the barn door. John gave them some loose ears of corn as a treat. "Hook that lead on his halter, Porter and lead her into the barn. She'll stand still because she is accustomed to being ridden almost every day. Your mount will have to be tied to that post until he gets accustomed to you. Take that halter off and put on her bridle and bit." After Porter put on the bridle he grabbed a saddle blanket and put it across her back. Next he picked up the saddle. It was heavier than he expected and he wasn't sure he could throw over the mule's back. He pulled the stirrup over the top of the saddle and heaved it over his head and over the back of the mule. Had the mule moved, it would have landed on the ground. The mule just stood there, she didn't seem to care one way or the other.

John clapped him on the shoulder, "Great job, I was wondering if you could figure it out on your own." From there they cinched the saddle up and put the leather strap across her chest. This was fleece lined, John explained that for some reason the strap seemed to chafe her without the fleece. Next he put on some saddle bags. Porter ran to the Rokon and got the jug of jerky, "I've got something you can chew on while you ride."

"Thanks Porter, I'll sure take you up on that, now let's go pick out your ride." Porter chose the last mule and gave him an ear of corn; he figured it would be a good idea to get on his good side. This mule knew the ropes, he looked as old as the hills and smelled terrible. He nuzzled Porter, almost knocking him down. They took the jerky to the house and filled up a canvas bag for John to carry with him. Porter watched from the porch as John rode out of sight heading north.

That night just as he promised, Charlie made contact with a ham operator near Jonesville, LA. They knew Coony Jones and verified that he was alive and well. They promised to get word to him about the fate of his son and family and that Porter was alive and safe with his friend Charlie Cross. They agreed to have Coony radio back in several days or to have a message for them then. Porter was relieved to know his grandfather was ok and agreed to help on the ranch unless his grandfather told him otherwise.

His mule's name was Dollar and would come when Porter called his name. An ear of corn or a biscuit helped reinforce the action and ultimately the bond. Dollar would even come into the barn without being led and allowed Porter to saddle him up with no problems. Dollar let Porter and Sandy ride double around the ranch house. Once Ally saw them she had to ride also. Porter figured she was family too, so he gladly gave her rides. Porter ask Mr. Charlie how come the mule was named Dollar. "Well you see, I bought a string of mules for my guide business 20 years ago. He was just a colt who's mother up and died. They threw him in for a dollar. I had a mare that had just lost a week old colt and she adopted him. Sometimes they won't accept a strange colt, but she did, so that is how we came to have Ole Dollar."

Most of the days were sent performing chores. Porter found he could split and tote wood. The firewood was harvested from along the rivers and streams on the property. Most of the ranch was semi-arid. It took many thousands of acres to support a small herd. Antelope abounded on the high ground and deer thrived in the river and creek valleys. The windmill powered pumps watered cattle and wildlife alike. Wild hogs wallowed in the mud holes around the water tanks. It was the ideal way of life.

CHAPTER 14

THE JOURNEY CONTINUES

The next day was pretty much uneventful; Dix started the day with coffee again and made more pancakes. He used honey for syrup and felt a little better after eating. He allowed the pups one each and kept an eye out for game. There weren't many deer or squirrels left after several months of hungry people hunting everything that moved. Occasionally he saw people on shore fishing. Once some people beckoned to him to stop, but he couldn't take the chance. He could hear his mother's voice in his head saying, "We need to check on Sister." The little Yanmar diesel ran on without fail. It was burning about ten gallons a day. He had more than enough fuel to make it up the river and to return if necessary. When running downstream his fuel use was almost nonexistent. All he had to do was keep enough power on to position the boat in the current.

He didn't make it all the way to the Big Black that day or the next two; but he did make it north of Natchez on the third day and was able to get into the old river just north of town. He knew that there were camps on the lake, but the river was very high and he knew that most of the camps would be abandoned. He motored in and found an old man running trot lines. The old man looked up surprised to see someone in a boat. He asked, "Want to buy some fish?"

"Whatcha got?"

The old man answered, "I've got about 30 river cat, I can't eat em all and there ain't no place to freeze em."

Dix's eyes narrowed, "I've got a hundred dollar bill in my pocket for a mess."

The old man looked up and smiled, "I still got some toilet paper, what I need are bullets."

Dix looked at the .22 rifle lying across the boat seat and the .22 pistol on his belt. "How about I give you five bullets a fish? I could use five."

"Deal," the old man agreed. They made the exchange and talked for a minute.

"How have you survived this long, old man?"

The old man slyly grinned, "I live in one of the camps up at the Old River boat landing, it's about 20 feet in the air and I can pull up my stairs. The river has been up almost the whole time and my place is junky enough to ignore." Dix counted out 25 bullets and took the fish.

The old man offered, "I'll skin and clean them for ten more bullets." Dix smiled, "That's a Deal."

Dix didn't need to waste the ammo on the fish, but he needed a friend if he made it back this way. Dix let him know, "The Chinese are landing in New Orleans; you might spread the word to everyone around that a battle is coming, and this battle will be just as bad as or worse than what's already happened. The Chinese are bringing bombs. By the way, my name is Dix Jernigan; I don't believe I caught yours?"

"I'm Bob Boyer most people call me Beagle Boyer. I've spent my whole life fishing and selling fish around this country, you any kin to Eugene Jernigan?"

"That's my Dad, he grew up over around Jonesville, LA."

"Why, I knew your Daddy my whole life, he was about ten years older than me. Yep, we're 3rd or 4th cousins on his mother's side of your family."

Dix smiled, "It's a small world."

The old man had the fish cleaned in the time they were talking; you could tell he had cleaned many a mess of fish in his day. Dix said, "Throw the heads and guts in this can and I'll cook them for the dogs."

"Your dogs eat as good as most people nowadays; I've had people swap me things for the guts they'll eat 'bout anything when they're starving."

The sun was setting and the old man said, "I need to get back before dark."

Dix offered, "If you tie up, I'll motor you on down to your camp."

"No, I find it better if I don't run any motors around when I can help it. A running motor attracts the wrong kind of attention, if you know what I mean."

Dix needed to know, "Will I be ok here tonight?"

"The only way someone can get here is by water, either from the river or from the lake up past my camp. Those Cur dogs should alert you if someone is trying to sneak up on you."

Dix watched the old man slowly paddle the old aluminum boat back down the lake until he disappeared into the night. A light fog was floating over the top of the water. Dix dredged the fish in corn meal and fried them up. He boiled the heads and skins and fed them to the pups, they didn't turn them down. Later that night, as he lay awake in his bunk, he heard a gunshot from way down the lake. He wondered if the old man was ok or if he was hunting or if some bad guy was now floating in the lake. He drifted off to sleep and once again dreamed of trying to save someone in his family. This time it was Jake who needed to get stitched up.

When he woke up it was already light, the sun was shining and it looked like it might be a pretty day. One of the pups spotted something in the water. A gentle current was flowing out of the lake and towards the river. A large man was laying face down in the water and drifting along in the current. A small red hole, just above and in front of his ear, came into view as he slightly bobbled in the water. It was the size hole that a .22 long rifle round would make. Dix took a boat hook and rolled him over in the water, his pockets were wrong side out, it looked like old man Beagle took care of business last night. Dix shoved the body into the current and watched as it drifted down the channel and out into the river. It would join countless others on its way to the Gulf of Mexico.

Dix cooked some more pancakes and he and the pups ate. The pups had figured out that pooping in the cabin was not a pleasant thing to do, particularly when they were caught in the act.

The little diesel cranked right up, Dix made a slow wide circle pulling the fishing boat and headed out into the river. He glanced down the river and found it empty so he headed into the middle of the channel and slowly made his way north. It was middle of the afternoon before he found the mouth of the Big Black River. He kept running up the river until he found a cut running into the Big Black, he estimated that he was somewhere near Grand Gulf, MS. He found a very isolated place where he could tie up and leave the catamaran. It was out of sight of the river, someone would have to be in a boat to reach his spot. He tied limbs all over the cat and camouflaged it so that at a glance you wouldn't notice it from the river or the bank. He cross tied it so that it could rise and fall with the river without having the rope sink it. He hoped that a falling river wouldn't set it on a stump or sand bar in case he had to come back. He spent the night on the catamaran and spent the empty hours packing up the equipment he might need.

Dix loaded up his fishing boat with the gear that he organized the night before. He had two magazine pouches with six thirty round mags in each. He put in the Springfield and a bandoleer of ammo. He also put in a can of .223/5.56 ammo for the AR15 and a can of 30-06 for the Springfield. He had his Browning 9mm and four 13 round magazines for it. He would wear the Browning in a shoulder holster with a magazine in it and two attached to the holster. The fourth he would put in his bugout bag. He put in three cases of MRE's in the front compartment of the boat and had seven loose in the bugout bag. He had a tool box in the boat, duct tape, flat fix and pump for the four-wheeler, electrical tape, etc. in the boat. He had a fold up hunting knife in his back pocket and a Kbar on his belt. He had to make the assumption that he may not make it back to the fishing boat or the catamaran.

He was finally ready; he topped off the fuel in the boat and put the remaining cans of gas in the bottom of the boat. He topped off the oil in the automatic oiler for the two cycle outboard motor and stowed the rest for later use. He slowly motored away from the camouflaged catamaran and headed up the Big Black River. The river was up as it had been raining. The fact that the river was up would work to his favor; a lot of the stumps and logs would be submerged below the depth of his motor. His motor had been set to tip up in the event it hit a stump or the bottom. Ben and Frank weren't sure about the boat at first; but were soon standing on the bow barking at birds. Dix kept the speed dead slow, he was going no faster than a fast walk.

He consulted the GPS and compared it to his map as he tried to determine his position. The weather was still cold, it was late February, and he had his cold weather gear as well as a sleeping bag and a big tarp. He would be camping at least one night on the river maybe two. He didn't stop when he passed near Port Gibson or when he passed under the bridge on the Natchez Trace. There were some people on the Natchez Trace Bridge. They stood for a moment and then ran off down the road. Dix kept looking over his shoulder and saw that several men had joined the one that ran away. He was far enough upstream that they were foiled in whatever plans they were concocting.

Dix was surprised to see a doe and two yearlings cross the river, he thought the deer population was surely decimated by now, but it would take more than a year to kill them all. Life goes on sometimes.

He found a sandbar on a bend in the river about 20 miles northwest of Port Gibson. He built a very small fire just up from the boat. The pups slept plastered up against him during the cold night. Only once in the night did they growl. Dix woke up and listened, an owl off in the distance hooted, somewhere back down the river another answered. Ben and Frank growled real low. A reassuring pat quieted them as they lay in the darkness. It was a bright starry night. Far off to the north an airplane's flashing light slowly cut a path across the sky. During normal times, you could find a jet's flashing lights in almost any direction at almost any hour. A meteor flashed almost overhead and fizzled out. Dix thought, "I guess I need to make a wish." He thought a minute and wished, "I wish I could wake up from this nightmare." He dreaded dozing off because with it came the endless nightmares and the horrible loneliness that followed.

The nightmare came to a head around daylight this time, the first man he killed was coming for him and he had to get a shot off before the killer could raise his shotgun. Dix woke up standing by the bed with his pistol in his hand. Ben and Frank looked puzzled. Dix shook his head; it had been a bad one this time.

Dix washed up in the river and broke out a couple of MRE's. He ate one and let the pups split another. He fed them the one with the omelet, he hated those but the pups didn't mind at all.

The river had dropped a little overnight and he had to rock the boat back and forth a little to free it from the sand bar. He ran the boat around logs and debris and through deep quiet sections. According to his GPS he was not far from a road that would take him to his sister's place in the country. All he had to do was find a place where he could off load the four-wheeler and drive it off the river.

He found the spot where cattle had been coming down to drink. It was a small landing where someone kept an aluminum boat. He ran the boat sideways to the bank with the four-wheeler facing the bank. A large tree was halfway up the bank, he could get it off here, getting back on would be another story. Maybe he could load it back if found some big boards. He ran the winch line over to the tree. He got back in the boat and on the four-wheeler and cranked it up. He put it in low and started taking up slack with the winch. The boat tipped a little and that was all that was needed to allow the four-wheeler to go over the side. It scratched and gouged the aluminum rail pretty bad, but having a pretty boat just wasn't important any more. A working boat was what was important at this period of time. After unloading the four-wheeler and hooking up its trailer, it was time to load up. He could easily travel the distance to his sister's place. In addition to food and various gear from the boat, he loaded a tool kit along with an axe, wrecking bar, and bolt cutters. He topped off the fuel tank and put in four extra cans of gas in the trailer. He wore the AR15 and Browning 9mm. He strapped the Springfield on the four wheeler gun rack. Once again he had to assume that he might not make it back to the boat so he had to go heavy. He would abandon gear if necessary but not until it was necessary. He tied the boat on a long line and shoved it out into the river; hopefully the boat would still be floating after the river dropped. A small river like this reacted to rain or the lack thereof with big swings in its depth depending on how much rain it receives.

He drove slowly up the trail leading out of the river bottom. He wanted to let the little catahoulas run until they got tired. It wasn't long before they rode up behind a big barn. Dix eased around it and found nothing special. The puppies tanked up in a tractor tire track full of water. They were still young enough that they squatted when they peed. He chunked one in the trailer the other on the back of the four wheeler, they caught on pretty quick and loved the ride. All the time in the boats helped. He pulled the GPS out of the bugout bag and turned it on. He punched his sister's address in and waited. Luckily the satellites were still functioning; a time would come in the near future when they would go quiet. He was only 11.3 miles from her house.

Dix saved the location in the GPS but also found a broken bottle and some beer cans and he left them next to the road where he entered the road. He stopped and took in his surroundings. He could see the top of the barn from here and noted that a large pecan tree was standing in the field directly south of his location. He had driven this road before, but had never stopped to notice anything. He fired up the four-wheeler and headed down the road. All was quiet, no roadblocks, he headed around a curve and found a wrecked pickup in the ditch. A dump trunk was sitting on the side further down. He passed a small farm with a double wide house-trailer; there was a man on the side running a tiller in his garden. He never heard them pass. Dix thought, "Letting your guard down like that could get you killed in these times. But you never know, his wife could be sitting under a tree with a 12 gauge.

When he got to the driveway gate of his sister's house he found it open; that was not a good sign. There were also the skeletal remains of a man near the gate. The skull had rotten teeth; it wasn't the skull of anyone he knew. He ran down to her house and found it open and ransacked. He found a note taped to her oven door. It simply said, Dix: We have taken the kids and grandbaby and have gone to the camp. Lucy...............

He noticed that there were spent cartridge casing on the floors, and bullet holes in the wall. However, there was no dried blood. Knowing Lucy, she probably cleaned it up before they left. Dix was relieved; they didn't try to fight it out here. In all probability they were alive and well. He started to head back to the boat; but the fact was he didn't know for sure if they were ok. He checked his Mississippi map and consulted his GPS. It was about a 75 mile trip one way to their camp. That was easily doable on the four-wheeler.

He topped off the tank in the four-wheeler and drove down behind the barn to where the bulk fuel tanks were kept. He tapped them with his foot and from the sound thought there might be some left in one of the tanks. He slid a shovel under the back and tilted up the rear of the tank. He kicked a brick under it and went back to the front and unscrewed the pump. He cut a piece of water hose from the spigot on the barn and poked it to the bottom. He was able to drain almost five gallons from the bottom of the tank. He had a full tank and four full cans in the trailer. That should be enough to get him there and back. He filled his canteens from the pond, tied down his gear and loaded up the pups. Three months ago Dix would not even considered traveling in broad daylight. But he really didn't give a damn at this point. If someone wanted to take him so be it, they just better hope they can hit what they were shooting at. Dix took the back roads avoiding the interstate. He didn't want to be exposed from the air. The Chinese would soon be patrolling by air; he wasn't exactly equipped to fight aircraft.

He was surprised he hadn't run across more people. He passed a few obviously abandoned homes and there were lots of abandoned cars. He came up on a farm with a lot of activity. They had the road blocked and waved him down. The guy stopping him had a gun on his hip but left it holstered. Dix rolled up and asked, "How you guys making it up here? I'm Dix Jernigan from Gulfport."

The guard answered, "I'm Alan Johnson, we have a group of 100 families living here and farming about 1000 acres. We are what's left of about five church groups who forted up here."

Dix asked, "You don't happen to have Pete and Lucy Jackson in here with ya'll do ya?"

Alan shook his head, "I know Pete and Lucy, they left out for the deer camp about the time we were forting up here. The food stamp crowd went absolutely berserk when the food ran out. We're the only law enforcement in the area. How do you know the Jackson's?"

"Lucy's my sister, my entire family was murdered several weeks ago, I've been fighting almost nonstop since. I'm making this run to check on Lucy and her family, if they are ok, I'll be making a run down into Louisiana to check on some of my mother's people."

"Do you need to rest a few days, we're chronically short of food other than corn; but, I can offer you some corn bread, we have an entire silo full of corn. We have fuel for tractors and tillers as we travel mostly by horse. We wound up with all the horses that the food stamp junkies didn't eat."

Dix nodded, "I appreciate the offer; but, I'd like to try and get up to their camp before dark. I don't know if you have a short wave or have heard; the Chinese are landing. Our wonderful communist President has invited them in. I ran into them in New Orleans a week or so ago."

"We're working on a defense right now; the Chinese are already running into resistance. Saboteurs sunk one of their ships in the middle of the Mississippi river at New Orleans. Did you see anything?"

Dix chuckled to himself, "I thought I heard an explosion after I passed the city. I suggest you mine all the bridges around here so you can limit their movements, you might leave a main one up in order to channel them into one spot for ambush."

Allen nodded, "I'll pass on your suggestions."

"Is there anything you know of that I need to avoid up the road?" Allen thought for a minute, "There is a group of folks about 40 miles up the road you'll run in to. We have an agreement, you'll need to put a piece of this yellow police tape on the front and back of your rig or they'll shoot first."

Dix tied the tape on and waved goodbye. As expected he was stopped about 40 miles further down the road. They were friendly enough and knew Pete and Lucy and in fact had been trading with them. Dix topped off his fuel and proceeded to the camp.

A one lane dirt road led up to the camp; it was located on about 1000 acres and was very isolated. Half way up the hill there were two posts, each had a human skull on top, a warning to whoever came this way. Dix was greeted by a big black lab barking through the metal gate.

Pete stepped out from behind a tree, "Lucy said you would probably come checking on us. Where's the family?"

Tears welled up in Dix's eyes, "They're dead; all of them are dead. I've been fighting almost nonstop for the last few weeks." Lucy came running up and threw her arms around him. Dix sobbed, "They're all dead, and I couldn't save them, even with all my preparations."

Lucy held on tight, "How did you get away?"

Dix stared off into the distance, "I didn't. I killed the raiders, chased them down and killed everyone I could find."

Lucy gasped, "How many?"

"I don't know I didn't count. There were dozens, I just kept killing and chasing until I couldn't find any more to chase and to kill. I went home, buried everyone and laid up until I was healed enough to travel."

How badly were you hurt?"

Dix shrugged, "Just a cut and a bullet through my leg, it's about healed now."

Lucy said, "You'll stay here with us."

"I'll stay a few days and rest up, but then I've got to go check on Uncle Bob and Uncle Joe."

Lucy shook her head, "I don't see how they could have survived, if they went through what we went through, I don't think they could have stood the stress."

Dix frowned, "Maybe our cousins helped them; otherwise, they couldn't have fought off all the human predators."

"You were absolutely right, when you said all the welfare folks would go crazy and boy did they!" Lucy continued. "We had to shoot three in the house, it was something everyday. We couldn't even sleep, if it weren't for the dog warning us, we'd be dead."

Ben and Frank made friends with the big lab and were soon running around the yard as Dix and Pete walked out to the guard post. "The Chinese are landing in New Orleans according to the shortwave. They are rounding up the healthy and killing the old and very young."

Pete scowled, "They won't be rounding us up, I already have two remote locations on the property set up as hidden bunkers; we've been working on them since we got here. We only had one set of intruders; a couple of their skulls are on those posts."

Dix spent three days at the camp, he gave a lot of thought to staying, but at this point he realized he was going to war. He had absolutely nothing to lose, war was coming. He could either wait or take the fight to the people who caused this disaster.

Pete killed a large wild pig on the second day. They cooked him over a spit. The fellowship was great and Dix slept soundly the night through. Ben and Frank piled up next to him as usual. He ran his hand over the loose skin and felt their soft puppy fur. This was the first night that he slept without the horrible nightmares. Maybe it was the decision on what he had to do. He would head south and take the battle to New Orleans. There were ships to sink and bad guys to dispatch.

CHAPTER 15

THE JOURNEY SOUTH

The next morning he packed up and enjoyed some more pig. Lucy didn't want Dix to leave and tried her best to get him to stay safe with them. Dix appreciated her trying; but, he had made up his mind.

He left them two cans of gasoline and the rest of his MRE's. He had seven in his bugout bag. He had enough fuel in the four-wheeler and in the one can to make it back to the boat. He ran back through the two roadblocks without incident. The folks with all the corn gave him eight pones of corn bread in exchange for a half a box of .22's. He ate one before he left. He stopped at the old barn and pulled off two long boards that he could use to get the four-wheeler back on the boat.

The boat was still floating and undisturbed. The river had dropped about a foot and that actually helped with the angle of the boat in relation to the bank. Dix tied the front and back of the boat so that it was positioned sideways to the bank. He took the boards and made a ramp over the side. He slowly drove the four-wheeler up the boards and over into the boat. He almost went over the handle bars when it dropped into the boat. An injury here could be fatal even if it were minor. He unloaded the trailer and stowed everything on the boat. He then upended the trailer as before and tied it down on top of the four-wheeler. He was still running off the 12 gallon tank on his boat and had not had to get into the large 20 gallon tank. He swapped tanks so that in case he had to open up and run fast he wouldn't have to worry about running out of gas at an inopportune moment. Topping off the oil in the oil reservoir, he loaded up Ben and Frank and headed downstream. He was feeling guilty about bringing them, where he was going they would be in danger too. He needed them as much for companionship as he did for their ability to help him stay alert. They both had a favorite stick to chew on as they lounged on the back deck.

Dix was losing track of time, he knew spring was close as flower bulbs were trying to bloom. He almost reached for his cell phone to check the date before he remembered he no longer carried it. It didn't much matter one way or the other, his mission wasn't tied to a calendar or clock. His mission was simple. He was going to kill bad guys and destroy their equipment or steal it if possible.

He camped on the same sandbar that he slept on a week earlier. He pulled out his fishing rod and used a piece of pig liver that he kept from Pete's slaughtered pig. He gave most of the liver to Ben and Frank, who made short work of it. He cast a small piece of liver on a hook into a deep hole near the far bank. He let it sit on bottom and waited. He had a small fire going behind him and the sun was going down. He was surprised when the line started running out. He gave it a jerk to set the hook and pulled in a nice two pound catfish. He fashioned a tennis racket shaped basket out of willow limbs so he could hold the fish over the fire. He gutted and skinned the fish and held it over the fire in the basket. It was crispy on one side and flakey on the other. The texture was interesting but it didn't taste bad. The night was uneventful, and the nightmares returned, which was no surprise. He was extremely lonely, especially in the morning. He missed his family, and he found that he wanted to get even with the people who were the cause of this. If he survived the coming battle with the Chinese communists, the next battle would be with the American communists.

The next day as Dix made it under the Natchez Trace Bridge he realized that there was a rope across the river. It snagged his boat and stopped him dead in the water. He still wore his pistol and had his AR15 strapped on his torso. It rode behind him under his jacket. He pulled out his Kbar knife and reached to cut the rope, bullets started hitting all around him. He dove behind the four wheeler and turned to see several men on the bridge. He rolled onto his back in the bottom of the boat and started shooting with the AR. He hit two of them, they fell forward off the bridge, and the other fell back. One landed dead on the back of the boat almost on top of Ben and Frank. They both jumped on the body growling and biting. For three month old puppies they were doing a good job.

The boat was leaking water through the bottom but it wasn't anything the bilge pump couldn't handle. He would have to try and patch it when he could get it out of the water. Dix cut the rope and let the boat drift down the river and kept an eye out on the bridge. The idiots couldn't hit what they were shooting at. He rolled the dead man off the side of the boat after cleaning out his pockets of any gold or silver. He fired up the motor and ran on downstream past Port Gibson before stopping to rinse off the blood and puppies using a bucket and river water. Coming to a sandbar not far from the Mississippi River, Dix ran the boat up on it. He got out and used the butt of his Kbar and knocked the aluminum on the bottom of the boat back in shape where the bullets had passed through. He whittled plugs out of a piece of cypress and pounded them into the holes. He hammered them in as far as he could, then trimmed the plugs off close. The plugs would swell once they were wet under the boat and would last until he could weld the aluminum. The boat had a double hull with foam filling; it wouldn't sink, even if the bilge pump didn't work. The problem was: it wouldn't maneuver well if it had a lot of water in it.

He ran out into the river and back up to the cut where he hid the catamaran. It was just as he left it, he almost felt like he was coming home. He unloaded his gear and dumped off the camouflage and tied his fishing boat behind it. It was almost dark, so he decided to spend the night. No one could really sneak up on him here. They would have to come through the woods on his west side to approach and Ben and Frank would not miss the noise that would make. If they came from the river they would have to be in a motor boat.

The catamaran had a shower; so, Dix fired up the water heater and bathed. He took a pone of cornbread and mixed up some powdered milk to pour over it. It wasn't especially good, but it was very filling and the dogs absolutely loved it. He spent the evening listening to the shortwave. The Chinese were still trying to remove the ship from blocking the port. They were forced to land at smaller ports and were meeting heavy resistance in some areas.

American troops under loyal commanders had seized control of the US government. A provisional government had been formed, their stated goals were to restore the constitution and free elections would be forthcoming once the foreigners were expelled. They had liberated several FEMA camps and replaced the prisoners with congressmen and any lobbyist they could identify. A number of governors and state representatives were also being rounded up.

One of the main problems facing the American troops was the lack of men, many of them had deserted and gone home to save their families. A lot of them had formed bands of raiders like the ones Dix had recently killed. Still others were in the local militias. The radio also said that a lingering major problem was the bandits that were still running loose, robbing, killing, and raping. And of course, there were the ones who agreed with the Communist President and still supported him. These were mostly still in the Washington area and were helping guard the old government with the help of the Chinese.

The Chinese were coming from the West Coast moving east and also from the Gulf Coast moving north. The short wave station would only broadcast about 3 minutes at a time before they moved. The old Federal employees in the FCC and in some of the loyal Federal police agencies were trying to shut the independent short wave stations down. The Feds were trying to keep the state media up and running. NPR never left the air. CNN stayed on until some Patriots hit their satellite uplinks and took out their broadcasting studios in three locations. After that they couldn't get anyone to work.

Dix shut off the radio and tried to sleep, he was glad there was resistance besides himself. He had to decide if he would try to join a militia or go freelance. He looked in the mirror as he brushed his teeth. He didn't recognize the man looking back. He had lost all the extra weight he had carried for years, he was wind burned and bearded and there were deep lines around his eyes. What would Mattie think if she could see him now? He thought about his mother and dad and wished he could see them just one more time. He cleaned Jake's rifle and wiped down the Springfield. He broke down his Browning and cleaned the dust out of it. He also pulled out Jake's Browning and cleaned it, he would always be ready. Sleep didn't come easy.

The next morning he split another pone of corn bread with Ben and Frank. It was a cool rainy day when he cranked up and headed down the river. The rain and mist almost obscured the catamaran out in the middle of the stream.

Dix found a grounded tug on a huge sandbar in the river. He motored over to see if there was anything of value on it. He tied off to the tug and called out, "anybody home?" He beat on it with the back of an axe to see if he could get anyone's attention. It was then that he noticed a trail in the sand heading away from the tug and across the sandbar. He climbed on board and found the tug abandoned. He pumped diesel out of the tanks and once again had his tanks on the catamaran topped off as well as all his empty five gallon cans and the 55 gallon drum full. That gave him about 150 gallons of diesel. He also cleaned out the galley of canned goods, oil, flour and other items. The crew quarters were empty of clothes and personal items, it had apparently been abandoned. Dix found the Captain's log and read the last entry. It simply said, "Beaching below Vicksburg so Captain and crew can walk home. Radio reports indicate that Chinese troops have taken New Orleans and are confiscating tugs and imprisoning crews as they arrive."

The tug was firmly aground, unless the river rose, which it would sooner or later, this tug wasn't going anywhere. Dix had no idea if he could operate the vessel, he didn't know if he could even crank it. He found the generator controls and gave it a try. The generator roared to life. He then located the controls to the starter engines and fired them up. He engaged the transmission and clutches that engaged the main engines. The big engines started to turn, black smoke started coming out of the stacks and soon the big engines were running. Dix shut everything down but the generator, secure in the knowledge that he could crank and run the beast.

He didn't find anything else he could use, space was limited on the catamaran and he was tying stuff on the deck as it was.

The tug had a washer and dryer so he used the opportunity to do laundry. This was the first time in weeks that he felt human. You don't realize how disgusting a man can become with dirty clothes and a dirty body; until you're inside that body. Next he ran a water hose from the tug to the catamaran and refilled the water tanks. The one luxury aboard the catamaran was a toilet with a shower, it sure beat sitting on the rail and going over the side. The refrigerator ran on propane; but, Dix didn't use it, instead he saved the gas for cooking. He didn't even use the gas for heat but relied on warm clothes and the ability to get out of the wind and weather in the cabin. He found a gas grill strapped to the railing next to the pilot house. Evidently they liked to cook out when they had an opportunity. He relieved it of its propane bottles; he would use them when the tank he was using on the catamaran ran dry. He cast off the catamaran and continued the trip south.

He found the Old River outlet on the Louisiana side of the river at Natchez and motored up into Old River. He ran slow hoping to catch a glimpse of old man Beagle Boyer. A couple of miles down the Old River he came to Old River boat camp. He found the old man working on nets under his camp. Beagle hollered out, "You ready for some more catfish? I've got a fish box full."

Dix smiled, "You betcha." Ben and Frank enjoyed running up and down the bank and splashing in the water, while old man Beagle had a mess cleaned and ready for the fryer. The price was the same, twenty five .22 bullets but he exchanged the cleaning for one of the pones of cornbread.

Dix asked, "Do you mind if I leave my boat here a few days, I want to travel over to Jonesville to check on some of my people."

"You may have a little trouble getting past Ferriday, they pretty much clean out anyone passing through."

"Who's doing the cleaning?"

Boyer scratched his head, "The old mayor has set up a little fiefdom over there, he's using the town marshal and police to enforce a road tax; if you put up a fuss they kill you or put you on the chain gang. Otherwise they let you leave with your clothes and nothing else."

Dix shook his head, "I'm surprised the locals are tolerating it. Where have they set up the stop?"

"They have three places, one on Hwy 84 east of town, one on Hwy 84 west of town, and one on the highway heading up to Clayton."

"How many men does it take to accomplish this?" Beagle thought for a minute, "Oh, they've got at least 25 or 30."

"Has anybody just tried shooting them?"

Beagle chuckled, "They keep a sniper hid back that takes out any resistance that the traffic stop can't handle."

Trying to think of all the angles, Dix asked, "Can I negotiate with a prepayment to let me pass?"

"Oh sure, you can pay them up front then they clean you out when you show up to go through anyway."

Dix decided, "We're at war, and as far as I'm concerned, they are the enemy."

"Well boy, I agree with you. The mayor was a tremendous supporter of our new communist President. In fact, he delivered more votes for him than we had residents in the Parish."

Dix nodded, "Enough said. I'd just as soon do battle here as anywhere, the reason my family's dead and buried is because of bastards like him and his minions. I'll start in the morning."

Beagle wanted Dix to be sure of what he was taking on, "Do you have any idea of what you're up against?"

Dix told him, "In the past six weeks I have killed more men than he's got; in fact, I think I killed that many in a day!"

CHAPTER 16

ONE MAN WAR

The next morning Dix slept until he woke up. He cooked enough pancakes for himself, Beagle and the pups. Dix told Beagle, "I've got a proposition for you: I'll give you a box of .22's if you'll watch the pups until I get back in a couple of days. You can eat what you need, and in the event I don't make it back you can have my boats and gear, with the understanding that you take care of Ben and Frank."

"You got a deal, son. I wish I could take the bastards out myself, I think my brother is in a work gang in there."

"I'm not going to stop until I kill them all or get killed." Beagle proudly shook his hand, "Well, good luck son."

Dix decided not to take the four-wheeler; but, to go in on foot. He took his Springfield, a bandoleer that held 25 cartridges, and put five more boxes in his pack. That gave him 125 - 30-06 rounds. He took his Browning 9mm with four extra magazines. He also put his 22 Beretta pocket pistol in his pocket. He had a fold up knife in his pocket and a Kbar on his belt. He figured to scavenge an assault rifle from the police if he needed one. He put on his hunting camouflage clothes and picked up a small pair of binoculars he had been packing around for years. He also put a backpacker filter bottle as a canteen on his belt and put four MRE's in his pack. His standard pack had a first aid kit, duct tape, multi tool, etc. He then cut three willow sticks about three foot long and tied them together with a small strip of paracord which would come in handy later.

He crossed over the levee and started hiking toward Ferriday. There was no traffic on the road, he saw a few people in their yards. A couple of men saw him and started in his direction, when he pulled the Springfield around and cradled it in his arms, they stopped and retreated. He walked until he could see the checkpoint in the edge of town. He crossed the road and walked into the overgrown field. It was still full of cotton plants that had never been harvested. The white cotton was drooping and mildewed, some of the seeds were sprouting in the boles.

Sitting in the cotton obscured him from view. He sat and watched as people came and went. They had five deputies working the barricade. People they knew could go through; they were mostly pickup trucks with trailers hauling stuff into the town. He watched one car drive up and the driver and the passenger were executed. One of the deputies took the car and drove it through the barricade; two more deputies drug the bodies over to the ditch and shoved them in. Dix raised his binoculars and carefully surveyed the area for the sniper back up. He soon spotted him sitting on a platform on the side of the old cotton compress building. He was about 400 yards away. He spent another 30 minutes making sure there was only one sniper.

Dix took the three willow sticks and opened it as a tripod. He then used the fork created on the top of the tripod as a rest for the barrel of the Springfield. He cranked the Trijicon scope up to

9x power and sighted in on the sharpshooter. Dix wanted to put the 150 grain bullet somewhere in the torso of the sharpshooter. The rifle was sighted dead on at 200 yards. He estimated about a six to eight inch drop at this distance. From this angle he placed the crosshairs on the sniper's chin and ever so gently squeezed the trigger. The big rifle barked and a scant heartbeat later the sharpshooter's heart turned to jelly. Dix didn't wait for him to drop; he knew that the shooter had made his last shot.

He quickly sighted in on the men at the barricade, they had heard his shot but it had not occurred to them that they were the target. They were only about 300 yards away. Dix could only see the head of one of the deputies. He put the crosshairs directly on top of the man's head and squeezed off another round. The man never knew what hit him; his head exploded showering his companions with its contents. The others dove for cover; he could see a portion of a leg hanging out from behind a tire they were using in the barricade. Dix put the crosshair just above the knee. The 150 grain bullet hit the leg about an inch below the knee. He jumped when the bullet struck and rolled into full view. The next shot went long ways though his body. The contents of his stomach and bowels were dispersed in a spray like pattern over the remaining two deputies. The only shot he had of the other two was an elbow sticking out from behind a tree. He hit it and reloaded.

He figured they would have radioed for help by now and that help was on the way. Dix got down on his hands and knees and crawled through the cotton patch until he was close to the road that intersected the highway where they had their barricade erected. As expected an SUV full of deputies arrived from in town. Just as they pulled to a stop, but before they could get out, Dix started shooting 150 grain bullets through the cabin of the SUV. The windows and metal doors offered little resistance to the fast, heavy 30 caliber bullets. They passed through the SUV, through the passengers and out the other side. Only two made it out of the doors and they were not on their feet. All but one of the deputies just had a 30-06 caliber bullet pass through their bodies. Dix found the uninjured deputy trying to drag his comrades out of harm's way. He dropped him like a sack of potatoes. He looked and found the last one, the one missing an elbow. He was crouched behind a pile of tires Dix put him down with a shot through his midsection.

Dix had cleaned out half of their forces in less than 20 minutes. He reloaded and refilled his bandoleer from his pack and headed south toward the road leading to the barricade on the west side of town. He would be traveling through a section of town where he didn't expect to find any friends. This section of town was dominated by welfare recipients living in government housing. There was no way to know if they were friendly, hostile or indifferent. Dix stuck to the west side of the road as this was an industrial area and he could retreat into an area of cover. The government housing was on the opposite side. Most of it looked abandoned. The poor fools probably starved to death when the food stamps quit working. They blindly voted themselves free benefits only to find out that they had voted themselves out of groceries.

Once again Dix slowly worked his way around until he was within sight of the next barricade. He knew that each checkpoint was covered by a sharpshooter. He crawled under an abandoned 18 wheeler where he could look out from behind the rear dual wheels. They would also provide a little protection if they were taking shots at him. He soon spotted what he was looking for. The sharpshooter was on top of the old farm supply store. He was on alert as he had gotten news of what had happened at the other checkpoint. Dix counted five more deputies on the ground behind the barricade. He wondered how much help these would get once the shooting started. He noted the location of each of them which was a good 350 yards away.

Their sniper was a about 50 yards closer. He was facing away so Dix placed the crosshairs on the nape of his neck. The bullet struck about two inches below and passed through his upper chest. He pitched forward and fell from his chair on the roof. His rifle rattled as it fell down the metal roof. Dix's second shot hit two of the deputies on the ground. One was hit through the mid section, the bullet continuing on and hit the next one in the arm just above the elbow. Since no one could help him with a tourniquet, the blood loss quickly killed him. The third shot went through the neck of the one trying to see where Dix was shooting from. It was obvious that they had become accustomed to relying on their reputation and numbers. Dix knew he had two more to go but they weren't sticking their heads out.

He decided not to move because they hadn't spotted him yet. He looked around to make sure that he wasn't being flanked by anyone bringing up the rear. They apparently didn't have the numbers or the will to follow up. He sat quietly and took a swig from his water bottle, waiting. He could hear them hollering at each other; but, couldn't make out what they were saying. At once they bolted for their pickup. When they were in and cranking it, Dix started firing rounds through the cab. He knew that all five rounds had gone through the cab. One round went through the passenger door, through both legs of the passenger and burned the top of the driver's leg. The last round went through the back wall of the cab and entered the driver just under his left shoulder blade and continued through his shoulder, destroyed the left arm socket and exited the cab on the far side. Although they escaped the scene both would die from massive blood loss before they traveled a half mile. They ran the truck into an old store front and never left the vehicle. Dix once again reloaded his rifle and refilled the bandoleer from his pack.

Dix thought to himself, "Surely this crowd was not so inept that I could kill 16 of their number and not have one of them even take a shot at me." Evidently they never saw him. He went over to the barricade and found one of their radios. He listened as someone was barking orders. The speaker was ordering them to come at him from two angles. Apparently they weren't sure where he was. Whoever was barking the orders was practically panicking. Dix figured it was Mr. Mayor.

Dix's luck had been nothing short of a miracle. He kept telling himself that the old Springfield rifle was giving him good luck and he had been holding up pretty good. Other than a lot of joint pain he figured he was good shape. His one man war had been a roaring success so far.

He listened to the radio and learned that they were going to converge on his suspected location from two sides. He walked about 250 yards towards town and spotted a large azalea next to an abandoned house. He crawled under it and waited. One group of the mayor's men was going to approach from the east and the others were coming from town. Dix hoped they would be driving. Not quite two minutes later a police cruiser came barreling in his direction down the road from town toward the barricade. When it was within about 350 yards of the barricade they pulled to a stop. That put them at 100 yards from Dix; you might as well say point blank range. Once again he started putting rounds through the passenger compartment of the car. It was a shame they had taken it out of gear and killed the engine. The 30 caliber bullets cut through the car and the passengers and as before, no one walked away. The mayor was practically screaming in the radio when he got no response from the car.

The group coming from the east had stopped and gotten out of their vehicle out of sight of Dix. He reloaded and refilled his bandoleer. He waited; this spot was as good as any. He could see them milling around the barricade and they cautiously approached the shot up car. One of them called the mayor, "Mel's men are all dead. There must be a bunch of them, everyone's dead." The Mayor fell silent for a moment, "get back here! They might be heading this way." They retreated to their SUV accelerating wide open when they flew past Dix's position.

Dix didn't take a shot until they were past and heading away. He shot at the retreating SUV, trying to put the round through the driver's side of the vehicle. The bullet went through the back window, clipping the left ear of the deputy in the back seat. It hit the steering wheel narrowly missing the driver's hand and then through the windshield which became opaque on the driver's side because that's what happens when safety glass becomes a maze of zigzagging lines and miniature pea gravel sized pieces.

The vehicle was traveling about 70 mph when the bullet hit it. The driver panicked, lost control and flipped the SUV. None of them were wearing seatbelts and most were ejected in the street. From about 400 yards Dix shot the ones that tried to get up. He reloaded and headed toward city hall.

The Mayor called back over the radio "How come you ain't here yet."

Dix keyed the radio, "We're coming boss, just hang tight." Dix walked by the overturned SUV and used his pistol to dispatch a couple who were still breathing. He swapped the magazine in his Browning 9mm for a full one and continued to city hall and the police station.

He took his time as he approached the main intersection of town. He cut around the houses to where he could see the checkpoint on this end of town. It was empty as he suspected. He stood out of sight in case the sharpshooter on this end was still in position. Dix sat tight and waited, time was on his side. The Mayor got back on the radio, "Milton, you seen anything yet?" A voice that Dix assumed to be Milton came back on the radio, "I ain't seen nothing yet, I heard some shooting down the road, but nobody or nothing has come by here."

The Mayor ordered, "Stay put, don't you be moving, they'll have to walk right by you to get here."

Dix thought, "Thanks for the tip. That was probably the sharpshooter on this end."

He turned the radio off so as not to expose his position, squatted, got down on his belly and ever so slowly crawled around the corner of a house and under an old Arborvitae tree. From here he could see up the street to the barricade on the north side of town. Milton's sniping position had to be where he could cover the barricade and the road to the City Hall. Dix thought and looked and methodically covered every square inch of the area. From where he lay Dix figured this was one of the only spots that he could cover both locations.

The Mayor got back on the radio. It startled Dix as he thought he had turned the radio down. That's when Dix realized that the voice was not coming from the radio in his hand but from Milton's radio on the porch just above and to the right of where he had crawled. Unknowingly, Dix had crawled up next to the porch where Milton was waiting in ambush.

This was one of those times that he took the luxury of thinking about his family and why he was here. He eased his 9mm out of the holster; it was not cocked so he held the trigger down with his right hand and pulled the hammer back with the other. Ever so easy he released the trigger and then eased the hammer back down. He had silently cocked the pistol. Milton once again told the Mayor to be patient. Dix rolled onto his side. He could see Milton sitting on the porch through the limbs on the Arborvitae. Dix waited. He had the patience of Job. After what he estimated to be an hour, his bladder felt as though it would burst. He could not take a chance of being discovered so he urinated in his pants and waited. He didn't have to wait long. Milton set down his rifle and walked over to the edge of the porch to pee. Dix waited until Milton had his hands full and killed him with the Browning 9mm. He kept firing until the gun was empty. Milton didn't die easy, but he got off a shot from a pistol Dix didn't see, it cut a gash across Dix's head. Dix replaced the empty magazine in his Browning and retreated around the back of the house. He ran his fingers through his new hair part, other than bleeding a little it wasn't hurting yet.

It was about that time the Mayor called Milton, "I heard the shooting, did you get him?"

Dix answered, "Yea boss I got him. I'm hit though I need some help."

The Mayor answered, "We coming boy, hang on."

Dix rolled Milton off the porch so that his body landed and rolled under the Arborvitae bush. Dix sat on the porch in his urine soaked pants and drank from his water bottle. A little blood dribbled down behind his ear. That idiot mayor was hopefully going to come up and Dix was going to kill him too.

It didn't take long for the Mayor and two men to drive up. They were in a big white Cadillac. As soon as he saw the driver put the car in park and kill the engine, Dix fired. Once again they couldn't get out quick enough. Dix had five rounds through the car and them before they could even move and by then it was too late. He reloaded and shot the bodies one more time before coming out from under the shadows on the porch. He called on the radio, "Anybody listenin', the mayor's hurt, we needs help." There was no answer. Dix pulled the bodies out of the car, he noticed people looking out of their windows. He hopped in the car, drove down to city hall and slipped in the back door of the jail.

To the surprise of the guys in jail, Dix opened the door to the cell block shouting, "Who we got in here?" At that moment he recognized his childhood friend, Butch. "Butch, do you recognize me?"

"Damn Dix, you are the last person I expected to walk in this door, it's been over 30 years since I've seen you."

Dix unlocked the door, "I liberated the town, now you're in charge." Butch asked, "Where are your men?"

Dix laughed, "You're looking at the men. I just took my time and killed the S.O.B.'s until I ran out of people to shoot. I'm going back to my camp and I'll be coming back through in the morning so don't shoot me. I'm sure all those men had family so look out, go look at all the bodies and see if any are missing and I'll leave the cleanup to you guys."

They shook hands and Butch grinned, "See ya in the morning."

CHAPTER 17

BACK AT THE CAMP

Dix pulled up in the Cadillac to the boat launch and was greeted by Ben and Frank. Old Man Beagle said, "I see you met the Mayor. I could hear the shooting from here; I figured you were dead and I had me a fancy boat for sure."

Dix told the old man, "Ferriday is cleaned up unless there are some out scavenging that I don't know about."

Beagle nodded, "They're probably all dead; but, if any come back I doubt they'll be sticking around."

Dix cleaned up and shaved his head and face. He smeared his head wound with antibiotic ointment. He looked at the old man, "Can I make it to Wildsville without much trouble?"

The old man pondered a moment, "I haven't heard of anything major, but you never know." With the old man's help he unloaded the four-wheeler and its trailer.

That night they ate fish, beans and cornbread. Dix broke down and opened a bottle of bourbon and for the first time in months mixed a drink with some cola he had found in the tug boat. He slept soundly that night, the events of the day did not weigh on his mind. He had a pleasant dream about him and Mattie making a trip in the motor home. He woke broken hearted again and couldn't help but wish he was dead too. Once again the weight of the world was on his shoulders. He wanted to kill a thousand communists and their enablers for every member of his family that had been killed. His future was destined; he would kill until there were no more to kill or until he was dead.

He opened a big can of sausage, cooked some more pancakes and brewed a pot of coffee. He, Beagle, and the pups ate heartily. The old man told Dix, "If I keep hanging out with you, I'm going to have to go on a diet."

Dix grinned, "Watch my stuff, eat what you need and hopefully I'll be back, if I don't ever come back, use what you can."

He finished loading up the four-wheeler, thought about taking the Cadillac but figured there would be a lot of people who would recognize it as belonging to the Mayor. He didn't want to get shot by someone thinking they were shooting the Mayor. He put the Springfield on the gun rack and put Jake's AR15 on his back. He also had six AK47's and about a 100 full 30 round magazines he found in the mayor's trunk. He brought these in case his uncles and their kids were still alive. He knew they could use more guns and ammo.

He headed out with his usual full battle pack, two magazine pouches with six thirty round magazines in each, a full bandoleer for the Springfield, knifes, Browning 9mm and four full magazines for it. He loaded all the cases of MRE's he could get on the trailer. He was close to using up his supply and really couldn't spare any; but, he had to take care of his Uncles, if they were still around. He gassed up the four-wheeler from gas in the Cadillac.

He also filled up two empty five gallon cans and carried them with him.

When he got to Ferriday he found the barricade manned by guys he had seen at the jail. They eagerly waved him through. Dix waved, "Where's Butch?"

They yelled, "He's on the west end." Dix made it to the west barricade about five minutes later.

Butch slapped him on the shoulder, "We rounded up the two you missed. You left one hell of a mess."

"The President has brought in the Chinese and they're rounding up citizens. I know the Chinese are in New Orleans, I saw them a couple of weeks ago."

"Dix, you're shitting me, right?"

"Butch, I suggest ya'll start planning a defense and put together a militia. Anyone who stands in the way, kill them. I cleaned out Ferriday for obvious reasons. Don't let anyone join your militia that was a supporter of the old government, they are the enemy, just like the Chinese. I would be prepared to blow the bridges around here, or at least funnel them across just one where you can ambush them."

"I'll get started Dix, where are you going?"

"I'm on my way to Wildsville, to check on my uncles, with a little luck, I'll be back in a few days or weeks."

The ride over to Wildsville was pretty uneventful. Dix had made this drive on many occasions over the years. Occasionally, there were abandoned cars and signs of life at some houses; but, most appeared abandoned. Others were burned to the ground. He found the country road leading to his Uncle's House, turned the four-wheeler and headed down it. About a mile down that road he came to the one lane gravel road leading to the farm. Seeing the house in the distance, he turned down the long driveway, going slowly so as not to alarm his uncle or cousins. When he arrived he found what he feared, the house was empty, there were graves in the yard, and a skeleton out under the tractor shed in the back. Dix wasn't sure who the skeleton belonged to, the bones had been scattered. From the size of the shoes, Dix assumed it was one of his Uncle's grandsons. Dix dug a grave next to the others and counted, there were 12 graves; that would account for his two uncles and their families.

The house had been ransacked, all the food was gone as were the guns and ammo. It was a sad day, and once again Dix wondered if he had tried harder could he have made it here in time to save them? Just as with his daughter and husband, had his actions or inactions, led to their deaths?

He fired up and headed south to where some other cousins lived. He found their home burned to the ground and no sign of anyone. He drove down to the family cemetery, there were no new graves. All that remained were memories, so he turned back north and headed toward Jonesville. He didn't try to cross the bridge into Jonesville but first ran down the levee to try and get a look at the other side of the bridge. As expected there was a manned barricade. He watched through his binoculars and observed the activity for several hours. He ate an MRE while he waited.

Apparently it was shift change at the barricade. Through his binoculars he recognized the man arriving as the sergeant from the hospital in New Orleans. He fired up the four-wheeler and headed on in. The Sarge was surprised, "I never expected to see you again in this life, how's Maggie and Doc?"

Dix could hardly get the words out. He whispered, "They're dead along with the rest of my family."

"I am so sorry, Dix. Thanks to you, I got to my family and with my brother we made it home. My family is secure on Dad's ranch. A group of us reformed some military units based at Fort Polk near Alexandria, LA. Some of our officers have set up a provisional government based on the original constitution. We had to battle some of our own troops commanded by some of the President's loyal officers. They folded pretty fast."

It seemed that the only time the communists prevailed was when they had an overwhelming advantage. They didn't have the desire to fight to the death, as those on the American side did. The communists were holding the major cities but the countryside was still open. The Chinese were entrenched at the ports of New Orleans, Houston, and on the West Coast. The Sarge told Dix, "They were delayed in New Orleans by a ship that sunk in the channel."

Dix grinned, "I sunk the ship."

"How in world did you sink it?"

Dix told him about the electric drill, five gallons of gas and some armor piercing bullets. He also told the Sarge about the tug boat on the sandbar north of Natchez in the river.

"Do you have any high explosives? We can probably bring down a bridge or sink the tug in the channel or both and slow them up to give us a chance to kill more. If we can get if off the sandbar, I believe two men and I could run it. I'm sure we could blow a hole in the bottom and sink it in the river or use it to ram a ship or we could pack it full of explosives and take down a bridge. If we could round up enough barges, we could sink them under the bridges and block the river to navigation." "I'll run it back up the line Dix, what are you going to be doing?" "I want to make a run up the road to see my parents." Concerned the Sarge asked, "Do you think they are ok?" "I'm traveling up to the old cemetery in the country." The Sarge understood, "Be careful, but I don't have to tell you that."

The Sergeant gave Dix a pass to use at the checkpoint on the other side of town. He headed north up the highway and turned down a road that went west out into the country. Here again there were scattered signs of people gardening and trying to go about their business. Everyone was armed, Dix was certain there were still bad guys running loose; but, their numbers had thinned out considerably by now. He finally wormed his way around the country until he came to the cemetery. It was somewhat neglected and could have used a good grooming. There were no fresh flowers and all of the solar lights were gone or dead. He spent about an hour sitting on the family headstone and finally broke down and collapsed. He was utterly alone, his sister and her children were all that was left; there was no one else. He had failed to save anyone but himself. He felt himself to be a complete and total failure.

If he went to his sister's, he would be a drain on their resources as soon as the supplies he could carry ran out. Once again he had two choices, he could hole up somewhere and try to hunt and fish like old man Beagle Boyer or he could join the war. He still found himself consumed with taking down the people who had destroyed his life and family. He couldn't help it; it was what drove him. He gathered himself and headed back to town. On the way he ran by his grandfather's old farm house. The old house was still there just as it always had been. The big pine that his uncle had planted 60 years ago was still standing over the house. The barns were gone but the pecan trees planted by his grandfather were still standing.

When he got back to town he found Sarge and told him, "I'm going to continue the fight."

"I figured you would, some guy cleaned out Ferriday a couple of days ago; so see, there are those like you out there."

Dix pointed to the four-wheeler, "See that old Springfield, that's what I used to clean out Ferriday."

Sarge shook his head, "I should have known, head down to the motel, we've commandeered it for housing, we've got a natural gas generator to run the hotel and our command post. We've got water pressure and lights, not much else."

Dix shook his head negatively, "I would feel trapped in the hotel or a house. I've been living out so long that I don't know if I could stand being hemmed up inside. I'm going to travel back to my Uncle's house and camp there. I'll come back in the morning and decide where I'll take a stand."

Back at his Uncle's house he found fresh sheets and drug a mattress into the front room. The propane tank still had gas so he turned on the space heater and warmed up the room. He barricaded the doors and settled in for the night. He ate dinner on the bar in the kitchen. He found some of his Uncle's old paperback books and selected several of the Louis Lamoure westerns to put in his pack. The early evening was uneventful. He finished off the last pone of corn bread and went to bed. He fell asleep and as usual his nightmares returned. This night he was hiding from the mayor and his men, he woke and thought he heard something. Dix turned off the gas logs that were warming the room. The gas logs cast a small amount of light across the room which would enable anyone peering in to see him in the twilight. His four-wheeler and trailer were backed under the carport out of sight, but anyone seeing him come in would covet his supplies.

Dix slipped out a back window of the house. A bright moonlit night enabled him to see. He quietly eased out behind the pump house and spotted two men working on stealing the four-wheeler and trailer. Once he was down on his belly behind the pump house slab, he called out, "If you leave now I won't kill you." They answered with a shotgun blast into the night towards the sound of his voice. Dix instantly spotted the muzzle flash and opened up. He killed one and wounded the other with Jake's AR15. He ran around the back of the house and came at them from the opposite direction. He had no way of knowing he had killed one, but he could tell from the breathing that the other one was hit in the lung. He watched and listened in the dim light as the raspy breathing increased and the man rolled over and was soon quiet. He waited another 30 minutes before moving to make sure that they didn't have any help coming or waiting. He flipped on his green cap light and found what he expected. Two unkempt men lay dead, one had a shotgun he recognized it as his Uncle's. He relieved them of their guns and ammo. He reloaded his AR15 with a fresh magazine and topped off the one he used. He then used the four-wheeler to drag them up to the head of the driveway so everyone would know what would happen if they tried to do the same thing. The rest of the night was quiet.

The overwhelming sadness returned and the firm resolve grew clearer when he woke. He topped off the fuel tank of the four-wheeler and headed to town. The bodies were still lying where he left them. When he arrived he found the Sergeant at their command post. Sarge told him, "Captain Miller wants to see you."

"Who is he?"

"He's our new commander, the old commander's in the brig."

Dix was curious, "What happened to the old commander?"

Sarge explained, "The idiot decided to start confiscating guns to make the town safer, our new government is reinstalling the original constitution, he violated the 2nd amendment, so now he is under arrest. He'll be court marshaled, and executed if convicted."

Dix nodded in agreement, "I can't wait to meet the new guy."

Sarge led him to the motel restaurant where they had set up a command post. Captain Miller looked like a kid with a three day beard. To Dix they all looked like teenagers. Captain Miller looked up, "Are you Dix Jernigan?" Dix nodded yes, and the

Captain stood up, "I want to shake your hand. I've heard what you've been doing."

"I've mostly been trying to keep from getting killed and getting even, I haven't done anything to earn praise. All I have been doing is making people pay for what they've done to me and mine."

Captain Miller nodded, "I'm not concerned with your motives; I'm prepared to offer you a battle field commission if you want to enlist."

Dix chuckled, "I'm too old to enlist, I just want to keep killing bad guys. I would just hinder or hold back a bunch of young guys. I can operate at my own speed and time and be pretty effective. I couldn't even pretend to keep up with you youngsters."

Captain Miller replied, "If you enlist, I'll put a half a dozen men under your command, and you'll conduct a Gorilla action against the Communist Americans and against the Chinese. Our forces have secured a satellite control facility and have diverted satellite control to our headquarters at Fort Polk. A communications man will be part of your team. I can also redirect equipment and troops when available, just don't count on much any time soon, we're doing good just to eat. Constitution troops are still purging their ranks and securing facilities."

"Did Sarge tell you about the tug on the sandbar?"

The Captain nodded, "Do you think you can get it down stream, Dix?"

"If I can get it off the sand bar I can get it down stream, I just don't have a lot of room on my boat for six men and myself. I can take three. What I need are three men who grew up on a farm or around a mechanics shop."

Sarge, who had been silent up until now, spoke up, "Dawson, Jacobs and myself grew up ranching and farming, I've seen the way Mr. Dix operates, I'm sure they'll volunteer."

Captain Miller asked, "Captain Jernigan, what do you say?" Dix shook his head, "I'm not going to join, I'll act as a civilian contractor without pay, and I may need supplies from time to time, but other than that I just want to get even with those bastards."

Captain Miller agreed, "Fair enough, I am putting Sergeant Taylor, and Privates Dawson and Jacobs at your disposal, what do you need?"

Dix thought for a minute, "I need 50 gallons of gasoline in five gallon cans, other than that I need the three men outfitted with rifles, ammo and gear. I've got enough food for the mission."

"Done, when can you start?"

"We can start as soon as you guys get your gear together." Meet me at the first checkpoint in Ferriday. I'm dropping some equipment off to my friend, Butch, and his friends."

Dix topped off the gas in his four-wheeler with his last can of gas. He loaded up and headed back to Ferriday. He found Butch and some of the guys at the checkpoint. Dix asked, "Any problems while I was gone?"

Butch shrugged, "All's quiet now, we finished rounding up the rest of the Mayor's people and all his elected officials. We tried them yesterday and are going to execute them this afternoon."

Dix pointed to his four-wheeler, "I've got five AK47's on the trailer and about 2500 rounds of ammo in magazines for you guys; don't waste your ammo." Butch and his guys eagerly accepted the gift.

Dix told them, "You need to run over to Jonesville and see Captain Miller and tell him you guys are forming up over here, so you can coordinate your efforts. They're part of the new Constitution Army. Also, there is an old man over on the river named Beagle Boyer, keep an eye on him for me, if you can."

Butch nodded, "I remember the old man; we get catfish from him when we can."

About that time Sarge and his men came driving up in a Humvee. They followed Dix over to the boat launch and unloaded their gear. The man driving waved, left the three men and their gear, and headed back in the Humvee.

Dix found old man Beagle paddling back to camp. He called out, "They haven't got you yet?"

The old man grinned back, "They haven't outsmarted me yet."

Dix said, "I want you to unload most of my canned goods, I'm taking these guys on a trip and we won't be taking time to cook. It looks like the river is rising."

"Yep, it's been easing up a little every day; snow must be melting up north."

"I need you to do me a favor, Beagle. I need you to watch Ben and Frank for a while. They might get hurt on this trip."

They unloaded all the food from the catamaran and left enough MRE's to feed them for a week.

Dix called the old man over, "I've got something for you." Dix handed him the 6th AK47 and ten full magazines for it.

"Thanks, I'll take good care of Ben and Frank until you get back."

"I'm leaving the four-wheeler and a can of gas, it's about half full of gas now. That should get you and the boys away in case you have to make a run for it. If you go to Ferriday ask for Butch Erwin and tell him I sent you, he'll help you out if you need it."

"I remember Butch. He's been over here a time or two." "Do you have time for some fried catfish, I just caught a mess."

"You bet, there's always time for a mess of fish." Dix knew that this may be the last time he or the troops would have a hot meal or any meal for that matter.

CHAPTER 18

WATER WAR

They loaded up the gasoline in the fishing boat and tied it behind the catamaran. Ben and Frank had to be tied to keep them from following Dix. Tears were silently running down Dix's face as he motored down the lake heading for the river. He let Dawson and Jacobs run the boat while he wiped down his rifles. He took the Springfield down and gave it a thorough cleaning. Lastly he took his Browning and cleaned it. He slept with the Browning in his hand every night; it was an important part of him.

Dix took over running the boat as they entered the narrow bayou that was the outlet from the lake into the river. He went dead slow out into the river. There was no boat traffic to be seen. They arrived at the location of the tug before dark. The tug was still on the sandbar, but it was visibly higher in the water. Only by firing it up and trying to use the wheel wash would they know if it could be floated free.

Dix ran the catamaran up on the sand bar downstream of the tug and dropped the anchor of the fishing boat. They climbed on board the tug and found it just as Dix had left it. Dix cranked the generator and showed Sarge how he figured out how to crank it. "I think we need to have one of us sleep on the catamaran in case we can't control the tug, that way we can evacuate to the catamaran."

Dix slept on the catamaran that night, while the Sarge, Dawson and Jacobs stayed in the crew quarters on the tug. They took turns standing guard. This was one of the few nights Dix had slept alone since getting the pups; he dozed after a while but didn't sleep well. He kept having the same nightmare over and over. Each time he would wake from it; but, as soon as he dozed off the nightmare resumed where it was. He finally gave up, got up and made a pot of coffee. If this had been any other time or circumstance, the early morning on the river would have been wonderful. Purple martins were swooping down and skimming their bills in the water to drink. The river current was producing whirlpools that seemed to pause in place before moving on. Whole trees could be seen out in the river, casualties from a storm somewhere up north.

He walked over to the tug and joined Sarge, Dawson and Jacobs. They all sat quiet and ate their MRE's. Dix cranked the starter engines and got the big engines turning over. As before, the exhaust stacks started pouring black smoke before clearing up when the engines started firing on their own and getting hot. Dix found the water temperature gauges and watched as the temperature climbed. He disengaged the starter engines and turned them off. The big engines were running on their own. Dix had Dawson take the catamaran with the fishing boat behind it out into the current and upstream to wait. If for some reason they were unable to get the tug free of the sandbar or if they lost a crewmember overboard, it would his job to pick them up.

Dix and Sarge figured out how to engage the drive motors. This tug ran like a locomotive. The huge diesel engines ran generators that, in turn, ran electric drive motors. This tug was operated by joy sticks and computer. Dix tilted the joy sticks back and they could feel the drive engage. The tug vibrated as the propellers sucked river water and blew it under the tug. Red lights blinked, Dix wasn't sure but thought that this was an indication that the front thrusters were inoperable. Sarge kicked up the throttles a bit and the tug ever so slowly backed into the current. The red lights went out as the tug settled down into the water. When they were 100 yards or so out in the river, Dix gently bumped the joysticks forward and to the left. The tug slowly changed direction and pivoted in the river. Once he was pointing the tug in the right direction he pushed the sticks forward and the vessel headed down stream. Dawson dutifully followed in the catamaran keeping a respectable distance behind. Jacobs called up on the ship's intercom and reported no fires or leaks.

Their goal was to once again block the river below New Orleans. With the river blocked below the Port of New Orleans, that would pretty much close the river for days or weeks. It would make the Chinese have to detour to other ports with less capacity or defenses. Every bump in the road or delay was a rock in the shoe to an invading army.

Dix told the Sarge, "You and Jacobs need to figure out how to sink this puppy, there has got to be a sea valve or a pump we can use to flood it." Dix found that there was a cruise control of sorts on the console. He found a setting where he could freeze the speed and direction. He started pulling out manuals. First he turned on the radar and now knew what was beyond his eyesight ahead.

Dix had Jake's AR15 with him and was still wearing the Browning. He noticed a blip on the radar coming fast up the river. Dix looked forward and realized that it was a helicopter traveling about 100 feet off the water. Dix saw that it was one of the Chinese army helicopters. He called down to Sarge and Jacobs, "We've got some company, a Chinese helicopter." It came over the tug and made a lazy circle around it. Dix took off his shoulder holster and stepped out of the door and waved. The helicopter stalled to a hover, Dix could see a camera in the hands of a passenger. At that moment Sarge and Jacobs opened up on the helicopter. Dix reached inside the door, grabbed Jake's AR15, and concentrated his fire on the engine compartment.

They must have hit something important because the helicopter lost power and went into the river. Its blades chopped the water not 20 feet from the tug. Water splashed upwards by the helicopter drenched Dix at the wheelhouse. The huge propellers quickly distorted and then disintegrated as the momentum of them hitting the water tore them apart. Dix could see the surprised look on the cameraman's face when he realized that they were going in. The helicopter disappeared under the water with its occupants still inside.

Dix got back to the controls and continued downstream. He hoped that the Chinese died before they could report or transmit a photo. Dix replaced the empty magazine with a full one from his magazine pouch. Sarge arrived shortly thereafter still on an adrenaline rush. Dix was munching on an MRE snack and drinking some coffee. Sarge looked at Dix, "How can you be so calm?"

"It's easy, we haven't seen anything yet. You guys still have a will to live. I, on the other hand, have a will to kill. I look at every one of them as just another roach in the kitchen."

They continued on down the river the rest of the day, although they had the radar, it would have been difficult for the catamaran to follow in the dark. So, they found a barge canal off the main river below Baton Rouge. Dix pulled the tug into the channel and brought it to a stop. He set the controls to a hold position. The big engines idled and the generator ran on. The thrusters held the tug within a ten foot GPS determined spot in the middle of the barge channel. Dawson pulled the catamaran around the front of the tug and they waited for the morning to come. Dix suggested they take the fishing boat down the river for a look see in the morning. It could travel light and fast.

The next morning Dix and Sarge left Jacobs and Dawson guarding the tug and the catamaran. They had 50 gallons of extra fuel on the boat. Dix took the Springfield with the bandoleer holding the 7 remaining armor piercing cartridges. He also had his usual full battle pack including Jake's AR15. Sarge had an M4, a lighter pack, an assault vest with six 30 round mags, a Beretta 9mm and body armor. Dix had nixed body armor some time back, it was all he could do to pack the weight of what he carried now. Besides, he wasn't worried about getting killed, he was living to kill and he figured today was as good as any to die. Death would simply end the endless nightmares and never ending agony of remembering his family.

The big fishing boat was 22 feet long and eight feet wide, Dix wished that it was some color other than white, but he had no way to paint it. The fishing poles and landing net sticking up around the center console may give someone enough pause for them to pass or delay their thought processes long enough for Dix to kill them.

They ran for about six hours and Dix stopped long enough to top off the main tank. He didn't want to be in the middle of an escape and run out of gas. He topped off the oil in the engine oil reservoir and they continued downstream. As soon as they came to New Orleans, and were within sight of the ships in the river, they pulled to the side and looked through Dix's binoculars and the scope on the Springfield. The ship was still sunk in the channel; but, a dredge had cut a channel on the other side of the river. A ship was slowly making its way through the new channel.

Dix told Sarge, "We need to sink the tug there or ram what-ever is coming through there. If we open the sea valves and set the thrusters to hold position we should be able to position it in the new channel. We'll sink it there first thing in the morning."

They fired up and headed back the way they came. They ran flat out until it got too dark to safely see logs and debris in the river. They got back to the tug and catamaran around midnight.

"Let's hit the sack and leave at daylight." Dix didn't sleep this night.

The next morning Dix laid out the plans, "We can leave the Catamaran downriver from here in a cut off the river that I stayed in when I came through before. At that point one of you will run the fishing boat and the other three will stay on the tug until we get it into the channel, the sea valves open and pumps turned off. I'll set it on hover, we will hop on the fishing boat and haul ass. If there happens to be a ship in the channel, we will ram it full speed. We'll have the sea valves open as a precaution any-way. Also, I think we should destroy the river dredge if we can work it into the raid."

They paused long enough to hide the catamaran and to top off the fuel and oil tanks in the fishing boat. They put the fish-ing boat on a long bow line behind the tug so as not to waste its fuel. This was all the gas they had or may ever have until the oil refineries were put back on line. When they were within sight of the port Dawson transferred to the fishing boat and stayed a safe distance away.

Luck was in their favor this day. The river dredge was working on the channel around the sunken Chinese ship. Dix increased the speed of the tug and headed for the dredge. He was within a quarter of a mile of the dredge before they realized he was bearing down on them. He called down to the Sarge, "Open the sea valves and get out of there." Red lights came on as Dix killed the circuits feeding the bilge pumps. Sirens sounded as water reached warning sensors in the bowels of the vessel. Dix noticed that the big engines were revving in an effort to maintain speed as the boat filled with water. The dredge operators were frantically waving and sounding their horn. Dix continued to bear down on them.

Suddenly the glass on the bridge started shattering as bullets tore through the tug. They were being fired upon by someone at the Port. Dix stayed at the controls. He glanced around and saw that Jacobs had taken a round through his shoulder. He was down and the Sarge was stuffing a rag under his body armor. Dawson was alongside now, and Dix ordered, "Get him in the boat; I'll get in as soon as I'm finished here." Dix turned his attention from Sarge and Jacobs back to the tug and dredge. Bullets were still spattering around the wheelhouse but to no effect. Dix braced himself as the tug caught the dredge amidships. The tug rode up on the side of the dredge, shoving it under the water as the far side tipped up. Water was pouring through the open doors. Nothing on this Earth would stop its inevitable plunge to the bottom of the channel.

Dix put the tug in hover mode and ran down to the waiting fishing boat. Jacobs looked pale but gave Dix the thumbs up as they raced up the river. He and Sarge opened up on the Port where they suspected the gunfire was coming from. They stopped the boat once they were out of the range of the small arms fire and looked back on the damage they had dished out. The dredge was out of sight and the top third of the wheel house of the tug was sitting in the middle of the channel where the tug sat firmly on the bottom. The river was closed at that point to all traffic for the indefinite future. It would take a team of maritime engineers and crews to open up the river. There would be no more ships unloading men and equipment at the Port of New Orleans.

Sarge reported to Captain Miller over the satellite phone that they had completed a successful mission and would be returning to base. Other than it raining, the trip back to the catamaran went smoothly. They saw several Chinese helicopters in the distance; but, none came towards them or even indicated that they were spotted.

When they got back on the catamaran they took a closer look at Jacobs wound. The bullet had gone all the way through his shoulder, and the wound had stopped pouring blood. Sarge and Dawson put a pressure bandage on him just in case and put him in a spare bunk. He could still feel his fingers in that arm; so apparently, he would get by with some scars to show his friends.

When it started getting dark they found another cut off the river and again spent the night. Dix slept pretty good, no nightmares haunted him this night. Exhaustion had taken its toll.

The next morning they topped off the fuel in the catamaran and proceeded back up the river. They were just entering the bayou that led into Old River where Old Man Beagle lived when the satellite phone rang. Captain Miller called Sarge and told him to get back ASAP. The Chinese were making a run northeast out of Houston, TX. They were apparently planning on capturing the Constitution forces operating out of Fort Polk. Forces out of Fort Hood in Texas had defeated the pro communist forces under command of the President. They were in a good defensive position; but would be unable to mount an offensive for several days. Constitution troops from Fort Polk were to intercept the Chinese and bottle them up until troops and tanks from Fort Hood could re-enforce them.

They pulled up at the old man's camp and offloaded. The soldiers hopped in the Mayor's Cadillac and raced to rejoin their unit. Ben and Frank gave Dix the greeting of his life. Dix watched the Cadillac disappear over the levee. Old Man Beagle couldn't wait to be filled in on the action.

"Ain't you going to fight the Chinese, Dix?"

"I can't keep up with the young guys putting to the field. I am perfectly competent to hide and shoot. Besides, I want to lay out a few days and rest. We'll listen to the short wave and decide what we need to do as the battle unfolds."

CHAPTER 19

HELL COMES TO THE RANCH

A week later Cooney Jones was on the shortwave and Porter actually got to speak with him. Porter gave Cooney a rundown of what had happened to the family. You could hear the sadness in his voice when he acknowledged the death of his son, grandson and daughter in law.

He told Porter, "I want you to stay put, all hell is breaking loose out here and it would be impossible to cross all the lines. I'm backing up the Constitution Army. Your orders are to obey Charlie and Bonnie. The Chinese may be coming through there either on their way across the country or retreated from here. If you and I live to spring, we'll decide what we'll do, for now put Charlie back on the radio and leave the room. And Porter, I'm proud of how you've handled yourself and I love you."

Charlie kicked Porter out and got on the radio with Cooney. He mashed the microphone key, "What's the scoop, Sarge?"

Cooney told him, "We're going to be catching hell, we've got a small group of Constitution troops here; the local sportsmen are doing the heavy lifting. We've had one old guy about our age who has been cleaning house, remember the name, Dix Jernigan. His family was wiped out and he has literally been a one man army. I took a bad hit from a stray bullet 30 days ago. It broke the femur in my right leg; I'm in bed right now out on my farm. It was a real bad break, it is healing mighty slow. It's a good thing I had some penicillin on hand that I kept for the cows."

Charlie laughed, "Yeah that cow medicine is good for about anything. In fact, you might want to think about using some of that Udder Balm on your leg, too."

Cooney chuckled, "We have an old retired doctor and a vet out here in the country that patched me up. Some of the boys brought the radio out here so I could call. I've had them moving all my supplies down to the old boat camp back in the swamp. I've had a big old house boat down there for years. They'll be moving me down there tomorrow."

"I figure I'll be hearing from you come spring then. The hair is thick on the deer this year, I fear it will be a winter to remember. It's already snowed here once."

"It snowed here too, the first time in at least 10 years. Train the boy, give him that deer rifle I keep there as a spare when I come. It's a shooter, in fact if I hadn't spent $1,800 on my new rifle, I'd suck up my pride and keep shooting my old gun. The day is going to come when that boy may need to kill somebody and I want him trained."

Charlie interrupted, "That boy has killed six men that he knows for sure and possibly another. His cute little blond girl-friend has killed one; if they survive to have kids, we're going to have one hell of a bunch of little Rangers on our hands."

Cooney answered, "Train him well, you're going to see some action; I'm afraid he's going to have to skip being a teenager, I'll be out of touch for a long time. When I get back on my feet I'll be back in touch, good luck guys..................signing off."

Charlie told Porter, "Your grandfather is retreating to the houseboat back in the swamp. He's recovering from a gunshot wound to his leg. It is healing and he has friends and supplies. He is safe and well and you heard his orders."

Porter nodded, "What do we do now?"

"The first thing we do is get you some training. Come with me, I've got something for you in the basement." They walked down to the basement and on a shelf in the back Charlie retrieved an aluminum gun case.

Charlie handed him the case, "This is what your grandfather wanted you to have and to learn to use." They sat the case on a table in the middle of the room and clicked on an overhead light. Charlie unlocked and opened the lid. Inside was an old Remington bolt action rifle. Its stock was well worn but the blued metal was clean and oiled. A large scope set on the top.

"That AK47 you pack around is a fine military weapon. It is designed so that a man with a little training can consistently hit a target about the size of a soccer ball at a hundred yards. It is also designed to operate in a dirty and neglectful environment," Charlie told Porter. "On the other hand, this rifle is designed to hit an object the size of a nickel at one hundred yards. The scope on top is a ballistic scope. The large center cross hair is dead on at 100 yards. The next smaller one is set at 200 the next smaller one is 300 and so on. It is chambered in .308 caliber just like the rifle you see me carrying. After lunch we start your training, we're also going to make some suppressors for your rifles and pistol. I have a metal lathe in my shop, my boy Sam is a whiz at working with metal. We'll let him outfit your guns tomorrow."

CHAPTER 20

TRAINING

After another hearty Texas lunch, Charlie and Porter went out to an improvised shooting range down behind the ranch house. A picnic table was set up with some sand bags on the top. Targets were attached onto wire frames that held them steady. Charlie taught him how to breath and how to squeeze the trigger so that he didn't jerk the trigger. After a hundred rounds Porter could put a bullet in a spot the size of an orange at 300 yards. With his AK 47 he could hit a target the size of a washing machine at 300 yards. Porter smiled at Charlie, "If I have multiple moving targets at less than 75 yards I think I prefer the AK47. But for everything else give me the long gun!"

The next morning, Sandy didn't wake Porter with a kiss; instead, Charlie had him up before dawn, "Porter, we're going for a little run before breakfast." Porter got dressed, Charlie told him to leave his jacket he wouldn't need it.

"Grab your AK47, your magazine pack, shoulder holster with pistol, and put on your big knife." Charlie already had all of his on. "Come on down to the basement." In the corner were a half dozen pair of old leather boots that the boys had outgrown. They selected a pair with decent souls that were about the right size. They cut paracord for new laces; Porter laced them up while Charlie filled a wash tub with water. "Put em on, lace them up and come stand in this bucket of water; as soon as your feet are soaked let me know."

They proceeded at a fast trot down the hill and down the trail. Porter was having trouble keeping up. Charlie didn't stop but slowed to a walk and turned south. Charlie called out, "Leave those boots on until they dry out this afternoon. Your feet won't smell good but those boots will be a perfect fit." Porter caught up still breathing heavy. They walked for perhaps another 400 yards and Charlie picked up the clip to a trot again and headed back towards the ranch house. Once again he slowed to a walk and let Porter catch up and they both walked back to the house. Porter huffed, "I'm sure am out of shape."

"No you're not, you are carrying about half the muscle mass that I have and carrying the same weight. By this time next month you will weigh another 8 or 10 lbs and will be able to keep up with me," Charlie explained. "You will be able to take that long gun and kill a mule deer at 500 yards and will be on your way to being able to hit a man at 1000 yards. In addition, you will be able to hit a target the size of a man's head with that Beretta at 30 yards. And with the Kbar fighting knife I'm going to give you; you'll know how to throw it up to 20 ft and will know where to cut so a man will bleed out in less than 30 seconds."

Every night was spent listening to the shortwave. They got bits and pieces of the battle. The things that had them worried were the reports that the Chinese were making a run from Los Angeles across to Houston. The Chinese were receiving little resistance crossing through California, Arizona and New Mexico. Troops from Fort Hood in Killeen, Texas, were bottling up the major highways and interstate. The worry they had was that their ranch was on one of the known crossing points on the river, in fact Porter and the girls had crossed it.

That night Sam was home and with Charlie, planned their defense. They figured that 4 men with rifles scattered out in hidden positions could pretty much lock down the crossing. They decided to put Porter on the north stand. They figured that the north stand was in the roughest terrain and the least likely direction for them to make a run. Porter had the least experience with long range shooting and he was the youngest. Porter objected, "Don't cut me any slack just because I'm young."

Charlie chimed in, "Porter, the boys and I have killed over 100 robbers and looters in the past 6 months. I've killed many dozens in Vietnam. We are putting our assets where we can most use them. We'll continue your training in the morning and then we're going to dig you a shooting blind on the North Slope."

Sandy asked, "Can I help?"

"As a matter of fact you can, you can help Porter stand watch. We'll only man two stands until or if they try and cross. There are still bad guys who may try to get us. We'll all have radios and we'll be in constant communication."

The next morning they loaded up the Rokon. Porter had already unloaded and taken the food and added it to the family stores. The cow hide was stretched to dry on a rack on the wall. They were using the Rokon because it could be laid down and hidden. Dollar would have stuck out like a sore thumb standing out in the open. The trailer held shovels, picks, boards and a roll of tar paper roofing. Charlie and Porter spent the morning digging out an elaborate shooting pit. Using rocks and boards they put a roof on it and covered this with the tar paper. On top of that they threw the dirt and rocks they excavated from the pit. There was plenty of room for a cot to stretch out on and for two folding chairs. The top sloped away from the front so it would not be visible from the field of fire. In the front they drug up weeds and scrub and tied it to the shelter using olive drab paracord. Unless you knew the shelter was there it was invisible. Porter wondered if he could find it again if he ever left. Someone would have to walk up and almost be in it to see it. They returned to the ranch, cleaned up their equipment and to Porter's surprise, Charlie put him through the same exercise regiment as the day before. That night Porter slept better than he ever remembered.

The next morning Charlie woke Porter for the same exercise routine and finished with a lesson in hand to hand combat. Charlie finished by taking Porter for a walk behind the barn. Sam let one of the stallions out of his paddock and in with the mares. In no time flat he found the one who was in heat and mounted her. Afterwards, Sam caught him up and led him back into his paddock. Porter was terribly embarrassed. Charlie looked at Porter and said, "Porter I didn't mean to embarrass you; but, I want you to explain to me what you just witnessed."

Porter stood there red as a beet, "I watched you breed two horses."

"Do you understand that the horse just stuck his penis into the vagina of that mare and the result of that action will produce us a colt sometime next year?"

"Yes sir."

Charlie continued, "The purpose of all this was not to teach you where horses come from; but to explain to you where people come from. You're going to be spending a lot of one on one time with a beautiful young lady. I consider you a full grown man. You've earned your manhood and I am not going to tell you what you should or shouldn't do. But until things settle down, it is not a good idea to take a chance on bringing a baby into the world. If you think things may get out of hand with the two of you being out there alone, tell me now. The time alone together can be good for a young couple; but, not if it distracts you from the mission or gets Sandy in trouble."

Porter nodded, "I think I can control myself."

"Good man, that will all come in time and if you have any questions concerning young ladies, Sam here has consented to answering them."

He and Sandy took the Rokon out to the gun pit and stocked it with a cot, chairs and food for several days. He lay the Rokon on its side and covered it with some scrub weeds and a few rocks. They spent the day looking at the horizon towards the crossing through the binoculars and through the scope on the rifle. Porter had 200 rounds of .308 for the rifle. He also had his AK47 with a battle pack and as always he had on his Baretta 9mm. Sandy was wearing her Chinese pistol, her SKS and her belt knife as well. The only thing they saw was a small group of antelope.

As directed by Charlie, Porter dug the pit out a little better and made a 3 foot deep hole under the cot so that in the event the enemy was able to lob a hand grenade in, all they had to do was kick it into the hole. Porter didn't enjoy the prospect of having Sandy out there with him and possibly in harm's way. But he caught himself dozing a time or two and woke to see that Sandy was still awake.

Before dark, Sandy took the Rokon and headed back to the ranch while she could see the trail back. He could still feel the goodbye kiss down to his toes. About 45 minutes later she called on the radio and said she was safe in the house. He built a small fire down in the pit. It quickly warmed the area. He gathered some large flat rocks and used them to reflect the heat towards the bunk. He took one last look into the distance and saw nothing but darkness. It was a very cold night and the sleeping bag felt good. The fire was out and there was nothing but stars as far into infinity as he could gaze. He awoke several times during the night and peered into the distance. The only sound was from the wind, there were no sounds of men or machinery in the distance and no light from vehicles or fires.

The next morning he woke to snow and wind, winter was taking hold. The radio crackled as Charlie radioed, "How you making it out there?" Porter answered, "So far so good, I was surprised by all the snow."

Charlie came back, "You are going to have to be on your own today. Until this snow stops I don't want Sandy trying to ride out there. It's easy enough to get lost out here when it is not snowing." Porter agreed with him. "It's easy to get disoriented in the snow, especially if you get snow blind. If you find yourself getting a headache, quit looking out for a while and focus your attention on the inside of the blind. Keep a small hot fire going in those big rocks we piled in there. That will keep you good and warm all day and night."

"Yes sir."

"I don't expect that you will see anything Porter, it will be hard for man or beast to travel in this weather. You should have plenty of food and water for several days." Just as Charlie predicted, there was no activity from man or beast.

It was on the third morning that Porter was awakened by the sounds of a helicopter coming in low from the west. He radioed Charlie who answered, "We see him, as far as he is concerned we are just one of many ranches scattered across the country. Everything is buried in snow and the stock is in the barn hidden from view. Just hang tight unless I tell you otherwise. That is just a scout looking around. We won't start shooting unless he tries to land." Porter pulled out his binoculars and peered off into the distance. From the direction of the river he caught some movement. A small herd of deer were moving up out of the river bottom and up towards some timber on the bank of a large hill. Something had spooked them from the way they were running. Porter was expecting to see coyotes or wolves. He was surprised to see a foot patrol of Chinese troops. He put down the binoculars and put his grandfather's deer rifle across the rock ledge of his blind. Through the high powered scope he verified that they were indeed Chinese troops. Their travel was slow in the heavy snow. He radioed Charlie and told him what he saw. "The boys have confirmed that there is a patrol that has crossed the river. It appears as though they are alone. They will probably head towards the ranch house. I don't want you to do anything until you hear us shoot. I want to catch them in a four way cross fire. They are coming up through a shallow valley; we are all on high ground so we will be shooting down on them. They won't be expecting 5 snipers hitting them all at once."

"Yes sir, I'll wait for your signal."

"I don't want them within rifle range of the house, so I will be going out to meet them. Keep your scope on them and have your cross hairs on the first one you want to hit. Have your second and third target in mind before you pull the trigger. Once you squeeze off your shot, go immediately to your next target. Don't wait to see if your first shot connected. They should be about 300 yards from you when the shooting starts."

Porter decided to take the one that was the nearest first and then the next two in line. He counted 20 men. The men were scattered out about 20 feet apart. The one in front stopped and raised his hand. Porter held the scope on the nearest man's chest and had the safety off and his finger tight on the trigger. He was not scared or nervous because he knew that the ranch and girls depended on what he did next. A shot echoed across the land and was followed by a volley of four more. Porter didn't wait to see if his shot was true; but, did as Charlie said and continued looking for targets and squeezing off rounds. He shot and reloaded three times for a total of 12 shots before he could no longer find a target. He reloaded a fourth time and waited. He pulled out the binoculars and saw no movement. Charlie got back on the radio and called, "Is everybody all right?" Everyone called back an affirmative. "Keep your eyes peeled, any survivors will pop up and make a break for it. There is no way of knowing which way they will go. They will probably make a run back in the direction they came from, but you never know."

Porter leaned the AK 47 up next to himself so he could grab it in an instant. He heard a long gun from one of the boys fire but could not see what he was shooting at. A moment later three Chinese were up and running in his direction at less than 75 yards. One fell in his direction from the force of a bullet hitting him from behind and a loud boom echoed a couple of heart beats later from one of the long guns. Parker pulled out the AK 47 and opened up on the running Chinese. One collapsed and the other returned fire. A spray of automatic gun fire tore through Porter's blind. Porter continued to fire his rifle in semi-automatic mode and soon had the soldier down. It wasn't until it wall all over that he realized that he had been hit. A ricochet bullet had caught him in the side. Another bullet had passed through his shoulder. He was hurting like the devil and was bleeding profusely. He dropped back in his seat and was about to get back up when he heard several more reports from the long guns. He was getting light headed but recognized the sound of Charlie's rifle. He tried to get up to peer out but that was all she wrote.

Porter woke up lying in the bitter cold blind. He had no idea how long he had been out. He was stiff from the cold and he hurt so bad he could barely move, but move he did. When he got to his knees he could see out of the blind. The Chinese soldier was laying about eight feet from the entrance.

Porter was bitter cold and he could barely feel his hands and face. He couldn't move his left arm because of the pain in the shoulder. He could barely wiggle the fingers on his left hand. He found some coals still alive under the ashes of his fire. He put on some tender and soon had a fire going. Once he had the fire burning he warmed up enough to move a little. He eased off his coat and felt the wound in his side. He didn't know if the bullet had nicked anything important inside, the only pain was from the entry wound. He couldn't take a breath without pain. Being high on his side, it may have busted a rib. It didn't penetrate his chest cavity or he would be short of breath. He drank from his canteen and slaked his thirst.

The radio was in a thousand pieces, having been hit by a bullet. He thought about the family back at the ranch house. They must be in trouble or they would have come for him.

The bullet went clean through his shoulder. There was a lot of blood in his coat and on the floor. The full metal jacket had passed clean through and fortunately the blood clotted and stopped flowing before he died. He could feel the entrance hole but could not reach around to check the exit wound. He had to do something; the family was in trouble or dead. He gritted his teeth and with tears streaming down his face he forced his arm into the bloody coat. The broken ribs were nothing compared to the wounded shoulder. The pain had a surprising effect on him. At that moment a strength he didn't know existed in him boiled up from within. Whether it was from the pain or the adrenaline coursing through his system, Porter was fortified with renewed strength. A meanness welled up from his very soul. The thoughts of what could be happening to Sandy, Ally and the others flooded his every thought. He took a deep breath and buried the pain deep in the recesses of his mind. The hate was boiling up within, just as it did when he killed the murderers back at his home. This time it was controlled, he was not guided by blind fear and rage; but by stoic reasoning. He suddenly knew what he was going to do and what it would take to do it.

He loaded up the backpack and put in 8 magazines for the AK47. He had the magazine pouch around his neck. All total he had 14 loaded magazines and one in the gun. It was a heavy load. He also had his pistol in his shoulder holster and a Kbar knife on his belt. All he could think of was Sandy and Ally and the rest of the family. It was still daylight so he headed back towards the ranch. The snow made travel slow but Porter's strength did not fail. After two hours he reached the top of a ridge where he could see the ranch house off in the distance. It was dusk and he could see the house lights and smoke coming from the chimney. His heart jumped into his throat as the realization set in to what he was seeing, the lights would not be on if the family were home and ok. There had to have been more than the 20 troops that made the initial attack. He couldn't believe that he had failed everyone when they needed him most. It was just like the attack on his family, he let them down and they died. The sun was going down so he continued to within about 300 yards of the house. He pulled out his binoculars and saw what he feared. Chinese troops were on the porch and in the buildings. They had guards posted out about 100 yards from the house. There were four that he could see, there were probably more. They had a number of bodies laid out on one side of the house; in the fading light he couldn't tell if the bodies were family or soldiers.

The nearest guard was sitting next to a 5 gallon bucket with a fire in it. He poured in diesel that probably came from the family's only tank of fuel. The diesel made the flames jump and the sparks from the wood dance high into the sky. The soldier jumped back in surprise, Porter heard the guards on either side laugh at the antics of their comrade. The guards were sitting looking at the fire and warming their hands. Porter was lying prone on the ground and decided to let the cold and boredom work on the guards. Although it was cold his jacket and wool stocking cap were keeping him warm. He shoved up a small wall of snow on one side that blocked the wind. He waited until he saw the guards starting to settle in for the night.

He kept stretching his left arm and shoulder so that they wouldn't stiffen up. The pain had long since just become a thing, it was no longer part of him; it was almost like the shoulder and side were supposed to normally feel like that. The wind would soon become his friend. The scrub bushes rustled and masked the sound he made crawling towards the nearest guard. His rifle was on his back and the Kbar knife was in his right hand. When he was within 20 feet of the guard, he paused and raised up to where he could see the guards on either side of the one directly in front of him. Both were sitting blindly looking into the fire, huddled onto themselves to stay warm. The guard in front of him was sitting with his back to him, none of them wore helmets. They were wearing what looked like stocking caps with bibs. Porter had spent weeks working with Charlie on hand to hand combat, throwing knives and shooting. Porter was very good with the knife, with one motion the big Kbar left his hand and a moment later it landed with a thunk in the back of the guard's head. The guard slumped to one side. Porter quickly closed the distance and took the guard's seat. One of the other guards looked up and Porter just gave him a quick wave and nod. In the darkness the guard mistook Porter for his comrade who lay face down in the snow. The guard turned back to staring at his fire. Porter got up pretending to go to the bathroom. It took a little effort but he pulled the knife from the dead man's skull. He wiped off the knife and put it back in the scabbard. The snow was deep enough that the other guards didn't see their comrade laying dead.

He sat for a while to let everyone get back into their stupor watching their fires. He added a piece of wood to the fire. He affixed the bayonet on the dead man's rifle. He pushed the body into a seating position and using the bayonet, propped the body up. He retreated on his belly back into the night and snow and repeated the process 3 more times. This took the better part of four hours; his methods became quicker with practice. He knew it would just be a matter of time before they changed the guard. At each spot he was able to warm up by their fire buckets.

He finally crawled up to the bodies in the yard. He crawled down the top of the line and discovered that they were all dead soldiers except the one on the end. The one on the end was Charlie's son, John. Although sad, he was relieved that there were no other family members. That did not mean that they were not captive. With the guards dead and propped up by their bayonets he was free to move about the yard. He took his time and moved around the grounds. He first went to the barn. If the family got away it would probably be on horseback or using some as pack animals. One of the horses had been slaughtered. Its carcass was hanging from a rafter. The skin and meat had been stripped away, a pile of guts were in an old washtub underneath. Half the horses were missing along with saddles and gear, there was still hope that they escaped. Two soldiers were asleep in a bed of hay. He remembered the suppressor Sam had made for the guns. He retrieved the one for the Baretta pistol from his pack and screwed it on the barrel. He walked to within 10 feet of the sleeping soldiers and popped each one through the head. He hoped that no one heard the shots. Although not silent, the suppressor muffled the blast so that it was improbable anyone heard it outside of the barn. Porter found that all the buildings had been ransacked but the contents were largely intact. He dispatched three more sleeping soldiers in the other building and replaced the magazine in the Baretta with a full one.

The rest of the soldiers must be sleeping in the house as he found no others in any of the buildings or on the grounds. He took the time to carry wood around to the dead guard's fires to keep up the appearance of them hard at work. He went around to the basement doors on the side of the house and listened. He did not hear anything so he tried them. He was surprised to find them unlocked. The family may have escaped this way. He quietly eased down the stairs; a lamp in the corner lit the room. He found three more soldiers asleep in the basement. Music was playing upstairs; that was a good thing, they wouldn't hear three quick shots. He clicked off the lamp and made his way to the

stairs. The door at the top of the stairs was open. The smell of cigarettes filled the air. A layer of smoke was hovering about head
high in the room, as a fire roared in the wood heater. An empty
bottle of whiskey rolled on the floor. Tied to a chair in the middle
of the room was Sam. He had obviously been beaten senseless as
he appeared unconscious sitting in the chair with his head hanging forward. He could see a guard standing by the door.

A Chinese office speaking in broken English was arguing with
an American soldier. He screamed, "What is wrong with these,
what you call Texans, don't they know we have them beat?" "I
don't understand it either, the people in California were almost
happy to see us." Porter thought to himself, "That's because they
were like my mother and grandmother." Porter waited long
enough to make sure that those three were the only ones in the
room. The 1st floor of the home consisted of a large room that
held the living area in the front, a large country kitchen with a
table and a big pantry to the side. All the bedrooms were upstairs
and in the loft of the big old house. It had been a ranch house for
many generations of the Cross family. He rolled his bad shoulder
again to keep it working and proceeded into the room. A shot
through the head of the guard dropped him in his tracks; his next
shot hit the Chinese officer square in the chest. The officer fell
back and the American ran for the back door. A bullet between
his shoulders sent him sprawling. Porter turned back to the officer who was rolling around on the floor trying to get his pistol
out of his holster. Two more shots, one to the chest and one in the
head, stopped the attempt. A shot across the room to the back
of the head of the American on the floor put him down. Porter
replaced the magazine in the Baretta and using his knife cut the
bindings that held Sam to the chair. Porter eased him to the floor
and turned his attention to the stairs.

The music was still playing on the radio so Porter turned it
up a bit and proceeded up the stairs. Room by room he killed

the men inside, only once was he discovered when one came out of the bathroom in the hall. Charlie's training of Porter paid off when a quick offhand shot to the man's head from 20 feet came off with a snap. By the time Porter had finished he had emptied another 15 round magazine. He now had the last full magazine in the pistol. He made one last walk around the property to make certain he hadn't missed any one. Sam was coming around by the time Porter got back in. The sun was coming up and they got on the radio. Charlie, Bonnie, Steve and the girls were taking shelter at a small hunting lodge about 5 miles away. It was one that the family used as part of their guided hunt business. Charlie and Steve had both been wounded in the fighting but would recover. Sam was in no shape to travel, so he put him on his cot by the heater. Porter hooked up the hay wagon to the tractor and made the trip to the lodge. Charlie, obviously devastated by the death of his son, grabbed Porter and hugged his neck. A large bloody wound on his leg was wrapped in duct tape, he was standing; so, it was evidently a flesh wound. He said, "Thank you, son." Sandy and Ally each took one of Porter's hands and clung to him. Sandy hugging him proclaimed, "You're bleeding, you're shot!" The shoulder wound was seeping again, the pain was raw but he kept up the practice of moving the arm and shoulder to keep them working. Against his wishes they pulled off his coat and shirt, and insisted on cleaning and bandaging him. When Sandy spotted the wound in his side she said, "I can see your rib moving when you breathe." She became pale and Porter grabbed her as she wilted.

Ally looked at it, "That looks nasty, does it hurt much?"

Charlie, grimaced, "I can tell you, it hurts like hell. Douse it with some whiskey from the cabinet, cover it with a piece of cloth and tape it down with duct tape; we'll do it right when we get back. We have a lot of work to do."

Steve had been hit in the head. A bullet had hit him high on his forehead, traveled under the scalp and exited out the back without penetrating the skull. It did however; knock him out cold as it gave him a concussion and probably cracked the skull. He joked, "That's what you get when you don't keep your head down."

The trip back was uneventful. The family got back and started the grim task of cleaning out the house and burying John. The Cross family had a family cemetery up the hill and under one of the few big trees on the property. It was a sad, mournful time for John's wife and the rest of the family. Steve and Sam hauled all the dead Chinese and the communist American out to the crossing and piled them up like cordwood at the gate. Bonnie and the girls patched and stitched all the wounds and secured all the buildings. All the livestock had survived but the one gelding that the Chinese killed and ate. The dogs and all but three of the chickens were accounted for; so, life was soon back to normal.

Chinese troops didn't try to cross the ranch again, the short-wave indicated that troops from Fort Hood had routed them and they were unable to join the Houston invasion. But, that didn't mean that more of them weren't on the way. After all, there were over a billion of them and more were being flown and shipped in every day. The communists in the US government and military had castrated the U.S. Armed Forces.

CHAPTER 21

QUIET BEFORE THE STORM

A great sadness hung over the house, but Bonnie and the girls managed to decorate the house for Christmas. They hung stockings on the fireplace and built a large fire in it. The house was heated by the wood stove next to it. In old days meals were cooked in the fireplace, the old cast iron hooks and racks were still in place. The snows came off and on for the next week and Christmas came on schedule. With nothing but the light from the fireplace, Charlie recited the "The Night before Christmas" and the kids all got ready for bed. With tears streaming down their faces, they sang Christmas carols and enjoyed some homemade eggnog. All the adults including Porter and Sandy had a little bourbon in their drink. All was quiet on the ranch and Christmas came. That evening Santa came on time, Porter and Sandy helped put out the gifts. The three granddaughters, two grandsons and Ally had homemade outfits and homemade toys. There were hand carved toy guns and handmade baby dolls. Porter had made hand woven bracelets from paracord for everyone. He made Ally and Sandy head bands as well. On Christmas day they had a day of feasting that included venison, turkey and ham. Bonnie and the girls broke out canned pumpkin and dehydrated apples and made pies. In the midst of disaster and loss they had a day of joy and, if only for a moment, they were at peace.

The day after Christmas, Charlie limped up wearing all his gear and woke Porter up. "Porter, it's time for your training to continue".

"You up to running with that leg, Mr. Charlie?"

"No, but this may not be the last time we're wounded. Every day we sit around is a day we're getting weaker." Steve and Sam were ready and geared up also. Sam's eyes were still black and blue, but his lips were somewhat healed. Steve still had a funny looking cowlick in his hair and winced when he pulled the stocking cap over his ears. Porter and Charlie helped them saddle up the mules so they could resume sentry duty on the range. Charlie and Porter saddled up Dollar and Charlie's horse, Dolly, too. They headed out to Porter's blind to retrieve his rifle. The ride out was cold but the snow covered landscape was beautiful. They reached the blind; the dead Chinese were still lying where they fell. While Porter retrieved his rifle and bandoleer Charlie tied a rope around the necks of the dead Chinese and gathered up their rifles. He tied their guns, magazines and gear into a bundle and stowed them on the back of the saddles. They towed the dead bodies down to the pile of frozen Chinese dead and added them to it.

Porter said, "I know this sounds crazy, but I want to kill more of them, a lot more. Something came over me back in the blind, I can't explain it."

Charlie nodded, "You went from being a boy to a man, I can tell it in the way you carry yourself and the way you look. I am sorry it had to happen because you will never be the same or look at the world in the same way again." They rode back in silence and spent the afternoon cleaning all the weapons and checking the sights on Porter's rifle. By the end of the afternoon, Porter could disassemble and reassemble an AK47 with his eyes closed.

The next morning he was awaken by Sandy with a welcome, good morning kiss. "Can you teach me and Ally about the guns and how to shoot?"

"Sure, I think it would be a great idea."

"Do you think Ally can shoot?"

"Sure, I have just the weapon." That day Porter taught Sandy and Ally how to assemble and disassemble the AK47s. He also taught Sandy how to handle the AK47 and to shoot the Remington rifle. He broke out his .22 rifle and showed Ally how to shoot it. The stock was a little long for her; so, he taught her how to shoot from the waist. It took a while but she became very adept at hitting a snowman at 30 feet. He made up a back pack for each of them out of those salvaged from the Chinese. He loaded the packs with supplies and made them bugout bags. They laundered some sleeping bags and rigged up a saddle for Sandy.

Charlie was back in the house with Bonnie and they watched as Porter taught his ladies to shoot and handle the weapons.

Charlie nodded toward Porter, "A boy went out on the range, a man came back; do you have any idea what it took for him to clean out this house? That boy slipped in here and did what no man I know of could pull off. It's not easy killing up close and personal; it's one thing to look through a scope and pull a trigger, it's something else entirely to use a knife and shoot men at point blank range."

Bonnie put her arms around Charlie, "I know."

"Our boys were trained from young boys," Charlie continued, "Porter grew up in L.A. for God's sake and only shot a .22 rifle before this started. I never taught him tactics or how to approach a situation like he faced. In the time it took us to evacuate to the lodge, he crossed the range on foot, infiltrated an armed camp, and methodically killed 18 men. He was also shot through the shoulder, had two broken ribs and is probably still carrying a bullet. He never even winced when we stitched him up. I had to clean pieces of his coat and shirt out of that shoulder and side wound."

"He's a brave young man, Charlie."

Charlie was still amazed at what Porter did for the family. "He can throw a knife better than any man I have ever seen. He just has a feel for it. We are lucky to have him, Sam would be dead for sure, and I don't think I could have come back and killed all of them without getting killed myself."

Bonnie sighed, "As far as I am concerned, he is one of our boys, and the girls are part of our family, too. There is no doubt that he is Cooney Jones' grandson."

That evening Porter took Charlie aside after supper, "Can I take one of the mules for Sandy to ride? I'll be glad to pay you for Dollar and one of the other mules."

"Your money is no good here, Son, you are one of my sons as far as I am concerned and I consider Sandy and Ally mine also. Go ahead and get her outfitted out and teach her to ride. I'm glad you're teaching them to shoot. Just don't let Ally cut herself on a knife, her hands are still small."

Porter embraced him, "Thanks Mr. Charlie, I feel like they are my responsibility, do you mind if I fix her up with John's old mule, Daisy?"

"Sure, she is the gentlest animal we have, she would be perfect. The Chinese cleaned out our smokehouse; in addition to the gelding, they ate up most of the sausage and ham. Do you feel up to some hunting for the next few days? It will get us some exercise and we can get the smoke house fired back up. Steve and Sam will be on the lookout for game while they are on watch."

"Sounds great to me, Mr. Charlie."

Patting Porter on the shoulder, Charlie nodded, "We'll start in the morning."

Morning came and Porter was once again waken by Sandy, this time with a kiss and a cup of coffee. Porter had grown accustomed to drinking a couple of cups a day. In fact he looked forward to a morning cup and a mid afternoon cup. Charlie laughed when he came down the stairs and saw Sandy give him a wake up kiss on the cheek. "I can think of worse ways to get woke up."

Porter snorted, "Yeah, like getting punched by a crippled old man with a piece of firewood." After hauling in some wood they had a hearty breakfast, that once again included heavy cream and butter. Afterwards they headed out to the barn. As usual they were packing pistols, rifles and knives. Instead of the Chinese AK47, Porter carried the Remington long gun. Charlie was packing his .308 battle rifle with a 20 round magazine. Porter asked, "Why don't you shoot a long gun like mine?"

Charlie hefted his rifle, "Sometimes you just wind up with a gun that is a shooter or rather, a gun you are proficient with. I found that I can hit with this gun without thinking. I just sort of know where the bullet is going to hit. For example, when you throw the Kbar knife, do you aim? Or do you just know where it is going to stick?"

Porter answered, "You're right, I never thought about it, it's just a feeling. I sort of have it when I shoot my pistol also. When I shoot my rifles I have to concentrate."

They rode out about 5 miles into the hills overlooking the river bottom. Using their binoculars, they glassed the tree line looking for deer, pigs and antelope. They were about 400 yards from the river, for some reason sitting on horses did not seem to spook the deer they were observing. Charlie instructed, while passing porter a tripod to aim across, "Ease off Old Dollar and walk around just in front of him and set this tripod up. Take that long gun of yours and shoot that little buck on the right through the chest, shoot the next one to him also if you have time and they don't spook." Porter did as instructed and set up the tripod. The three poles were about 5 foot tall and were tied about a foot from the top so that when deployed produced a stable shooting platform. He flipped off the safety and peered through the scope. There were three bucks feeding under some scrub oaks near the river. The wind was still so all he had to do was hold on the little buck with the third dot above the center line. He squeezed the trigger and without waiting to see the result, moved to the next target and fired. Both of them died within 10 seconds of one another. They gutted both deer and filled the body cavities with snow to cool them down. They killed two more deer, a pig and two antelopes before the day was over. It was early evening by the time they hauled back all the carcasses and had them hanging in the skinning shed. The temperature hovered in the twenties so they left the meat hanging till morning. The next morning they skinned and quartered the deer and antelope and had the pig scalded and scraped. They took the deer and antelope quarters and wrapped them in cheese cloth and hung them from racks in the smoke house. They quartered the hog and hung it in cheese cloth also. The back strap and loin were also put in cheese cloth bags, but these would be used right away. Charlie built a fire in a small steel box connected to the smoke house, its exhaust fed into the smoke house. The hardwood and mesquite filled the structure with smoke and raised the temperature to a level that ever so slowly preserved and seasoned the meat. The pig supplied two great slabs from its abdomen that would become bacon in a few days. Another day of hunting had the 12 X 12 smokehouse brimming with meat.

The next month was spent guarding the ranch, working out and perfecting combat skills. Sandy became very proficient shooting and was fair with a knife. Ally could now hit a soccer ball size target at 30 feet with the .22 rifle with every shot. This was a quiet time on the ranch. The snow melted and new snow appeared a couple of weeks later. There was no sign of any more Chinese or hostile strangers. They spotted a helicopter in the distance once, but couldn't tell if it was friend or foe. Porter's wounds healed and although it felt stiff to Porter, he showed no outward appearance of weakness.

CHAPTER 22

THE WAITING GAME

D ix and the old man spent the next week eating catfish and drinking coffee; Dix even broke out his whiskey and the two men had several days of sipping whiskey, fishing, and enjoying the water. Ben and Frank were getting bigger, and chewing everything to pieces around the camp.

It was later in March when the short wave reported that the Constitution troops were at a stalemate with the Chinese. They were stopped at Lake Charles on the Calcasieu River.

The next day Butch Erwin rode up to the camp with news. "I wanted to give you guys a head's up, the Chinese and some of our communist troops are landing at the Natchez airport. It looks like they're going to try and cross the river at Natchez and head to Alexandria. We'll be caught right in the middle between the two armies."

"Do we have anyone on that side of the river, Butch?"

"No, the Mayor and most of the population over there were and are big supporters of the President. When the food ran out they went absolutely crazy, most of the old homes were either burned or commandeered by the locals. Those that weren't killed evacuated over here or out into Franklin County. Nobody in their right mind will try and cross the river into the area. They are as bad or if not worse than Ferriday was before you made your visit."

Dix shook his head wearily, "I don't feel up to taking on that job. I don't mind killing the S.O.B.'s, I just don't know if I have it in me to do it again unless I have to. Is Captain Miller still in Jonesville?"

"No they pulled out when the Chinese tried to break out of Houston. My guys and others have taken over. We think we can bottle them up in Jonesville. We can bring down four or five bridges and they can't get out of Catahoula Parish. It would be a blood bath; but, we can kill them all."

Dix nodded, "What do you want me to do?"

Shaking hands, Butch said, "You don't have to do anything after everything you've done, I just wanted you to know what our plans are."

"Then I'll be on the Jonesville side of the river with my Springfield."

Dix gassed up the four-wheeler and loaded it up with his last four cases of MRE's, an ammo can with 800 rounds of 30-06, Jake's AR15 with 12 thirty round magazines. He had his Browning 9mm with eight magazines. He had a 1000 round can of .223 and a can of 9mm with 800 to 1000 rounds. He added his camping gear, backpacker's water filters, sleeping bags, etc.

He went back to the Catamaran and made a list and a map of where he had buried his family as well as the spot where he buried the family pictures and personal items. In the note he had instructions on where to locate his sister, Lucy, where they were now and where their home was if they ever got back. He pulled out his sack of gold and silver. He put half of it in an ammo can, stuck a small handful in his pocket and the rest he handed to the Old Man and told him that this was his for taking care of Ben and Frank when he was gone. He told him to give the note and the balance of the gold and silver to his sister if he survived and if things became normal again.

"You ain't expecting to make it through this are you?"

Dix looked at the old man, "Four or five thousand Chinese and communist troops are going to be bottled up in Catahoula Parish. I figure I can put down a good many before they get me."

"Don't you talk like that," Beagle told him, "why can't you hang back a little? You've more than done your part."

"Look, these people are extensions of the very people who are responsible for my family being murdered, I plan on killing all of these troops and when I finish I'm going after the ones who caused all of this."

Old Man Beagle tied up the pups and Dix told them goodbye. He drove to Ferriday and told Butch that he was heading over into Catahoula Parish.

"Where are you planning on setting up, Dix?"

"I'm heading south towards Larto where I can find a place to camp. I'll snipe and kill as long as I can find targets. When I run out of targets I'll find you guys and you can point me in another direction."

Butch shook his hand, "Good luck and I'll see you after the fight."

Dix ran the four-wheeler at a fast clip all the way to Jonesville. He made a quick run around town for old time sake, then turned south down toward his dad's old home place. He rode down the highway on the levee. The old road next to the river was still intact in places. From up on the levee it looked like it was ancient, but this was the road his Dad taught him to drive on so many years ago. He had ridden down this road in the back of his dad's old 1966 green Ford pickup. They had come this way many a morning to get to the boat launch at the crack of dawn. The old green aluminum boat would hang out of the back of the truck, the little black Mercury outboard resting safe in the bottom between the seats. An ice chest with beer and Pepsi would be in the back. A paper sack between the seats held a box of crackers, sardines, potted meat and cheese with a red rind on it.

Dix ran down to the old abandoned cemetery where his great grandparents and his dad's mother were buried. Some of the graves were never marked, his dad had pointed out the spots where they lay. All the houses on the road were abandoned because most of the people had left years ago. Dix rode down to the old homestead, the original house was long gone. The house that had been built in the last few years was burnt to the ground. The whereabouts of the new owners was unknown. Dix walked down the lake bank to the old cypress tree, the one his Dad played under as a boy. He had come here on many occasions as a child and remembered catching frogs and crawfish under it. It would all come to an end, he was the only person alive who knew who lived, and played here. He had brought Jake here and showed him this wonderful spot. He had planned to bring his grandsons here one day. That day would never come. The memories would die with him and probably in the next few days. He placed his arms around the tree and imagined his dad running up and down the lake bank with two big old Catahoula Cur dogs named Ben and Frank.

He went back up to the old home place and stood under the giant pecan tree that his great grandfather had planted over a hundred years ago. On the back of the old farmstead a bamboo grove that covered a couple of acres grew. Sometime in the distant past some Japanese bamboo was planted for fishing poles.

In the years since it had been abandoned, it had grown and spread and had become an impenetrable maze. Dix wormed his way into it and opened up an area about eight feet across. He was sheltered from view from above. Even the wind had trouble penetrating the maze. He put up a tarp and rolled out his bed roll. He built a small fire from the dry bamboo. It made a hot fire and any smoke was dissipated by the thick growth of bamboo leaves.

He spent the night here and was awaken by helicopters passing overhead in the darkness. He had no way of knowing who they belonged to. A battle was shaping up and all he knew was that he was in the middle. He was certain they would be sending scouts and patrols out into the countryside, that's what he would have done if he had been in charge.

He left most of his gear and food at the bamboo campsite. Carrying his standard battle pack and gear, Jake's AR15 slung down his back and his Springfield on the four-wheeler's gun rack along with his bandoleer and a can of ammo, He drove about half way to Jonesville and hid the four-wheeler in the bottom of a silo with a large door just off the main road. He left the AR15 and the extra magazines and picked up the Springfield. He put 10 boxes of 30-06 cartridges in his pack. He had 25 cartridges in the bandoleer, seven of which were armor piercing. That gave him 225 rounds of ammo with him for the Springfield. They were uncomfortably heavy. He only put one MRE in the pack the other six he normally carried stayed on the four-wheeler. He had his Browning 9mm with four 13 round magazines in addition to the one in the pistol. He also had his Beretta 22 in his jacket pocket. It had seven rounds but no extra magazine. It was his final backup gun when all else failed. He had a large folding pocket knife and his Kbar knife on his belt. He was wearing his old Maine hunting boots with the gum shoe bottoms and an oil cloth cap with his green LED light on the brim. In his pack he had a lighter, multi tool and miscellaneous items such as duct tape, rope, string, etc.

By the time he finished loading everything, he could hear the helicopters. He peeped out the door and saw that they were Chinese and they were heading north toward town. Staying under cover of the trees, he made his way toward town too. He could hear gun fire in the distance, he knew it had started.

Chinese military vehicles came pouring down the highway and turning up the road that headed west. Dix guessed that they would split up and travel over all west bound roads in the parish. In that way they could spread out their risk of ambush as well as scout out the area and split up any enemy forces. Dix sat in the edge of the cotton patch with his tripod set up and his Springfield resting in the fork. From where he sat he could see the vehicles slowing to turn up the road. Each truck was full of troops. Dix took this opportunity not to stop the trucks but to kill troops.

He was about 400 yards in the edge of the cotton field, completely hidden. He put the crosshairs about a foot over the top rail on the bed of the next truck that was turning. He pulled the trigger and sent a 150 grain bullet through the side of the truck, through the troops in the back, and out the other side. One or more soldiers in the back of the truck were killed or desperately wounded. He fired through truck after truck after truck. The trucks didn't stop right away. He had stopped to refill his bandoleer before the first trucks stopped down the road and troops poured out. They fanned out in the field and started walking his way in an attempt to flush him out. If he jumped up and ran, they would have him in a minute. If he started shooting they would spot him as well. He simply lay down and crawled into the woods out of sight. He had gathered up the spent bullet casings and stuffed them in his pocket on his way out.

Dix walked until he came to a small bayou. He walked near the edge but not close enough to leave tracks in the mud. Finding an ancient log laying half in and out of the water, Dix carefully walked out on it, eased into the water and across the bayou. He disappeared into the buttonwoods and cypress saplings on the other side, sat down in the thickest part and waited. It wasn't long before he heard the troops breaking through the brush. The little bayou probably ran a mile in either direction. Dix had duck hunted here as a young man. He had shot squirrels out of the big cypress tree a Chinese soldier was standing under. Dix sat still and quiet, they couldn't see him where he sat, and unless they had dogs, they would never find him.

He carefully and silently took the empty bullet casings out of his pocket and placed them out of sight next to a log. He waited for three hours before he moved. He didn't go back to his previous position, if they were smart they would leave a shooter in the area to wait for him. He took his time and walked the mile or so around the southern end of the old bayou. He had walked up a good sweat and stopped short of the highway to take a drink. It was then that he heard the explosions that took out the Black River Bridge and the Little River Bridge. The battle was on, they were trapped and he was in the middle of the battlefield.

It was getting dark and he knew that they would have night vision capability so now was the time for rest. He went back to the four-wheeler and headed back to his camp at the old home place. Back safe in his bamboo grove he was hidden from the world. He opened an MRE and dined. He was glad the nights were cold because the mosquitoes were wicked in this part of the world. It was also good that the water was cold, as this was gator country. It was not uncommon to run up on them, twelve feet or longer. When it has an opportunity a twelve foot gator eats whatever it wants.

The next morning he was awaken by traffic on the road. He eased out through the bamboo with Jake's AR15 until he could see what was going on out on the road. A UN SUV with Chinese troops and a large black man were standing outside taking a leak. Dix killed them as they were trying to get back in the SUV. He shoved them in, heaving the driver into the back. Dix drove the SUV down the lake bank to the old boat launch. He left it in gear and stepped out. He started to take the radio but he didn't understand Chinese so he changed his mind. He took their four AK47's and the ten full magazines they had for each rifle along with a box of rations. He went through their pockets and kept any gold or silver. He pulled two full 5 gallon fuel cans off the back before released the handle on the parking brake and let it run out into the lake. It floated for a full 30 seconds before it sunk out of sight in the lake. He walked back to his hidden camp and broke out an MRE for breakfast. There is nothing that works up an appetite faster than killing bad guys first thing in the morning.

He took the four-wheeler back through the woods to an old fence line he remembered from his youth. Pulling out his bolt cutters, he opened up the fence. He traveled through the abandoned fields where he used to Dove hunt as a boy. The lake in front of the old home place was actually the most recent river bed that was abandoned when Black River changed course sometime in antiquity. The bayou he was skirting now was the river bed prior to the lake and the one prior to it was about 400 yards away and ran parallel to both of them. He was able to travel between these through what was at one time, a pecan grove during and after the civil war. Many of the ancient trees were still standing, others were missing and replaced by subsequent generations of trees. Dix had hunted squirrels and rabbits a lifetime ago on this land. Back then he had an old pump 20 gauge shotgun. It was the same gun that his dad had carried as a boy. Again the memories would die with him.

When he was within walking distance of the one lane gravel road that he knew lay ahead, he stopped the four-wheeler and picked up his Springfield. He left Jake's AR15 on the rack and picked up his pack and once again was ready for the hunt. This time he walked across the fields and behind the barns. He walked out around the end of Jones Bayou where his dad swam as a boy. He stopped while still in the woods and looked down the highway in both directions. All was quiet. He could hear gunfire echoing from the distance. Dix crossed the road and walked the two miles along the overgrown edges of a huge abandoned corn field. He came up on the bullet riddled body of young man. His Remington rifle was busted with a bullet hole through the receiver. 30-06 cartridges were scattered on the ground. Dix picked them up and got the ones out of his gun. Anything else of value was gone. The Chinese troops had cleaned him out.

Dix continued on trying not to give the young man much thought. He took out his compass and decided to cut diagonally across the corn field. As he crossed each row he stopped to look up and down the rows long ways as he traversed the field. He soon came out on the other side along the road where he made the kills the day before. He was about a mile further down the road from where he originally set up. He could see where they had set up a camp site across the road in an old cow pasture. They were occupying a farm house as well. If he fired from here he would be committing suicide. They could spot him by sound and he was probably within sight of a shooter. He melted back into the corn field to think.

He could hear a generator running over at the farm house. Gunfire was coming from every direction, apparently all the good old boys were picking away at them. He kept walking rows until he looked down a row and saw the generator truck. He pulled out an armor piercing round and replaced the bullet in the chamber. He set up his tripod and took aim at the engine block. Gunfire broke out nearby on the main road. This was a perfect opportunity to make a shot. He waited until the gunfire erupted again and squeezed off a round. He immediately fell to the ground between the rows and waited for the field to be swept by gun fire; but, it didn't happen. The shooting continued on the highway. The generator started smoking and quit. He moved over a couple of rows and traveled about a quarter of a mile further back into the field. Then he eased up toward the sound of the shooting. The shooters were some Chinese solders shooting off toward the river. They ducted behind their vehicles as someone was shooting back from across the river. Dix waited until one of them fired before he squeezed off a round. The first one folded up and fell. The others thought the shot had come from across the river. They hoped up and fired again, and Dix shot another. They returned fire one more time and once again Dix killed another. There was one left and Dix waited. He stood and fired again and Dix killed him. No one was the wiser.

Dix fished out the cartridges he had scavenged from the young, dead man and refilled the empty rifle and the empty loop in his bandoleer. If this battle was going to come to an end, he would have to keep killing the invaders. He melted back into the edge of the woods and hid. He could smell smoke and see a column of smoke rising on the far side of the field. The wind was blowing from the southwest. The Chinese were using the wind to burn the field. Soon the cover from the field would be gone, so he slowly retreated back to the bayou he had crossed the day before. Once again, he found the old log and crossed the bayou into the buttonwoods and cypress saplings.

He heard the water splashing further up the bayou. Several local men dressed in their hunting gear were scrambling across the bayou. They were making a lot of noise and being careless in their haste. He could hear more men on their trail. Dix crouched behind the log he had been sitting on. He took aim over the log as a squad of Chinese troops came into view on the far side of the bayou. They started shooting in the direction the Americans were running. Dix put a round through the soldier in the rear. The 150 grain bullet cut through his chest and before he hit the ground Dix had another round chambered and had hit the next one through the mid section. Once again he cycled the action, by this time the remaining five or six had taken cover.

They shot wild as they did not know where the shots were coming from. Dix hunkered down as close to the ground as he could get and waited. He was well concealed; so when he eased his head back up to see, they were oblivious to his location. He eased the rifle back over the top of the log and found one in the cross hairs. A shot now would only alert them to his location so he waited, stealth was his friend. He took the time and located all of them. He couldn't line any two up but at least he knew there were only five. If there were a sixth, he was well hidden or trying to get around him. No, if they knew his location they would be shooting at him. He heard the one in the middle bark an order, all together they jumped up and retreated. Dix killed the one who gave the order and threw a round through the tangle of men as they retreated back towards the fields. He knew he could expect artillery or mortar fire so he retreated in the opposite direction. He didn't just run wild but with purpose. He slowed to a near crawl when he saw the edge of the woods and the fields beyond. He would be exposed as he crossed the turn row into the cotton field. As he paused in the woods, he lay on his stomach and waited. About 100 yards to his right and to the west he saw the three men who had been chased. They had stopped in the open turn row and were tying up the arm of one of the men. He wanted to tell them to get under cover but wasn't about to reveal himself.

The arrival of a mortar round made the decision for him. One round landed between him and the men. Dirt and mud showered down on them. Dix crawled forward on his belly into the cotton field ahead and stayed down between the rows so that the raised row could offer him some degree of protection. It was every man for his self. The mortar rounds came in two or three at a time. One went off when it hit the trees behind him. A burning hot pain lit up his left leg, a piece of shrapnel had found him in the field. He kept crawling down the row until he was out of the field of fire.

He stayed down and in spite of the pain continued until he reached the road-way that ran down beside Jones Bayou. Only then did he roll to a sitting position where he could check his leg. A jagged bloody hole in his pants leg revealed the location of the wound. Dix pulled up his pants leg and found a jagged hole in his calf. He could feel the piece of metal about a 1/4 inch under the skin. He pulled a tube of antibiotic cream from his pack and liberally smeared the hole and area; then took out his folding pocket knife and smeared the blade with the antibiotic cream. He made a quick slit above the knot of metal under the skin. It popped out with a squeeze. It was bleeding profusely but not so bad as to warrant a tourniquet. He wrapped a hand-kerchief around it and secured it with a turn of duct tape completely around the leg.

He could move and flex his foot so there was no nerve or ligament damage. He was certain it would be stiff in the morning and he may even be stove up for a few days. Against his better judgment he decided to go back and check on the other Americans. He found them where he had left them. Two were dead the other was mortally wounded. He pulled the man back into the woods and sat with him until it was over. One of the men had a 30-06 so Dix scavenged the bullets. He took their guns and ammo and wrapped them in a garbage bag he had in his pack. He tied it closed with duct tape and stashed them next to a log where he could find them later if needed. He then left their bodies where they lay and made his way back to where he had hidden the four-wheeler.

He retraced his trail back to camp. He parked the four-wheeler, his leg was hurting and it was painful to use the toe shifter with the hole in his leg. He limped into his camp and started a small fire. He stowed the Springfield and laid Jake's AR15 within reach. He pulled out his first aid kit and properly dressed the wound. It had started raining and the temperature hovered in the low 50's, but for now he was secure and fed in his bamboo hideout. He could hear gunfire and explosions off in the distance. The weather got worse in the night with lightening hitting around the area. It didn't break for almost a week. He kept the leg loaded with antibiotic cream, letting it drain and was finally able to walk on it without limping. It hurt a lot worse than the gunshot wound he had previously in the other leg. Several times UN vehicles passed down the road in front of the camp. None stopped, evidently they were on patrol. If they had stopped Dix would have killed them.

CHAPTER 23

ENLISTMENT

I t was now March and the news on the shortwave was good and bad. Some areas were successful in repelling and holding the enemy, others were not. The cities were pretty much a mess, most people were dead or scattered out across the countryside.

Steve, Sam and Porter were out in the blinds keeping their eyes open for danger. A group of about 20 men came through the gap where the dead Chinese were piled up. Sam radioed in, "We've got twenty men on horseback with pack animals heading up the trail from the river crossing." Charlie answered the radio, "Do they look like ours or theirs?"

"They look American and they are not in a hurry. Do you want me to ride out and meet them?"

"No, I'll go out and meet them, Porter you come off your blind and ease up about 400 yards behind me with your long gun. I want you between me and the house. If a ruckus starts up, I want you to kill as many as you can see, then head back to the house and get the family heading for the lodge. Sam and Steve, I want you to get within rifle range so that when I meet them we will have them in a crossfire. If the shooting starts you know what to do."

Porter put on his pack and grabbed up his long gun and placed it in the scabbard on Old Dollar's saddle. He hung the AK47 behind his back and swung into the saddle. He watched as Charlie, on his horse, crossed from his left to his right in the distance. He let him get almost out of sight before he gently bumped his heals against Old Dollar. The mule started at a plod towards Charlie, he instinctively knew where Porter wanted to go. When they reached a point on a rise where Porter could see Charlie and the approaching line of men, he got off Dollar and set up his tripod and got out the long rifle. He set the rifle in the fork created at the top and peered through the scope. He cranked up the magnification to the 9th power which enabled him to see the men close up. He cycled the action, picked a target and waited.

Charlie rode his horse up to a point on the trail where he was above the riders and dismounted. When they were about 100 yards down the trail, he stepped into view with his rifle pointed at them from his waist. Anyone else would have to raise their rifle to eye level before making an accurate shot. Charlie on the other hand, could easily knock the lead rider off his horse by firing from his waist at this distance. The lead rider made no aggressive moves and only tipped his hat. He stopped about 20 yards away, "I'm Roger Daniels and I am looking for Charlie Cross."

"You got him, what can I do for you fellas?"

"We are on our way to Louisiana to join the Constitution forces fighting there. Cooney Jones told us to come through here on our way and check on you guys. He also said we could probably camp for a couple of days at your lodge. Without taking his rifle off him Charlie asked, "What else did he say?"

"He said you had his grandson Porter staying with you."

As he lowered his rifle, Charlie said, "Good answer." He pushed the button on his portable radio, "Guys, it's ok, stand down, they're on our side. Porter, meet me at the house."

Porter folded up the tripod and stowed it along with the long gun back on the saddle and climbed back on Dollar. They were about 5 miles from the ranch house so he turned Dollar towards the house. Dollar knew the way, Porter didn't have to guide him; he had been going home his entire life. Porter looked at the back of the mule's head as it gently bobbed up and down with each step. He flapped his ears and chomped at the bit a little, rearranging it in his mouth. Porter left the rains slack and let Old Dollar just do his thing. Porter beat the men back. They were down in a valley of sorts and it took longer on the trail to work their way up to the flat where the ranch house set. They were on the same trail that Porter and his girls were on when they drove up, months earlier.

When they reached the barn, Porter turned Dollar into the corral and went into the barn. He opened the side door and let him in, Dollar stopped near his stall and waited while Porter pulled off his saddle, blanket and bridle. Porter put some grain in the feed trough and some hay in the basket, there was water in a trough just outside the door. Porter took his long rifle under his arm and headed back towards the back door when the men came riding up.

"Porter, I want you to meet Roger Daniels, he is a Sergeant in the Constitution Army and he has been in touch with your Grandfather Cooney.

Porter brightened up, "Have you talked to him? Is he ok?"

"He's fine and getting around on crutches. I used to work for him before he sold his company. All of us guys worked in the oil patch with his construction company."

"I never knew what he did, I just knew he was retired and lived in central Louisiana in Catahoula Parish. I only spent a couple of weeks with him several years ago after my Grandmother died."

"That's a shame, kid; he is one hell of a man."

Charlie piped up about that time, "Roger, you guys follow that trail down behind the barn. About 5 miles down it you will come to a lodge. There's a corral for the horses and a tack shed that you can stow your saddles in. There's hay in the loft and a water trough. The lodge has wood stacked out back for the fireplace and wood stove. There are can goods already in the kitchen, kerosene lamps, bunks and blankets. We'll be down later with some meat. If you want showers, you'll have to fire up the gas hot water heater, we have a windmill well pump and the house has a solar powered water pump so you will have water pressure in the kitchen and bathroom."

The men disappeared down the trail. Bonnie and the girls were standing on the porch and looking out the windows as the men proceeded down the trail and out of sight.

"Charlie, who were those men?"

"They're Constitution Army volunteers headed to Louisiana. They are going to lie up at the lodge for a couple of days to get some rest and clean up. Why don't you rustle up a basket of fresh biscuits and a couple of pones of your cornbread? Porter and I will slice up some pork and venison and cook it up on the grill. It will be a little tough, but I bet it will go down good."

She smiled and turned back toward the door, "I'll have it ready in about 45 minutes."

She and the girls went to work on the bread while Porter and Charlie fired up the wood grill and cooked the meat.

"Mr. Charlie, you told me that if I hung around to spring you would travel with me to Louisiana; if Sergeant Daniels will let me, I would like to tag along and join the fight. With John gone, you're needed here."

"Have you thought about Sandy and Ally, what do you think they will have to say about you leaving?"

Porter sighed, "I don't expect them to be wild about the idea, but let's face it, there is a war going on and I know how to fight and kill as well or better than most men. We won't have much of a life so long as the Chinese and American communists are here. The best we can hope for is stay hid or be executed or enslaved; I'm not up for any of that. If we can clean them all out, we can start over."

Charlie looked at him, "That is one of the most mature and reasoned decision I could have heard. You need to talk to Sergeant Daniels and see if he would be willing to take you on. Let's load up the meat and bread and head on down to the lodge." They saddled up Old Dollar; Charlie had left his horse saddled, and they took the baskets of food down to the lodge. The snow was still on the ground but the stars were out and the moon lit the landscape. The horses exhaled their steamy breath into the night air, Porter and Charlie didn't talk the entire trip out. There was a column of smoke coming up from the stove and fireplace in the lodge. Several men, who served as sentries, waited on the outskirts of the yard as silent guards. Unlike the Chinese, they had no fire and were hidden from view. These were men who had spent their lives in the outdoors working, hunting and fishing. They held their weapons with a comfort that only comes from a lifetime of handling them. The men relished the food and didn't seem to mind that the meat was a little tough. They joked among themselves and enjoyed the evening. A card game was taking place on a coffee table and they all gathered around the short wave.

The person on the radio was relaying information about the fighting. A gasp of shock and indignation erupted when the operator gave the news about the nuke hitting Fort Hood. They were all silent as they listened. Finally Sergeant Daniels stated, "Guys we will have to travel south before we can travel east. There will be a trail of fallout blowing to the Northeast from there. Unless we can find some potassium iodate, K103, we're going to have to stay well south of Fort Hood.

Charlie broke the silence, "Guys, we have found ourselves in one hell of a fight. Roger, Porter and I need to have a word with you."

"What's on your mind?"

"Porter here would like to join your command and get in the fight."

"How old are you boy?"

Porter was embarrassed and answered in a low voice "fourteen."

"The youngest one in our group is 23, do you think you are ready to head into what could be hell on Earth?"

Charlie smiled and spoke up, "See that dart board on that far wall? Porter, stick that board with your knife." In one motion the knife appeared from behind Porter and landed with a "thunk" almost dead center of the board about 18 feet away. Roger Daniels let out a whistle from between his teeth, "Damn that was a good throw, but there is a big difference between hitting a target and actually killing a man."

Charlie smiled once again, "Do you remember that pile of dead Chinese you passed on the trail?" Roger nodded. "Two thirds of them were put there by this man. He quit being a boy a while back, in fact he showed up here already a man."

"We can use all the good men we can find, you willing to join the Constitution Army? I can give you the oath tonight. You will start as a Private, you won't get paid, you have to provide your own gear and we expect you to be in the Army for life. After we win the war you will remain on reserve duty until you are too old to get around, you ready to be sworn in?"

Porter grinned, "I'm ready."

"Then hold up your right hand and repeat after me, "Do you swear to uphold and defend the original Constitution from all enemies, foreign and domestic, as written by the founding fathers of the United States of America with the additional provision that every citizen automatically becomes a member of the militia at birth, so help you God?" Porter repeated every word and everyone patted him on the back.

"Private Porter, report here at daylight the day after tomorrow. You need to have full gear and rations, a pack horse would not be a bad idea either. You are now a member of Daniel's Devils, sounds vicious doesn't it?"

"Better than Daniel's Dancer's," Charlie piped up. They all had a good laugh.

Porter wasn't looking forward to telling Sandy where he was going. On the ride back to the ranch house, Porter asked Charlie, "I hope you don't mind looking after Sandy and Ally until I get back?" "I told you Porter, ya'll are part of my family now, not guests, family, do you understand?"

Porter nodded, "I feel the same way, I guess I sorta feel like Sandy and Ally are my girls and I expect them to be with me for the rest of my life. I didn't think I would be in this position until after I got out of college, but it doesn't look like I'll be heading off to college any time soon. I don't think there will be any colleges anywhere for quite some time."

"No, you went from being a pimple faced kid to man in a few months time. You still can't grow whiskers worth a dang, but you sure as hell can fight."

"Thanks to you, without your training I'd probably be dead."

"Don't be thanking me, I almost got you killed out there in the blind, but at least you got some dynamite scars to show your grandkids one day." They both laughed and headed back to the ranch.

The night was real cold, Porter knew that Steve and Sam would be spending the night in sleeping bags in their respective blinds. He would get to sleep by the fire for two more nights. After that, his life would be living on the trail far from the comfort of a mattress and good home cooked meals.

Sandy was waiting up for him when he came in. Charlie patted him on the back, "Goodnight kids" as he headed up the stairs. Sandy sat on the bunk next to him and started to cry softly, "I know you are getting ready to leave and you won't be taking me and Ally with you."

"How did you know?"

"I just know, I've been around you enough to figure out what's on your mind. I won't put up a fuss so long as you promise you'll come back for me. I don't know how to say it just right, but I love you and want to be with you from now on. I know we are too young to do anything; but, soon we will be old enough to get married and I don't want anybody else but you."

Porter gave her a kiss on the lips, "I feel the same way, but I know we can never have a life so long as the communist Chinese and the communist Americans are here. We would spend the rest of our lives living in blinds, running and hiding. We could never have a home and kids or anything. We would be nothing more than slaves."

"I know you're right. It's just so hard."

"I want you to stay here on the ranch, this is our family. I have you, Ally and my grandfather. With a little luck I'll catch up to him, I'll be in touch on the short wave whenever I can. I'll be leaving the day after tomorrow. You can help me get geared up in the morning. I'm taking Old Dollar and another pack mule."

Sandy started crying again and Porter said, "Don't worry you'll see Old Dollar again someday." She punched him in the stomach and gave him the best kiss he ever had. He hated to see her disappear up the stairs. He topped off the stove with wood, crawled into his bunk, and was soon asleep.

Morning came with Sandy kissing him on the cheek and his mug of coffee. The house was soon up and once again he had a hearty country breakfast. He laughed when he thought of how his mother wouldn't let them eat bacon, sausage or eggs. If he were back home, she would be giving him oatmeal or a bran muffin. He remembered his dad taking him down to Waffle house for the good stuff, of course he couldn't tell his mother or he wouldn't get to do it again. It seemed like so long ago, it was almost as if it were someone else's life. His hands were calloused and his body was scarred. He drank coffee and had a beautiful girl friend and could do things he could only have imagined a few months ago. The months seemed like years at this point.

Charlie told Porter, "Catch up that brown mule with the gap in her ear. We've used her as a pack mule as well as a saddle mule. She and Old Dollar get along and we've used them as a pair over the years. We call her Ruth, neither one of them have shoes, which is just as well, there won't be any blacksmiths where you are going."

Porter enticed Ruth up with a bucket of horse feed. Old Dollar wanted in on the deal so Porter slipped him a stale biscuit. Once in the barn, Charlie got out a pack saddle and showed Porter how to put it on Ruth, adjust and secure it. He helped him pack the canvas bags that mounted to it. The old mule could carry a good load, but Charlie stressed, "The more you put on her, the slower you will have to travel and the more you will have to stop and let her rest. We are going to concentrate on food, and basic supplies. I am going to stock you with 25 lbs. of hard tack, 25 lbs. of beans, 25 lbs. of meat, 25 lbs. of rice, a box of salt, pepper, 10 lbs. of sugar, a mess kit, aluminum pot, first aid kit, sleeping bag, 4 canteens, an extra AK47, 30 loaded magazines and 5 boxes of .308. We will limit her load to around 200 lbs. We'll have you, your backpack and rifles on Old Dollar. I want you to have a camel back water bag on your back. With you and your gear, Old Dollar will be carrying about 200 lbs. also. You'll need hobbles for them so you can let them graze at night. I would go thirsty and give them water before I drank, whenever you find water, let them drink their fill unless they have been running. You have to let them go easy on the water until they cool down. Take their saddles and packs off at night to give their backs a rest. Wipe them down good with the saddle blankets. If you have any questions ask the other guys, they seem to know about horses too." Porter nodded and packed and repacked the packs trying to balance the load between them. They took a file to the mule's hoofs to head off any splits.

"How long do think it will take us to get there?"

"At least a month maybe more, traveling cross country will not be easy, ya'll will have to stay off the roads as much as you can to avoid trouble until you get into the thick of it, then I expect you won't be able to get away from it."

Sandy and Ally cooked a big batch of cookies, and Ally helped fold up his clothes, they also wrote letters that he could open up each week. They were labeled week 1, 2, etc. The girls stayed close to Porter all day, they were living with the fear that they may never see him again. Bonnie cooked up the hard tack and a sack of biscuits and came up with a jar of honey. He had his compass and the atlas map pages of Texas and Louisiana tucked into the pocket of his jacket. That night they prepared him a going away feast and after supper they all sat around with him being the center of attention. Porter was obviously uncomfortable with all the attention so everyone took the hint and told him goodnight. Sandy and Ally sat up with him. Porter insisted, "Tomorrow is going to be a long day for me, so I guess we had better turn in."

Ally piped up, "Can we be quiet and watch you sleep?" Porter scooped her up and gave her a big bear hug and kissed her on the cheek. "Get into bed. I'll be back before you even miss me."

"We already miss you, and you ain't even left."

Sandy grinned, "She's already sounding like a Texan." They all laughed and the girls went upstairs to bed.

Porter lay back in his bunk and took a deep breath, he wondered what was happening to his house back in LA. He thought about his parents and little brother and the long journey getting here. He considered the journey ahead, it couldn't be nearly as rough as the journey behind him. He looked forward to the battle in front of him and he looked forward to seeing his grandfather again. He got up and filled the wood stove with wood and slipped under the covers. A short while later Sandy slipped back downstairs and slipped under the covers next to him. They didn't do anything but lay in each other's arms, there was nothing left to say. Porter woke up well before daylight and sent Sandy back to her bed. He reloaded the heater with wood and got dressed. Bonnie and Charlie were up and soon had a hot breakfast of pancakes, ham and eggs.

Charlie then helped Porter saddle up Old Dollar and Ruth. His long rifle and tripod was on the side of his saddle. An oil cloth drover's coat was rolled up around his bedroll on the back of the saddle. Saddle bags held odds and ends. He had a rope coiled and hanging on one side of the pack on Ruth. Her lead rope was secured with a snap ring to the back of Old Dollar's saddle. Porter had on a camel back canteen, his back pack and the AK47 slung so that it rode in front of him where he could get his hands on it. His pack held enough supplies to sustain him for several days in the event he became separated from his mules. He had six full magazines plus one in the rifle giving him 210 rounds for the AK47 rifle. He wore his Beretta with two extra magazines in a shoulder holster and his Kbar knife in a scabbard on his waist. Charlie handed him a hand drawn map that would take them off the ranch and then east and south so that they would parallel a roadway, but keep them out of sight for a few days. It also had water spots marked. "You may have to locate some locals to guide you to more water." Porter studied the maps so he knew where he was going and several routes to get back. He told everyone good bye and in spite of his shyness, gave Sandy one last kiss. All the ladies were crying, "Tell Sam and Steve goodbye for me."

"Remember what you learned and come on back when you get the job done," Charlie called. Porter swung into the saddle and headed off into the darkness. The mules knew the way to the lodge they had made this trip before.

CHAPTER 24

THE HUNT

Dix decided that the pain in his leg was too great to try and shift the four-wheeler, besides he wouldn't have enough fuel to get back to the catamaran if he kept running it.

The next morning he was waiting in ambush for the UN patrol to come driving by. He sat up down at the end of the road where they had to almost stop to make the turn. He was directly across the ditch and waiting in the bushes. Right on cue they arrived and just as they slowed to turn, Dix emptied a 30 round magazine from Jake's AR15. The driver punched it and drove off into the ditch. They never left the vehicle.

Dix dragged the driver out of his door and left him in the bottom of the ditch out of sight. He put the pickup into four wheel drive and backed it onto the road and back down in front of the camp. He siphoned off the gas and carried their guns and ammo back to the camp. They also had a case of Chinese MRE's in the truck. The meals were sweet tasting cookies in foil pouches. Once again he drove the truck down to the lake and let it roll into the water next to the UN SUV that was already there. It bobbed a minute and sank out of sight. At least he had some more fuel for the four-wheeler and there were three more dead Chinese soldiers.

Dix tried walking everyday to work the stiffness out of his leg. He remembered an old Crepe Myrtle tree near the side window of the old family home. Dix walked over to look for it. It was still there; but, the top of it was blown out. It was in sorry shape but there were green buds trying to put out. This was the tree that his father played under 80 years earlier. It had to be over 100 years old and it was hanging on to life.

Dix nursed the leg another week and finally felt he was ready to take to the field again. No more patrols came his way, but he could still hear fighting off in the distance. He ran his four-wheeler up to the east side of Jones Bayou and hid it in the brush. He once again picked up the Springfield and left Jake's AR15. With his standard battle pack he made his way around the bayou and across the road back into his old hunting grounds. He made it all the way across the fields and around to the break where he was wounded by the exploding mortar round. The dead Americans were exactly where he left them. Animals had pretty much consumed their bodies.

He quietly made his way around the end of the break. He didn't want to get the water in his wound unless necessary. Although his leg was hurting again it was not slowing him up. The dead Chinese were still lying where they fell on the other side of the brake. Dix made it across the big corn field to where he had killed the generator a couple of weeks earlier. The generator was still there but everyone else had moved on.

He went back to the four-wheeler and drove it down the road and towards town. The road was on top of the levee, so he turned off the road and went down to the bottom of the levee and stopped under some trees. Dix killed the motor and listened. There was fighting towards town. He got back on the road and stopped about two miles south of town. Once again he hid the four-wheeler off the road next to a pasture with large bales of rotting hay. He sat with his back to one of the bales and ate a power bar from one of the MRE packs. After washing it down from his water bottle he loaded up and headed toward town.

He stayed off the road and instead walked through the fields, meadows, and the back lots of little farms until he got into the town proper. There was a lot of shooting up ahead. He was traveling north into town and was near the river on Front Street. Dix stayed close to the houses. The battle lines were drawn with most of the Chinese on the north side of town. He ran into some guys sniping across the main highway into the old part of town. He was surprised to find Butch Erwin sitting under a tree smoking a cigarette and reloading his AK47.

"Don't you know cigarettes will kill you?"

Butch hollered out, "Hey boy, where you been, vacationing?"

Dix chuckled, "I've been camping and enjoying life, the hunting has been great."

"Have you thought about taking a bath? You look like hell, Dix!" After a good laugh Butch brought him up to date on the battle.

"We've been killing the S.O.B.'s for weeks. We've kept them bottled up. We stopped them at Lake Charles, and we're mopping up here. There are still a couple of thousand of them holed up in town. We're picking them off as we can; but, they're picking us off too. There are only about 200 of us; but, they don't know that."

Dix commented sarcastically, "If they knew the odds were so bleak for them, they'd surrender."

"Surrender is not an option at this point. We gave them that opportunity three days ago. They fired on our white flag."

"So," Dix asked, "Where can I set up?"

"That depends, how far can you hit with that Springfield?"

"I regularly make kills at 400 yards, if I can see 'em, I can probably get a hole in them."

"Good, we've got a boat on the river, if you can set up on top of the new bridge, you can probably see all over town. They don't have snipers that we know of."

"Sounds like a plan, my friend."

Dix caught a ride across the river and with the help of several of the Ferriday boys carried some bags of dirt and sand up to the top of the bridge where it ended. The rest of the bridge was in the river where it had fallen after the fuel oil IED bomb went off. He lay down with the Springfield across the bags and observed the town through his scope. He was sure to draw fire from up here. They hauled more bags up, put a board across the top and set more bags on top of it. That left him an opening about a foot square to shoot through.

He took his time and looked through the Trijicon scope. He dialed it up to nine power looked over every building and opening he could peer through. At last he found what he was looking for. A soldier was sitting with his back to the brick wall of the library. Dix estimated the distance at 500 hundred yards. He counted the bricks above the soldier's head. His bullet would probably drop a full 12 inches at this distance. The wind was still, so Dix took aim at the 4th brick above his head. He took a breath and let half of it out. He gently squeezed the trigger and was surprised when the gun fired. He looked back and didn't see the soldier. Where he had been leaning was a large bloody splotch with a chunk missing out of the brick where he sat. He cycled the action and got back on target. Another soldier ran to the spot where the first one fell. Dix squeezed off another shot. That solder fell against the wall and stayed propped up a moment before falling forward. He cycled the action again and continued his search.

He saw that soldiers were running across the street from one house to another. He noticed that they would pause for a moment at the corner before darting out and across the road. Dix aimed at the point where they glanced out before they came out. He didn't wait for the next one to glance out but squeezed off a round at the corner in anticipation of the next peeping around in time to meet the bullet. The round met the man's head knocking his helmet off. He then fired through the corner of the house in anticipation of someone standing behind the wall. He didn't see anything move so he cycled the action again. One hundred shots and 7 confirmed hits later, the Chinese had him spotted. About a hundred of them opened up on his location on the bridge. The air was alive with rounds zipping all around. Dix retreated back down the bridge keeping the roadway between him and the rifle-men. The sun was low in the sky when Dix came down off the bridge and met Butch.

"How did you do?"

"I know I hit at least 7, but I probably hit four or five more." Butch whistled, "Why did you come down?"

"I'm getting skittish in my old age. I had about a 100 rifle bullets flying past my head every second." Butch reached up and grabbed Dix's hat. "Did you know that there are three bullet holes at the top?"

"I guess they almost got me, again. I need to get my four-wheeler, run down to my camp and bring all my ammo and gear back up."

Butch asked, "Do you have any more ammo for the AK47's?"

"I sure do, I'll bring it back with me and see you back here tomorrow. Now, if you can take me back across the river, I'd appreciate it."

Butch dropped him off on the other side of the river and one of the other Ferriday boys gave him a ride to where his four wheeler was hidden. Dix cranked it up and made the run down to the old home place. He felt safe there so he spent the night in the bamboo grove again. The same nightmares haunted him and once again he woke depressed and profoundly sad. He packed up all the gear, guns and food and tied everything down. He made one last walk down to the old cypress tree. He wanted to firmly set its memory in his mind so that he would never forget it.

He climbed on the four-wheeler and headed for town. The knobby tires on the four-wheeler were starting to show wear from all the time on paved roads. He would have to start looking for a new set or a set from another four-wheeler when he had the opportunity. He met Butch where he said he would the day before. Dix handed him seven AK47's and a large pile of loaded magazines for them.

"How many have you killed since you've been over here?"

"I quit counting while I was still in Gulfport. These are just the guns and ammo I picked up that I didn't have to pack very far. I know where there are three or four more with ammo if you need them."

"Ammo is the main thing we need."

"We've been in touch with Captain Miller," Butch continued, "The Chinese have picked up reinforcements and will probably cross the Calcasieu River today. A nuclear bomb went off at Fort Hood. We think that our communist President gave up the nuclear command codes. Constitution forces had secured 95% of the nukes right away; but, we think this one came in on a cruise missile from a ship in the Gulf."

"It sounds like they have redirected the invasion to Houston."

Butch grinned, "Word is that they abandoned New Orleans when the river was blocked."

Butch and Dix were suddenly interrupted by paratroopers filling the sky and landing south of town. The question was: which side did they belong to?

Dix motioned to Butch, "Hop on." They drove over the levee and into the willows next to the river. Dix strapped the Springfield on the rack, put on Jake's AR15 and picked up the two magazine pouches that contained six thirty round mags each. He already had the pack loaded. He took out the 30-06 ammo and returned it to the ammo can. There was no use carrying the extra weight.

He and Butch made a quick run to the top of the levee. The sky was still raining paratroopers. Dix looked through his binoculars and to his horror realized that they were Chinese. Constitution forces would not be packing AK47's. Dix asked Butch, "Do we have any allies that would be coming in to save us?"

Butch shook his head, "I think our odds just changed and not for the better. I'm going to order our men to make a run for it."

Butch got on the radio and told the Americans what was taking place and to fall back into their former guerilla positions. The battle had changed back to guerilla warfare just as it had been up until yesterday.

"Damn it Butch, I wished I hadn't brought my gear up from my camp. At least they are on foot like we are. I wonder if they realize they are boxed in by the rivers and blown bridges?"

The Chinese troops secured the small local airport and started receiving parachutes that were landing heavy equipment. They quickly joined up with the Chinese in town. For the first time since everything started Dix was uncertain as to what he should do. He and Butch went back down the levee and melted into the willows along the river. The Chinese set up sentries within sight of one another up and down the levee.

"I can kill all of them within sight of us with the Springfield. I wonder if we can cross the river in your boat with my gear."

Butch drawled, "We could, if the boat was on this side, it's on the other side of the river, and the men who took it aren't coming back."

"Well then, I suggest we just park our butts on this river bank until dark. We can try swimming the river after dark or we can slip out of here on the four-wheeler after dark. Now if you're in a hurry to start fighting, we can start shooting from here and just fight our way south to open country. But I'm almost certain that this four-wheeler and the trailer will float. If we can wait until dark, we can slip into the water and float across or we can float downstream for a mile or so and get out."

"I don't see where we've got a choice, Dix. I don't want to take on a bunch of fresh troops right now." They sat quietly keeping their eyes on the two sentries closest to them.

As soon as it was dark they bumped the four-wheeler out of gear and eased it out into the river. It floated as planned and they hung on each side and steadied it so that it wouldn't tip over. They silently drifted downstream in the shallows. They could see the sentry's silhouetted on top of the levee as they silently drifted down the river. The water was cold and they were soon shivering uncontrollably. Fortunately the river was up just above its natural banks and they were able to stay in the shallow water.

Dix cranked the four-wheeler and it climbed out of the water with the trailer behind it. They climbed on and Dix headed back to his camp at the old home place. He and Butch drove back into the bamboo thicket and disappeared. Dix soon had a hot fire and in no time had his camp re-set up. He hung the tarp and using paracord had their clothes drying on it around the fire. They were out of radio range so all they could do was wait at this point. Dix cleaned his guns and inventoried his ammo and weapons. He still had over 500 rounds of 30-06 and a full combat load for Jake's AR15 and his 9MM. He topped off the gas tank in the four-wheeler. There wasn't going to be a lot of sightseeing taking place, unless he captured some more fuel.

That night they opened a fifth of bourbon, passed it back and forth and talked of times past and dead friends. Dix said, "If I survive this war, which is highly unlikely, I plan to buy this place back and come home."

Butch reminded him, "There's a good chance that nobody owns this place anymore. They estimate that 75% of our population is dead."

They dozed by the fire and the morning came. They ate a couple of MRE's for breakfast and loaded up. The sun was almost peeping over the horizon when they headed out. They were on foot as stealth was the order of business today. Dix led them back through the old pecan grove between the bayous behind the old homestead. They walked out behind Jones Bayou, across the road and north to town. They had an eight mile walk and it would take hours to get back. They couldn't walk down the road on top of the levee because they would be sitting ducks out in the open.

Butch carried his AK47 and the battle gear he was packing from the day before. Dix carried his Springfield; he realized that in open country fighting, the need for extreme long range accuracy was preferable to raw firepower. Jake's AR15 was better for urban fighting where you would be engaging moving targets less than 300 yards away. Dix was not a young man, and he didn't have speed and agility on his side, but he was in top physical shape for his age. All these weeks in the field had taken all the fat off his body. He would hate to see his blood pressure readings; he had run out of his medicine months ago.

About three miles from town they spotted the first Chinese patrol. Just south of Jonesville a road cut back to the west. The road made a meandering circled around and went back to the highway west of town. Dix and Butch sat back in the cotton field and watched as the patrol turned and walked down the road.

"Do you think we should try and kill them, Dix?"

"Let's see if you can raise your men on the radio first."

Butch keyed the microphone on the radio, "Is anybody listening this morning, this is Butch."

A voice came back, "We thought you were dead."

"Almost froze to death, but I'm still alive, where do we stand?"

Butch whispered to Dix, "That's my cousin, Carl."

"Everybody made it out last night. We are in our original campsites. The Chinese flew in heavy equipment out on Alexandria highway, repaired the bridge on that end and are getting ready to break out."

"Have you notified Captain Miller, Carl?"

"Yes, he said not to stop them, they have something planned. He wants us to regroup after they've left and prepare to repel them if they come back."

"Evidently," Dix thought, "they were going to hit them with something or they were going to blow the bridges at Alexandria."

"Butch, I'm heading back to camp and then to my boat to clean up and rest for a few days. I could use another five gallons of gas if you can round some up and you can help me float the four-wheeler across the river when I get back here."

Dix turned and headed back to camp. Once again he loaded up and headed back to town. When he arrived Butch had him a can of gas and the fishing boat was back on the Jonesville side of the river.

"They all pulled out about an hour ago, I'm going to let you drop me off in Ferriday on your way back."

Butch and Dix floated the four-wheeler and trailer across with the help of the aluminum boat and outboard motor and made the run back to Ferriday. Dix topped off the fuel and headed back to the boat camp.

Old Man Beagle Boyer couldn't believe his eyes, "Hot damn, I can't believe what I'm seeing; the stories coming from the battle were something. We lost a lot of people."

Dix nodded, "They lost more."

Ben and Frank knocked him off his feet and covered him up. "What you been feeding these boys?"

The old man laughed, "Lots of catfish, and don't make the mistake of cooking pancakes, they are the two biggest beggars that has ever been born."

Dix climbed on board the catamaran and kicked on the engine long enough to top off the batteries. He fired up the hot water heater and took a much needed and well deserved shower. He shaved his face and head clean. He put his clothes in a cut off plastic barrel that Beagle had on the dock. He dumped some detergent in and let them soak. He put on fresh clothes from the catamaran and boiled a pot of rice. He dumped some spaghetti sauce on top and stirred it up. Beagle came out with some fried catfish and they had a feast. Dix needed calories. One MRE a day was not enough to maintain a man in the field. Dix asked the old man, "What happened when the Chinese came across out of Natchez?"

"The Chinese made a run through Vidalia. They killed a few people who got in the way and a few people who didn't. Then the ruling Communist in Natchez felt it was time to extend their jurisdiction to this side of the river. They started to try and collect a toll from everybody this side of Ferriday. They left Ferriday alone because Butch's people were still running the show."

"Have they been by here?"

"They're charging me 50 lbs of catfish a week," Beagle grumbled.

"How many show up to do the collecting and what time do they normally arrive?"

"There are three of them, one who does the talking and two standing around with AK47's. They stop by here last thing in the afternoon every Wednesday, I think they have a fish fry after their political meeting. They even make me clean them."

Dix started thinking, "What kind of vehicle will they be in?"

"They'll drive up in a 4X4 Red Dodge pickup with four doors. They put all the crap they steal in the back. They'll have an ice chest for the fish. All I have to do is fill it up with fillets."

"Do they all get out at the same time?"

"Yea, they aren't worried about me putting up a fuss; they put the guns on me as soon as they get here."

"How deep is the water under the catamaran, Beagle?"

"It drops off to about 20 feet."

Dix nodded, "Well, at least I can sleep late in the morning." He cleaned his weapons and reloaded all the magazines.

The next morning they ate a good breakfast and Dix said, "Let's put Ben and Frank in the catamaran out of the way. When they arrive I'll be waiting out of sight behind that old boat. You give them the fish. When they get in the truck and turn it around, I'll kill them where they sit. They will be facing the other direction and will never know what hit them."

The day went as planned. Dix locked the pups up in the catamaran about 3:00 o'clock. He set up over by the old boat with Jake's AR15 and his magazine pouch containing six thirty round mags. He also had his Browning 9mm.

They arrived on schedule, a small man with braids and two huge guys with AK47's. They hopped out and called to Beagle, "Old man, fill it up, next week the tax is going up, we're going to need two ice chests full, we're having a party." Beagle filled the ice chest and they told him to put it in the back. Beagle struggled with the heavy chest but got it loaded. The biggest gunman shoved him and he fell on his back in the dirt. Dix watched as they got in and turned the truck around. As soon as they dropped it into drive, he opened up on them. He ran all thirty rounds through the cab and through the occupants. The driver hit the gas and the truck headed off toward the levee. It hit the levee, made it about half way up before it stopped and rolled back to the bottom. Dix walked over the truck and turned it off. The little one with the braids was still alive. Dix shot him through the head. He pulled the big man out from behind the wheel. He and Beagle went through the truck and saved anything of value including the catfish. He also drained the gas out of the gas tank and the oil from the crankcase.

Dix moved the catamaran away from the launch and tied it up on the side. He loaded the dead driver into the back seat and rolled the windows almost all the way up. He cranked the trunk, drove it to the edge of the ramp, set the parking brake, and stepped out with it in gear. The engine was knocking from the lack of oil. Dix tripped the brake release and the truck rolled into the water. It floated out a bit and sank to the bottom. He cranked the catamaran and repositioned it at the launch, completely covering where the truck sank. The old man dusted himself off, "What do we do now?"

Dix grinned, "We have an ice chest full of fish, let's eat. When they don't show up, we'll see if they send someone else. If they do, we'll kill them too. If they give us too much trouble, I'll go clean them out, just like I cleaned out Ferriday. I don't care one way or the other."

They let Ben and Frank out and fired up the grease in the Dutch oven. They even had an ice chest full of cold beer in the truck. Dix stowed their weapons and ammo, took their jewelry and precious metal and dumped them into the money box. The fresh eggs and milk would taste good for breakfast. They also had a case of coffee and all sorts of canned goods. The old man squirreled away the tobacco, Dix took the whiskey. Dix laughed, "I can't wait to see what the folks they send to look for them will have."

Dix was up early the next morning. They cooked and ate breakfast as the sun was rising. Dix figured they would be paid a visit that day and he wasn't wrong. They tied Ben and Frank up under Beagle's camp. Dix had reloaded his empty magazine and once again he waited over behind the old upended fishing boat. Sure enough four thugs showed up in a black Ford Expedition. They got out with short barreled shotguns and AK47's. The one driving had a Glock. They spotted Beagle, "Old man, did you see my men yesterday?"

"They were here at 4:00 o'clock yesterday afternoon. The last time I saw them they were in their red truck."

Dix didn't let them get too close; he stepped out and opened up on them. He had them killed before they could get off a round. Beagle complained, "I'm getting too old for this sort of thing, I need to sit down."

Dix looked in the truck, popped the back open, and cleaned out all their stuff. They had a box full of stolen jewelry and several cases of wine from the local winery. They also had several cases of buckshot, a box of Chinese hand grenades and a two way radio. He picked up their guns and picked them clean of their jewelry. They even had some gold and silver coins in their pockets. He took their knives and threw them in a bucket for trading later. He again drained the gas from the tank and the oil from the crankcase. He loaded them all up in the shiny truck and sent them to the bottom with their comrades in the red Dodge truck.

Dix said, "I hate losing these fine vehicles, but I don't want to advertise that we're doing the killing. We need to keep looking harmless." They turned on the radio, heard someone calling, but they gave up after not receiving an answer.

Butch ran by several days later, they had gotten word from Captain Miller that the Constitution Army had the Chinese bottled up between Alexandria and Lake Charles, Louisiana. They had a squadron of A10 Warthogs operational out of Bossier City that they had used to defeat the pro-communist police in the Shreveport - Bossier area. After the battle, our side was able to secure the air base, and support the squadron. "The A10's hit them this morning at Bossier and it looks like the troops that came through here are going to try and retreat to Natchez where they still have planes, and support equipment on the ground. Captain Miller wants us to take the airport at Natchez."

Dix was on the job, "I started several days ago. I've killed seven of the Natchez communists already. I'll get started on the airport in the morning." Dix loaded Butch up with more AK47's and ammo. "Is there anything else you need?"

"I haven't eaten in couple of days." Dix opened him a can of beans and Beagle dug out a couple of pounds of fried catfish.

The next morning Dix restocked his pack and loaded up Jake's AR15. He carried two magazine pouches with six thirty round magazines. He had his Browning in the shoulder holster and the four extra magazines for it.

Dix told the old man, "I'm going to stick around all day just in case they send another team of collectors out. They are awful easy to kill when they think they are facing an easy target. If they send another team great, if not you're going to take my boat and deliver me down the river and drop me off under the hill after dark. I'll go into the city and start softening them up." "I doubt they'll come over here once I start killing them in Natchez. Keep one of those shot guns handy or take the catamaran down the lake with Ben and Frank if you feel uneasy. Don't try to sleep unless you feel secure."

CHAPTER 25

LIGHT UP THE NIGHT

Beagle dropped Dix off under the hill below Clifton on the bluff. He took his time and made his way out of the river bottom. He was dressed in the same outfit he was wearing when he went into New Orleans to get Maggie and Bill. Once again he was haunted by their deaths. He had already convinced himself that they would have survived if it weren't for him. He had the feeling in his stomach again just like he felt when he found them all dead. For the long walk up Learneds Hill he was an emotional wreck. Luckily this road was seldom traveled and by the time he reached the top he had regained his composure. This was the town where he grew up. He remembered riding in the front seat of his dad's car and wondering if the car could make it to the top. He turned at the top of the hill onto Madison St. and again onto Linton. His rifle was under his coat and his hand was on the pistol grip so he could deploy it in a second. There was no power in the city and he slowly made his way down the sidewalk by the moonlight. He had become quite adept at moving around in the dark. He continued past the Victorian mansions until he reached the one owned by one of his friends.

He climbed the steep driveway and went to the back door. The back door stood open, he called out, no answer. He flipped on his green cap light and went in. His friend Tate was still there; his skeleton lay at the patio door. He recognized the cap and clothes. His house had been ransacked. Dix had hoped he had escaped to Louisiana where he had family. Dix walked out on the back porch and raised the hidden door to the basement. No one had found his wine cellar. It was still full and would be a great place to hide out in an emergency.

Dix left the house and walked down the driveway to the street. He worked his way back to the old bar on the corner. It was just down the street from the police station and the county jail. If the communists were in charge, they would be near here. He paused in the doorway of the bar and looked in. It stood empty with the doors open. He flipped on the green LED cap light and looked around. The floor was covered in litter and peanut shells. The peanut barrel was empty and all the beer and liquor was gone. There were just broken bottles behind the bar.

Dix set up a chair where he could sit in the dark and watch the street. He knew the police would be the bad guys here. He could hear a generator running and he could see lights on up at the jail. He left the old bar and walked up the street as a police car pulled up in front of the jail. They pulled a lady out of the back seat, Dix recognized her in the lights from the front of the jail. She was the granddaughter of one of his mother's best friends. She was about 40, if he remembered correctly. He raised his rifle up and killed the two cops. Before others could respond he grabbed their cuff keys off a ring and pulled her back into the shadows. He didn't stop with her until they were in the bar. By the time the other cops responded he had her out of the cuffs and told her to not make a sound.

The police were running up and down the street with spotlights on the patrol cars flashing. Dix stepped out of the opening and killed three more cops as fast as he could put the orange spot on them and pull the trigger. They were experiencing mass confusion. He replaced the magazine in the rifle and poked his head back into the bar.

"You coming with me or staying?"

"I'm with you."

They called her Rachel when they were growing up. Dix warned her, "When I stop you stop, do exactly what I say when I say, do you understand?"

She nodded, "Whatever you say."

They turned on Canal Street and starting casually walking. She whispered, "Shouldn't we be running."

"If we run we might trip over something in the dark. If we take our time, we have time to react and think; besides, it isn't easy running with the load I'm packing." They stopped in the shadows when a patrol car came down the street.

"Rachel, if they spot us, I want you to get down on the ground behind me, I'm going to kill them."

The car didn't stop so they continued on as soon as it passed. They walked on down Canal Street until they came to Madison, then turned up Linton Ave and went to his friend's house. They didn't speak until they were in the house. Rachel stared at the skeleton on the floor.

"Don't be afraid, my friend is dead but I am not going to disturb his body, I don't want anyone to know that we are hiding here." She stepped over the skeleton as Dix opened the door to the cellar. They walked down the stairs and closed the lid behind them. Dix had the green LED light on until he fished out a candle lantern and lit it. "You're Rachel Johnson aren't you? I'm Minnie's son, Dix."

"Oh, I remember you, but I didn't recognize you, you've changed a lot since I saw you last."

"A lot of time and a lot of miles have gone by since I left town."

"I remember when Ms. Minnie died, my grandmother talked about her all the time."

"What were the police dragging you in for?"

"The Party Chief in Adams County likes fresh meat every day. He has his goons pick up new entertainment every day."

"Who is the party chief?"

"Do you remember the old District Attorney?"

Dix thought for a minute, "Do you mean Damon Jones?"

"Yes that's him, but he goes by his new Islamic name, Assad Abdul."

Dix laughed, "I wonder how long it took him to think that one up?"

"What are you doing here armed for battle?"

"The Chinese are making a run back here to the airport. I've come in to soften up the resistance a little. You need to stay hidden here for a while. I'll leave you some food, there's plenty of wine and there's water in the hot water tank in the corner." Dix opened the valve and saw that it ran. "If you need to go to the bathroom, I suggest you go over in the back corner of the basement. If you have to go out, try not to travel in the daylight. I'll try and get back to check on you, but you never know what I'll run into." He handed her the .22 Beretta pocket pistol and showed her how to click off the safety. "I recommend you use this at point blank range only."

"Where is your family now, Dix?"

Dix looked back at Rachel, "They're all dead, that's why I'm killing all the good folks that enabled the communists to get and stay in power. I am working with the new Constitution Army." He unloaded all but a couple of the MRE's in his pack and headed up the steps. He called back as he closed the lid, "Good Luck."

It was after midnight and he decided to go take a look at the airport. He walked north through the neighborhoods, all was quiet in town. Once he heard a car coming and squatted down next to a pile of uncollected garbage on the curb. It was a police car. The car stopped up the street and the cop got out and went up the driveway into a home. Dix heard a woman arguing with him and watched as he came storming out. When he got back to the car Dix was waiting. He waited until the patrolman was seated behind the wheel and shot him. Dix rolled him over into the passenger's seat got behind the wheel and closed the door. He cranked the engine and pulled away in no particular hurry.

Dix cut through the neighborhood streets driving slowly along Martin Luther King Street and headed north out to Pine Ridge Road until he came to Airport Road. He followed it until he came to Artman Road, made a left turn and stopped on the first bridge. He pulled the dead deputy out of the passenger seat, took his Beretta 9mm and the extra magazines and emptied his pockets. He had a pocket full of wedding bands and several diamond engagement rings. Dix rolled him over the side of the bridge railing and listened as the body dropped about 30 feet to the shallow stream below. He took the car up to an abandoned farm house on the right hand side of the road and drove it into an old garage that was about to fall down. He listened on the police radio the entire time and never heard any chatter. It would be a while before they missed him.

He walked back to the road and casually strolled back down to Airport Road. He was less than a mile from the airport. The night was cool as he approached. He slowly made his way into a little recreation area with a pond that was located next to the airport. The airport was dark and there were no signs of life. He noticed the tip of a cigarette flare as the owner drew a puff. It was a sentry standing at the front gate. Dix continued his wait, kneeling beside a big pine tree. The clouds parted and let the moonlight shine through. He could hear a generator running somewhere behind the little terminal building. Another guard walked out of the front door of the terminal. He flipped on a light for a moment while he was fiddling with something in his hand. Dix couldn't see what it was. The light went out a moment later. A truck cranked up out in one of the hangers. The headlights flooded an area where a group of about 30 cargo planes were lined up next to the runway. The airport was small and they were parked where they didn't block the two runways which were long enough to land large commercial jets.

Dix remembered when George Bush Sr. made a political rally stop back in the 80's. All this Progressive New World Order crap was getting kicked off even then. It just took a communist President to use the groundwork laid out by those idiots to attempt an overthrow.

The truck pulled out and made a long slow run around the airport property. A spot light swung around the edges. Dix got ready to step behind the tree when the spotlight paused and a shot rang out. They were spot lighting deer on the airport property. While they were busy retrieving the deer Dix created an opening in the fence and slipped through. The entire airport facility was not fenced, just the portion around the roadway and around the main terminal. Dix slowly walked over to the first airplane and waited. He listened and watched as the deer hunters loaded the deer and returned to the hanger. After they drove past he looked up and flipped on his green LED cap light. He quickly found what he was looking for. The drain line on the fuel tank was under the wing near the fuselage. Dix opened the valve and let the fuel flow, he did the same thing on the other side. He made his way from plane to plane. There were several different makes and models but he managed to find all the drains. He no longer had to use his light to find the openings and valves.

The troop transport helicopters were American made, it took him a few minutes to figure out the valve locations. The wind was blowing from the south so the smell of jet fuel was being carried away from the buildings. When he finished he lit the dry Bermuda grass full of jet fuel under the plane on the end. He walked toward the hangers where they were cleaning the deer. It only took a few moments until the flames caught the second plane on fire. The doors flew up on the hanger and Dix killed the Chinese who had been butchering the deer.

He waited in the shadows of the hanger as the airport came to life. By now six of the planes were engulfed in flames and had the entire area lit up. A fire truck came out of the fire station. Dix waited until they were at point blank range and opened up on the cab where the driver and firemen were riding. The truck careened out of control and into the inferno. The truck just added to the conflagration. By now more than half of the planes were on fire.

Dix swapped the empty magazine for a full one, his secret was out and he came under fire from the gate guard. He ran back into the shadows and slowed so he would not trip or injure himself. He walked out from behind the hanger and shot the guard who was still looking for a target. By now the entire airport was ablaze. The garrison of about 100 Chinese troops was in full panic mode.

Dix created another opening in the fence, walked about 300 yards up the road, and disappeared into the woods. He crossed the road and followed a power line that led back around to Artman Road where he stashed the cop car. He crossed the bridge at a run and got back to the old farm house. Cranking the patrol car, he backed out of the drive. He turned south, went back to Airport road and took a right. He retraced his steps back to Tate's house where he parked the police cruiser in the garage and closed the door. He called out to Rachel that he was back. "I don't feel like sleeping on a cellar floor, so I'll drag down a couple of mattresses and blankets."

Dix took a few minutes and rolled his friend Tate up in the den rug and moved him into the kitchen out of the way. If he lived long enough and had the ability, he would bury him down at the cemetery. Dix went upstairs and brought down two mattresses from the bedrooms along with some quilts and pillows. They made pallets to sleep on and Dix was soon out for a while. He slept until after lunch.

Rachel woke him, "I've been hiding out of sight up in the front room, I don't know what's going on, but the police are all over the place. I haven't seen this much activity since they took over the town in the beginning."

Dix yawned, "They have 5 dead and one missing. All of the Chinese aircraft were destroyed last night along with a handful of dead Chinese. They are looking for the dozens of saboteurs' who are running around in their midst. By the way, I brought you something."

He dug into his pouch and brought out the Beretta 9mm and the extra two magazines. "The fellow who had these doesn't need it anymore." Dix gave her a rundown on the events of the evening.

Rachel laughed, "The last we knew you were selling office equipment, were you always working for the government and using the salesman thing as a cover?"

"No, I just got worried that we were headed for a financial collapse when we elected a communist president. I put together what I thought were adequate preparations to survive, that included food and weapons. The same thing has happened in every country in history that had a communist get in power. Our population was seduced by all the free government giveaways. They were also ignorant from all the subtle brainwashing by the main stream media and the idiots in Hollywood. Bad people started taking advantage of the innocent. They destroyed everything I had including every member of my family. I am doing what needed to be done to begin with; I'm killing every S.O.B. that needs killing. Right now it is the communist Chinese and their enablers here in the city. I plan on killing bad guys until they are all dead or I am."

Dix opened up a MRE and told Rachel, "Try to limit yourself to just one a day. If you find yourself in a position where you've got to move, do not leave any food. Try and stay long enough to eat everything you can't carry first. Your body will store the food until you need it. You haven't said much about your people, or what happened to you."

"I was married to Mitch Jones for about ten years. I never had any children because he didn't want any. He decided he wanted a younger woman about three years ago. I should have expected it, as he left his first wife for a younger woman when I met him, that younger woman was me. All my people had died before the collapse. My brother and his family were in Alaska working for an oil company. The last I heard from them is that they were heading to his fish camp and were stocking up while they still could. Knowing him he was ready. I wasn't so smart. I thought he was a nut. I put back a little food but I wound up at a FEMA camp. I escaped the FEMA camp when we realized that we were going to be shipped out to work in a factory in exchange for the food they give us. All they fed us for weeks was a small bowl of rice with a small spoonfull of salty beans. We were all slowly starving to death. I went under the wire with a couple of other ladies. I don't know where they went, because we split up."

"Where's the camp located?"

"Do you remember the prison down in Wilkinson County?"

Dix nodded, "Yes, what did they do with the prisoners?"

"They killed all of them."

"And then?"

"I hid out at my mother's old house until they found me looking for food last night. They told me if I made Assad Abdul happy I would get a good meal; that was when you showed up."

"Stay put while I check something out." Dix slipped out of the cellar and went out to the patrol car in the garage. He popped the trunk lid and looked in the trunk. Just as he expected, it was full of canned goods. It took him five trips but he unloaded all the food. He had struck pay dirt once again. "Rachel, do you mind staying forted up here for a while?"

"No, this food looks so good, I'm not going anywhere."

Dix waited until dark before heading out again. He once again carried what he considered a heavy battle load. His pack was restocked and he carried eight full 30 round mags for Jake's AR15. The two empty ones were in his pack. If he lucked up on some more .223/5.56, he would fill them again. He walked down Maple St. towards Main. It was pitch black dark and he drifted in and out of the shadows. There was some activity in a backyard on the west side of the street, a small fire was burning and you could see people sitting around it. He turned and walked down to the bluff and stood in the darkness overlooking the river. There were no street lights shining. He could see the bridge in the moonlight. A small light could be seen at the base of the bridge on the Louisiana side of the river. Evidently they had a barricade and checkpoint at that location.

Back in Natchez he saw a bonfire going, but couldn't tell much about it. A patrol car cruised down Broadway causing Dix to crouch behind the old gazebo and let it pass. It turned north on State Street and headed for the jail. He sat for a long time taking in the sights and smells of the night. He walked up State St. to within shooting distance of the jail. The carnage from the night before had been cleaned up.

The old jail house was still standing, he didn't know if they still housed prisoners in it or not. He thought about setting it on fire, but didn't want to take a chance on burning some good guys to death. Dix stood back in the doorway of an abandoned lawyer's office and waited until another police car passed. Apparently they had quit using the city police department and were working out of the new county jail. It was only about 20 years old and they had plenty of room. He figured fat old Assad Abdul was working out of city hall and probably living in Dickel Hall, Jefferson Manor or Blackthorn Place. All were immense antebellum mansions that had been restored and maintained in their original splendor.

He back tracked down to the old train station and cut through the parking lot. There were some abandoned cars with flat tires and a couple that appeared to be used on occasion. The tires were pumped up and the windshields were clean. He turned on Washington St. and walked down Wall St. to Orleans. He methodically walked down Orleans until it turned into Homochitto. The old drive in was still on the corner, it was probably vacant.

He walked in front of the old elementary school and was almost caught out in the open by a patrol car. He froze in place as they turned from MLK right onto Orleans and went in the opposite direction. He would have simply opened up on them and killed them had they turned in his direction. Dix found it amusing that instead of being paralyzed with fear as he once would have been, he looked at every encounter as an opportunity to finish the hunt.

He continued his stroll past the old high school and on to the old home called Blackthorn Place. It was a massive, antebellum mansion surrounded by columns rising up to the second story roof. As he expected, there was a guard house at the gate and a generator was humming away somewhere behind it. The house was lit up like the Governor's mansion it was. Dix crossed the street and hid in between a couple of old houses that had been abandoned. Patrol cars came and went. A big black Cadillac Escalade came in around 9:00 pm. The guard closed the gate behind it. Dix thought to himself, "Assad Abdul has evidently arrived."

The guard walked around to the side and took a leak hidden in the shadows of the guard house. Dix took this opportunity to cross the street and stand next to the little guard house. The guard came back in and resumed his duties. Dix stood quiet in the dark. The guard turned on a lively rap tune that grated at Dix's nerves.

Dix wished that he had taken Jake's advice and made silencers for their pistols. Dix didn't want to kill the guard with his Kbar; he much preferred to pop a cap on them. He slung the rifle behind him and pulled out the Kbar. He could see the guard through the window. He kept nodding off. Dix waited until he started snoring and timed each step with a loud snore. The Kbar was razor sharp. With one quick thrust he ran the knife through the guard's throat. The guard struggled less than a second and it was over.

Dix took the Glock 40 and the two magazines the guard had on his belt. He wiped the knife off on the guard's shirt and replaced it in its sheath on his belt. Something you never forget is the smell of hot blood squirting and steaming in the cool night air. The guard had lost control of his bowels in the final moments of life which added to the acrid odor.

Dix washed his hands from the water cooler standing in the corner. He walked out and eased the gate open enough to slip onto the grounds of the mansion. Making a kill is a matter of planning when possible. Sometimes he had to shoot on instinct, but most of the time it was no different than deer hunting. You orient yourself in a hidden position, you take careful aim and you execute your plans. You concentrate on the process not the results. The kill takes place because you carefully execute the chain of events leading up to the act.

Dix stayed in the shadows as he approached the house. He sat for a long time in the yard until he spotted a guard sitting just inside the front door. Dix saw him through a window when he got up to get coffee. He eased around the back and sat for a while and found a couple of Chinese officers sitting on the porch smoking. They were in heated conversation that Dix could not hope to understand. One of them smacked the table and the other hopped up, slightly bowed, and went in. Evidently they were not happy that all the aircraft were destroyed.

From his spot in the yard he could see up on the second floor. Assad Abdul could be seen though his bedroom window. Several scantily clad ladies could also be seen. In another bedroom he saw the lights come on and the Chinese officer who had just left walked into view.

Dix put the yellow dot of his Trijicon scope on the side of Assad Abdul's large head and squeezed off a round. The next shot went through the torso of the Chinese office that was still smoking on the back porch. The third shot went to the Chinese officer who had come to the window to see what the shooting was all about.

Dix didn't wait; but went to a spot where he could see the guard from the front door. He saw him pass in front of the bedroom window, in Assad Abdul's room. The guard bent over out of view; when he stood back up into view, Dix popped him through the back. Dix then hit the generator with about ten rounds and the lights went out.

He replaced the magazine in his rifle and proceeded out of the gate in the dark. He stopped at the houses across the street and hid in the shadows. Police cars rushed to the scene. When they stopped to open the gates, Dix riddled both passenger compartments with 55 grain, full metal jacket .223 bullets. One car took off, hit the other, and pushed it through the gates. Dix emptied a second magazine into both vehicles and reloaded again.

He walked down to Arlington Ave and back into the residential housing area in town. He continued down Washington all the way to Wall St. near the jail, he found it bustling with activity. They were all packing shotguns and rifles, their little world had been upset. Three cars sped away with lights and sirens on; evidently, they were rushing to save the mayor. Dix couldn't know for certain if the Mayor was dead, but if he were a betting man, he would bet that the Mayor was having his opportunity to meet Allah. Dix wondered how that "72 virgins" deal was working out for him.

One last car pulled up in front of the jail. The deputy in the passenger seat hoped out and ran up the steps of the Sheriff's office. He came out with a shotgun. Dix popped him just as he stooped to get back in the car. He then fired through the back window killing the driver. He paused a moment then walked over to the car while keeping an eye on the jail. He pulled the dead driver out and got in the seat. He put the car in gear and drove up to Pearl and headed back to Linton Ave.

He hid the police car in the garage behind the abandoned house next door to his old friend's house. He looked in the trunk and found a battle pack of 5.56/.223 NATO ammo, as well as more food. He went back to the cellar and was greeted by Rachel.

"I don't think the mayor is going to be a problem any longer, he had a tremendous headache the last time I saw him."

Rachel wanted to know, "Where are we with the kill count now?"

"They're probably down to less than two dozen if you include the ones manning the roads into and out of town. I shot two Chinese officers over at the Mayor's house on Homochitto."

"How did you know he lived on Homochitto?"

"You just have to think like they think. If you considered yourself to be the Governor of the region where would you live, then you'll want to live in the fanciest house in town."

Dix reloaded his magazines from the battle pack and ate some peanut butter and crackers. They opened a bottle of wine and relaxed. He pulled out the Glock 40, the extra two magazines and added them to the cache of food and ammo in the cellar. "We can hold up here for a few more days if we need to, there should be enough water in the hot water heater to last a while."

Rachel sighed, "I wish I could take a bath."

"I'm afraid you'll have to wait until I can get you to the catamaran."

"What's a catamaran?"

Dix explained to her about the catamaran and what he had been doing for the past couple of months. The only worry he had was if someone had seen him coming and going and told the police. The thought continued to bother him as he finished eating. Finally he sat up, "We're moving. I'm starting to feel trapped. We've got about two hours to go before daylight, let's load up the patrol car and get out of here." They loaded up all their supplies and headed down the driveway.

"I've got a wild idea, I know where there used to be a canoe in a friend's pond out on Artman Road. If we get that canoe, we can put it in the river somewhere north of town, cross the river, and get into Old River where my Catamaran is anchored. Otherwise, we'll have to find another place to hide or run the gauntlet by running the checkpoint on the bridge. Believe me, the last place you want to be is in a car being shot with rifles."

They drove out MLK to Pine Ridge Road and out Airport Road to Artman again. They parked in the carport of the old farm house. Dix closed the door on the garage and the cruiser was hidden from view. He told Rachel to stick the Glock 9mm behind her belt at the small of her back and to put the two extra magazines in her back pocket. She said, "I don't know how to shoot it." "It's simple, all you have to do is point it and pull the trigger." She grinned as she tucked it away and put on a black windbreaker they had found in Tate's closet.

"Do you ever take off your guns?"

Dix glanced over his shoulder, "I always keep a weapon on me or within arm's length."

"How many men have you killed?"

"I quit counting a couple of months ago; but, you don't want to know. Just know that I can and will tend to business if necessary. Now stay quiet unless there is something I need to see or know. I don't know if anyone still lives here or not."

"How do you know this place?"

Dix shook his head, "I built this house a lifetime ago."

They were silent as they climbed the hill; the house was empty, ransacked like most others. The big barn in the back was open. They walked through the barn and out the back door. A trail leading down the hill in the back led to a lake. At the bottom of the trail was an orange Coleman canoe with paddles. The sun was starting to come up and he looked across the lake. Tears welled up in his eyes as he remembered a father and two little kids paddling around the lake. He kept looking around for his old Catahoula Cur, named Champ, to come running down the bank. Rachel looked concerned as he grabbed the canoe and started up the steep trail dragging it. She grabbed the back and helped him drag it up the hill.

"There's no one here, I'll get the car and bring it up here and we'll tie the canoe to the light rack on top."

"What does this place mean to you?"

"My kids grew up here, we had dogs, and Christmas trees, and ...." His voice trailed off as he got choked up all over again.

She hugged his neck and went in the house out of the wind while he went for the cruiser. He parked it in the barn and went to check on the house next door. It had been burned to the ground, so no one was there to notify the police.

He put the canoe on top of the car and using some wire he found in the barn secured it to the light bar. They didn't have far to go so they were good to go. Dix went over the entire house. The furniture was still in the house. He went into his old office and into the closet. He looked up on top of the hot water heater in the closet and there it set, the little magnet key that would unlock the hidden closet door.

Dix placed the magnet over the hidden latch and the door popped open. Dix pulled open the door and flipped on the green LED light on his cap. A Remington 12 gauge 870 pump with an 18 inch barrel was right where he left it along with a bandoleer holding 20 rounds of #4 buckshot and five 12 gauge slugs. He left the 22 pistol and the carton of 22 bullets in the bottom of the little hidden closet, in case he had to ever come back. He gave the 12 gauge to Rachel along with the bandoleer. "Do you know what this is?"

"Yes, my father use to take me hunting, his 870 had a long barrel. We shot low brass #8's dove hunting." She put the sling over her shoulder, the bandoleer fit around her waist. Dix gave the old barn and pool house a once over but didn't find anything else they really needed.

They loaded the shotgun, hopped in the cruiser, and turned back to Airport Road. When they reached Pine Ridge Road they turned north and went up to a place the locals called, Anna's Bottom. The road went down into the river bottom which was now covered by backwater from the river. They unloaded the canoe in the ditch beside the road. Once they had all the gear loaded they climbed in and paddled down the ditch into deeper water. After about an hour they made it to the main river.

It was very intimidating, the river was huge and the canoe was small. Dix told Rachel, "If we turn over stay with the canoe, there is foam in the ends and the canoe won't sink. You just concentrate on paddling us across the river. I'll try to keep us lined up." Dix was on his knees in the bottom of the canoe and he pulled hard on the paddle as they crossed the river. Whirlpools grabbed them and pulled them around. One completely spun them around in the current. After a long 45 minutes they finally made it to the far side. They stuck close to the edge until they reached the bayou that would take them into Old River. Once in the bayou the current released them and they paddled into the lake.

Once again Dix came upon Old Man Beagle Boyer running his nets. The old man looked up at them, "You're the last person on Earth I expected to show up here in a canoe with a lady. The word on the street is that a commando squad has hit Natchez, did you see any of them?"

Dix shrugged, "I thought I heard a little shooting."

They paddled back to the landing and Dix fired up the hot water heater in the catamaran. After a round of hot showers, Dix cleaned his weapons and asked Beagle, "Have you heard from Butch lately?"

"He was by here this morning. The Chinese have stopped their retreat in this direction. Word is that a squad of commandos destroyed their aircraft on the ground."

Dix just laughed, "I opened the fuel cocks and let the jet fuel drain out in the grass. I took my time and went from plane to plane until I had them all draining. Then I lit the last one and the fire just went from plane to plane. I shot all the Chinese I could see and disabled the airport fire truck. Then all I had to do was slip out without getting shot."

Beagle shook his head, "It couldn't have been that easy."

"That wasn't the hard part; the hard part was rescuing the girl!"

Beagle laughed, "I haven't heard hide nor hair from the mayor's men."

Dix told him, "They are looking for a new mayor, the old one and about two thirds of his men didn't come to work this morning."

"Butch said you were absolutely ruthless."

"I admit it. I've been on a vendetta. They started it. All they had to do was to leave us all alone and let us live our lives. They destroyed everything that mattered to me and my plans are to destroy them and everyone who has enabled them."

After a big mess of fried catfish and beans from a can they called it a night. Dix let Rachel sleep in the catamaran and he slept on the deck on some cushions. Ben and Frank thought it was great. They both spent the night plastered up against him.

The next morning Rachel cooked breakfast. She used some of the eggs, grits and spam. She made biscuits from scratch after firing up the propane stove in the catamaran. They spent the rest of the day catching up on their rest and doing simple chores.

CHAPTER 26

CLEAN UP

The next day Dix hopped on the four wheeler and headed to Ferriday. He found Butch over at the police station. Butch looked at Dix, "What in the daylights happened in Natchez? We heard that a squad of commandos took out the Chinese forces at the airport and two thirds of the Natchez police and the mayor."

"I think most of the remaining Chinese troops are still alive; but, there should be less than a hundred left. All of the Chinese aircraft were destroyed on the ground. The mayor should be dead along with most of his men. I'm sorry I couldn't do more, but I had to evacuate a lady I rescued from the police. I had a funny feeling that I needed to get out while I could," Dix explained. "I'll go back in a couple of days if ya'll need me to."

"That's why the Chinese stopped their retreat and are now trying to make a run south to the coast. Captain Miller asked us to secure the Natchez Airport. They want to use it as an A10 refueling and maintenance field."

Dix nodded, "Well, the runways are open, but the open areas are a horrible mess. I think we can flush them out pretty easy. Ten good men with rifles could probably do it in half a day. With the aircraft destroyed there is no reason for the Chinese to stay. With their officers dead, they may even surrender. I killed three of them the night before last. Can you wrap up the rest of the Natchez police in Vidalia?"

"They cleared out three nights ago."

"Butch, have your guys shoot the ones manning the check-points on the river bridges. That'll be four or five more we don't have to worry about. We can land a squad below Learneds Hill from the river. The mayor's got a hole through his head and most of his coworkers are dead. I don't think their heart will be in defending the city."

"I'll have the team put together, when do we leave, Dix?"

"Tomorrow just before dark, meet us at the boat camp. I'll get Beagle to drop us off in my boat."

Butch asked, "You need anything?"

"I need a bottle of propane for the catamaran, I like a hot shower every week or so."

Butch laughed, "I'll see what I can do."

Dix ran back to the boat camp in time for lunch, Rachel had clothes drying on lines strung between trees. He hopped off the four-wheeler and asked Beagle, "Are there any of these camps in any shape to occupy?"

Beagle thought for a minute, "There's a houseboat about a half mile up the lake, it's in real good shape, I think there is even a 100 gallon propane tank on it still full. I can't move it by myself and you haven't been here long enough to help me."

"Let's go get it, I don't want to sleep on the boat deck again, I'm getting too old to keep sleeping on the ground or on top of things that were not made to sleep on."

They cranked the fishing boat and ran down to the house boat. It was sitting on pontoons and was about 30 feet long and about ten feet wide. They tied on to it with the fishing boat and cut it loose. They floated it down next to the catamaran and tied it off to a couple of big willow trees. It had a fresh water cistern fed by a gutter system on the roof. It also had a 12volt RV water pump, a propane stove and hot water tank. There was even a solar panel on the roof and some six volt batteries from a golf cart just waiting to be hooked up.

Dix looked at Rachel, "You now have a house unless someone shows up some day to claim it."

"Why don't you take it, Dix, I don't feel right getting the best house."

"I don't stay around enough to worry about a nice house. I just need a place to rest up between missions. If I have to, I can move the catamaran wherever I need it."

The house boat had a little diesel generator on the back. They cleaned out the fuel tank and put on a fresh fuel filter they found in a cabinet. Dix pulled the battery he took out of the brown bronco and fired it up. It ran great, the water system pressured up, fortunately someone had drained the water lines for the winter. The house boat also had a washing machine. Dix said, "go easy on the lights at night, we'll run the generator once a week to wash clothes and charge up the battery. I'll hook up the solar panel as soon as I have a chance."

The cistern on the back of the house boat looked like it held about 250 gallons and it was full. Dix poured some Clorox in the cistern to kill any bacteria and gave Rachel a filter bottle to drink from.

He told her, "Once we start using the water and fresh water is added from rain we won't have to worry too much about contamination."

He ran a water hose over to the catamaran and topped off the water tank in it. Beagle fried up some more catfish and they cooked some corn bread in a skillet. Then Dix went into the catamaran and fell asleep. He woke up middle of the afternoon; the nightmare had left him in a cold sweat, his hands were still shaking as he put his gear together. He found Rachel in her living area sewing.

"Are you taking in mending, Rachel?"

She laughed, "I found some clothes that are a little big. Beagle is going to help me go through some of these other camps to see if I can find some more clothes, dry goods and stuff. This houseboat has two bedrooms and the bed is a lot bigger than in the catamaran. You can stay here as well."

"I appreciate the offer, if I survive this mission I'll think about it."

"What mission, Dix?"

"I'm taking a squad in to do a little clean up in Natchez."

"Why do you have to do it, Dix?"

"I don't have to do anything, I'm going hunting, I take great pleasure in putting holes in bad guys. These people are tentacles of a great big octopus that caused everything that has happened. I plan on cutting off tentacles until the octopus is dead or I'm dead."

"Sooner or later, Dix Jernigan, you're going to have to realize that you are just a man and you can't hold the weight of the world on your shoulders. I know your family is dead, and everything is gone, but you are still alive and there are people who care whether you live or die. You saved my life, you saved Beagle, and those dogs love you, look at them sitting next to you. Don't keep trying to get yourself killed."

"If I don't do it, somebody like Butch who still has a family will have to take the chance. I'm almost an expert, I am one of the few men alive who can walk into the lion's den, kill the lions, and walk out with their food."

At that moment Butch and his men drove over the levee. "Are you ready? Here's your propane bottle." He reached over in the back of the truck and gave it to him.

"Thanks, the boat's ready."

Dix dropped his pack into the boat, slid Jake's AR15 over his head and put on his oil skin coat and his cap with the green LED cap light. Rachel handed him the .22 Beretta. He took it and put it in his back pocket.

He told Butch, "By the time Beagle gets back here, we'll be in position on Canal Street to kill any cops coming to the checkpoint rescue. You guys take the checkpoint communists out. We'll take care of any reinforcements. Ya'll come on across with our transportation. We'll be going to the airport from Pine Ridge Road. I want us to go at them from the back side. If we approach from Airport Road, I know they will see us and put up an alert. They'll have a generator going, so with a little luck, they'll be lit for a few seconds to give us a chance to shoot. I want us to crawl through the woods and grass using the destroyed aircraft as cover. If we can make it to the damaged aircraft, we can use them as cover to shoot from."

Dix opened the can of hand grenades he had taken from the police cruiser and passed them out among the six guys who were going with him on the boat. He recognized most of them from the Ferriday jail. Beagle dropped them off under Learneds Hill. The sun was setting as they spread out about 20 feet from each other in a line.

They made their way down the Bluff and along Canal Street. A police car pulled out down on Main turning in their direction. Almost as one they opened up on the car, the patrolmen inside never knew what hit them. The guys quickly cleaned out the car of guns and ammo and whatever else they could carry. They split up the food and by and large it was eaten by the time they reached the bridge. About that time they heard Butch and his guys take out the guards on the bridge. As expected, two police cars came from the east. Both cars were riddled and the occupants instantly killed. Once again the cars were cleaned out.

Butch and his group came over in two Chevy Suburbans. One was full the other had only a driver. All but two of Dix's men piled in the near empty one and they headed through town. They didn't run into any resistance. Two men with AK47's who didn't get in, positioned themselves to keep the bridge open.

When they got to the back of the airport, they parked their Suburbans, and listened while Dix told them where the buildings were and where the destroyed aircraft were resting. They scattered out about 20 yards apart, eased into the woods and made it to the open grass area around the airport. On their stomachs, they crawled across several hundred yards until they were among the wreckage of aircraft.

Dix was surprised they had not met resistance. He could see the front gate, there was no guard and the generator was not running. He motioned for Butch to hang back. Dix crawled across the next runway until he was next to the fence that separated the tarmac from the parking area. Dix once again created an opening with a pair of bolt cutters he kept in his pack. Once through the fence, he crawled over to the building they were using as barracks. He pulled a pin from a hand grenade and hurled it with all his might through the glass window. The old single pane window shattered and the hand grenade rattled across the floor. Dix was against the brick wall on the outside. The grenade went off; nothing happened. Dix went around front staying clear of the windows. He tried the door and found it open. Inside he found the building empty. He motioned for Butch who came running.

"I think they've pulled out. Get your men to do a sweep of all the buildings."

The Chinese had pulled out. They were either on the road or a transport came in and evacuated them. Butch radioed back to town and learned from the men in town that a caravan of police cars and SUVs just came down Canal Street and turned east.

"They are either heading this way or heading south to the FEMA prison in Woodville."

Butch got on his radio and spoke with Captain Miller and told him that the Natchez Airport was secure and that they would try to get the generator running and the landing lights working. One of the guys with Butch was an electrician.

Dix told Butch, "You saw how we had to approach the airport. Any bad guys coming back will have to do it the same way. Get us some eyes among those wrecks looking in that direction. Now that we have it, we need to keep it without getting killed. Let's head back to town, make sure the communists are completely gone and let whoever is in jail out.

"Let me assign someone in charge here and we'll head out. We're good to go, the Chinese must have left by air because they left several hundred rations and MRE's."

Dix nodded, "We had better take a couple of cases of food with us as any prisoners we find will probably be starving."

They loaded up and headed to the jail. They stopped several blocks away and approached the jail on foot. Everything was quiet. As expected the jail was empty. Dix and Butch went into the cell block and found most of the guys in bad shape. They let them out and passed out MRE's. One of Dix's lifelong friends, Jerry Wilson, was among them.

Dix asked, "How long you been locked up, Jerry?"

Jerry looked at him twice, "Dix is that you, what the hell happened to you, you look like hell."

"I've just been fighting for the past few months. I try not to look in a mirror if I can help it. You aren't exactly ready for GQ magazine yourself."

"We're the mayor's yard boys. They lead us out once or twice a week to work at Blackthorn Place or as the mayor calls it "The Governor's Mansion.""

"I hate to tell you this Jerry, but it looks like you've lost your job, the mayor retired suddenly with about 2/3rds of his men. I know you're here, what happened to your kids, Kelly and Matt?"

"Last I heard Kelly was in the FEMA camp south of here, I haven't heard from Matt since we lost communication with him at school. He was out in Logan, Utah, at an engineering school."

"Utah would have been one of the places I would have chosen, those Mormons believe in food storage and preparation."

"What about your family, Dix?"

"They were all murdered."

They just looked at each other in silence after that. Dix broke the silence, "Let's get you armed up. Butch, do you have some guns and ammo, these boys want to go hunting." "Do you guys need any help?"

Jerry shook his head, "You just show us the guns and ammo and get out of our way."

"You may run into some Chinese troops, if you do, send someone back so we can help."

Jerry and about 30 other former inmates armed up out of the mayor's arsenal, wolfed down some food, and headed out.

Dix warned them, "Be careful if you are driving, I killed most of these idiot cops while they were sitting in their cars, you're a sitting duck when you're in one. Five or six cars passed our guys heading east after we took out the bridge guards and three of their patrol cars with deputies. I figure they are heading to the FEMA prison. If they're smart they'll have a bug out location."

Jerry looked back, "They aren't that smart, they were just part of a political machine that we let get out of hand."

Dix and Butch watched as they headed out looking for cars and trucks to take them south to the FEMA prison. "Those guys don't look in any kind of shape to go fighting."

"They look just like us when we started, I'd hate to be on the receiving end of what they're fixing to dish out."

Dix sighed, "I'm tired, this fighting all night is about to catch up with me."

"Do you want me to have one of the guys run you back to your boat?"

"No, just run me up to a friend's house on Linton Ave. I'll sack out there for a while then I've got something to do." Butch's man dropped him off at the foot of the driveway.

CHAPTER 27

THE FINAL PUSH

The sun was just starting to lighten the sky in east when Porter reached the lodge. The sky was deep red, he didn't know if it was a good thing or not, but it was pretty. A light wind was blowing from the Southwest. All the men were packing up and cleaning up around the lodge. Charlie would find that it was immaculate. The bed clothes were already washed and hanging on lines to dry. All the men waved when they recognized him. Sergeant Daniels called out, "Porter, did Charlie tell you the best way to head out of here?"

"He said for us to follow this map, it has water holes marked, after that we're on our own and will have to find locals to point us to water."

"Porter you lead the way, I assume you have some idea where we are going?"

"Sure thing Sarge, the road leads straight out to the highway. We can take the highway or cross it and continue cross country, that's your call, I'm just a private."

"Okay guys, saddle up and follow Porter." With that, Porter gently bumped Old Dollar's sides and the mule started up with

253

Ruth in tow. The line between them stayed slack, she had followed Old Dollar before. They didn't go fast, the animals had a long way to carry them and there was no reason to tax the animals. They rode for several hours and came to a water tank by one of the windmills on the ranch. They let the animals rest so Porter set the packs off Ruth's pack saddle to let her have some relief. The other guys left their horses loaded but Porter didn't want to wear her down. They drank their fill and Porter spoiled them by giving each one a biscuit.

Some of the guys were curious how Porter was able to kill so many Chinese. "I don't know, I just did it, I thought my family was prisoner in the house and I had to get them out. So I figured I had to start killing them to work my way inside. So that's what I did, I just kept killing 'em until I ran out of targets. I didn't have time to count." An older guy named Bill asked, "What did you use son, I mean what weapon did you use?"

"I used everything, I started with my long gun out on the range, changed to my AK47 when they came in on my blind, and used my knife and pistol at the house."

"Damn, remind me not to get on your bad side." Everyone laughed and they mounted up and headed down the road. Another two hours had them out to the highway. They once again gave the horses a rest and studied the maps. The decision was made to go cross country as the terrain looked easy and there were several small rivers and creeks on the projected track. They travelled the rest of the day and stopped for the evening on a small creek.

A little snow remained and the night would be getting cold. There was some grass growing along the creek, so Porter took off the packs and saddles and put a halter on Old Dollar and hobbled them. Both seemed content to eat the grass along the stream bank. The troop set up camp, Bill was the corporal of the troop and assigned guards for two hour shifts so that everyone could get some rest. All the other horses were also hobbled along the creek so they could graze. Porter piled up some rocks to reflect the heat of the fire towards him. He built a small fire and rolled out his bedroll. He cooked some rice with meat, salt and pepper. It wasn't the best meal he had ever eaten, but it was filling and hot. The sleeping bag was warm and he was tired. He was woke around midnight for his guard duty. Nothing happened that night; he could see Dollar and Ruth in the moonlight grazing. They stopped after a while and appeared to be sleeping standing up. His father's watch had a soft glow and it read 2 am, so he woke the guy who would take over the guard duty and he went back to bed for the rest of the night.

He lay on his back looking up at the stars and wondered what Sandy was doing back home. A kick at his feet brought him to a sitting position. It was early morning and he didn't realize that he had been asleep. Sergeant Daniels said, "Jones, bail out, we got a long way to go if we are going to get into Louisiana in time to kill us some Commies." Deciding to eat a cold breakfast, he put some honey in a couple of biscuits, which with hard tack would be nibbled on while he rode. Old Dollar and Ruth were easy to catch, they were about as tame as you could get, and he had them saddled and packed in no time. Sergeant Daniels told him, "Porter, it's someone else's turn to ride point. You can eat dirt today and bring up the rear."

"Whatever you say, Sarge."

They headed out like the day before with Porter bringing up the rear. He stayed back about 100 yards to stay out of the dust. The wind was still coming out of the Southwest so it blew the dust kicked up, by the 30 or so horses in front of him, away to his left. It was good thing he was hanging back, because the helicopter gun ship that appeared concentrated its gunfire at the men in front of him. Horses and men died in the melee. Porter turned

Old Dollar and Ruth down into a draw with a lot of scrub and cover. He tied Old Dollar to a stout shrub; and proceeded to a point where he could see the helicopter and where he had some concealment. He flipped the selector switch on his AK47 rifle to full auto. The helicopter was hovering facing the men and firing its forward mounted machine guns and cannon. They were at a slight angle to him which gave him a view of the pilot and gunner. A door on the side was open with another gunner leaning out with a machine gun mounted to the frame. Porter estimated the range at about 300 yards and squeezed the trigger. The 30 round magazine was empty in a matter of seconds. He slapped in a fresh one and got back on target. Once again he ran the magazine dry and slapped in a third. When he got back on target he realized that the side gunner was sagging against his harness and his gun was silent. The third magazine had no effect, but the fourth one caused the helicopter to lurch violently to the right and it literally flew hard into the ground where it exploded into flames. Leaving his cover he ran to the carnage that lay before him. Men and horses lay dead and dying everywhere. Sergeant Daniels was pinned under his horse but was otherwise unhurt. He bellowed, "Get this horse off me." Without a word Porter snagged a rider-less horse and tied a rope around the dead horse's head, the other end he secured to the horn of the standing horse's saddle. He swung into the saddle and pulled the horse off Daniels. Once he was back on his feet, Daniels's orders quickly brought some order to the chaos.

The next 4 hours were a blur of activity. All in all they lost 12 men killed and, and two incapacitated with wounds. They had the two mules and 12 of the 30 horses. Every man with the exception of Porter had injuries. Most had minor wounds such as cuts and bruises from falling off horses. One man had busted ribs from being kicked by a panic stricken horse. The two incapacitated men would be out of the fight for months. One had a leg broken by a piece of shrapnel that was still in him. The other was shot through the arm, both legs and hand. He was still unconscious and had a goose egg sized bump on his head. There were a number of horses missing. Porter looked at Sergeant Daniels, "We need to get to where we have some water and can camp a few days, we are about 3 hours from where we camped last night or we can move on. The longer we stay here the quicker we run out of water."

"You're right, kid let's head back to where we camped last night. Some of the lost stock might head back there for water. The pack horse with the radio is one of the ones missing."

He gathered the men together and told them the plans. "Out of curiosity how many of you got off a shot at that helicopter?" They looked at each other and saw that Porter was the only one with his hand raised. "Don't look at me, if I hadn't drifted back to stay out of the dust, I would have been piled up with the rest of you guys."

Daniels shook his head, "How many rounds did you shoot?"

"Four-thirty round mags, sir."

"How did you manage to even hit it?"

Porter gave him a puzzled look, "It wasn't but about 300 yards away; back at the ranch, I could hit a target the size of a washing machine that far away, that helicopter was a lot bigger than that."

All Daniels could say was, "I'll be damned, Charlie was right."

The men made litters for the injured men so they could be dragged behind the horses.

"Do you mind if I go over to the crash site to see if there is anything we can use?"

"That's another good idea, kid; since our corporal is dead I'm making you the new acting corporal. Congratulations, you've been promoted to corporal the pay is still the same." Porter made his way over the crash site; in the meantime, the men buried their dead and butchered the dead horses so as not to waste the meat.

At the crash site, Porter found what he suspected. There were four dead men that he could count. There must have been a gunner on the opposite side he hadn't seen. He couldn't tell if they were Chinese or not, the flames had cooked them beyond recognition. There was nothing he could find that they could use so he returned to help with the dead and wounded. They took all the weapons and extra ammo and divided it among the living. Porter was able to replenish his spent magazines with ones from the dead men who had also been packing AK47s. They took the remaining weapons and ammo, packed them in a Gortex sleeping bag cover, and left them where they could find them. If Porter got a message to Charlie, he would tell them where to look. The extra food was packed away on the pack horses. Daniels and the other men were preparing to leave with the wounded to head back to the previous night's camp. "Porter, do you think you can look around for those runaway horses, especially the one with our radio, without getting lost?"

Porter just looked at him, "With the trail we've been leaving, it would be impossible for me not to find you."

Porter started riding in a circle around the ambush site. Each circle was a bit larger than the previous one. It wasn't long before he hit a set of tracks and then another. Before the afternoon was out he had found six of the missing horses including the one carrying the pack with the radio. He found two more that had been badly wounded; these he dispatched with a shot to each of their heads. He took the pack saddles off the dead horses and replaced the riding saddles on two of the remaining horses. He stopped long enough at the ambush site to pick up the cached weapons and ammo. He also loaded up the extra packs and saddles to carry back for the ranch.

He arrived back at camp with Old Dollar trailing Ruth and the other six horses. Daniels shouted, "By God, I'd promote you to sergeant, if we didn't already have one."

"I got your radio Sarge, let's radio Charlie and tell him what happened." They set some wire for an antenna and raised Charlie on the radio and told him what happened. Charlie radioed back to leave the injured, he and the boys would come get them and put them up at the lodge until they were ready to travel. That night they once again took turns standing guard. All was quiet, but the camp was sad from having lost so many friends. They hung around the next morning until Charlie and Sam got there. Daniels greeted them, "I'm not much of a leader, I've lost almost my entire command and I never even got a good look at the enemy, if it weren't for the kid, we'd all be dead!"

"I told you he could carry his weight."

"I've promoted him to corporal already, at this rate I'll be reporting to him."

Charlie took Porter aside, "Try to keep them alive until they can at least get a shot at the bad guys; at night start teaching them some of the things I taught you, it might keep them in the fight a little longer."

"Sure thing Mr. Charlie, I was just trying to follow orders the first few days."

"The main thing, Porter is to try not to get hurt or killed; I'd have two girls who would never get over it."

"I don't think I would get over it either," he laughed.

The small surviving troop left once again for Louisiana. Each man had a horse and led a pack horse. Porter still had Old Dollar and Ruth. The days turned into weeks as they wormed their way across Texas. The terrain was less arid as they passed between Austin and San Antonio. There were small farms and ranches with occasional windmill water pumps.

They met up with other Constitution forces near New Braunfels and discovered that there weren't a lot of troops available for combat. Due to the fact that these forces were protecting their families, their role was limited to defense. Only single or widowed men with no young children were free to go and fight. By forming local militias they had managed to fight off the gangs and defend against the Chinese. The pioneer spirit was alive and well in this country. Even the women were packing rifles and pistols. It was not uncommon to see older children armed as well. This limited the Chinese to the main roadways in and out of Houston. When the Chinese destroyed Fort Hood, it stopped the main offensive drive against them in the region.

There were still bands of thieves and gangs, although their numbers were greatly reduced. There was word that the country was dotted with small fiefdoms where local chiefs set up shop and ruled with iron fist. Porter figured that they would be the next to fall, if the Chinese kept landing troops, even the Constitution forces would fail. This was a war of attrition, the goal was to make taking and occupying the country so expensive the Chinese would have to give up.

It was mid April by the time they made it near the Louisiana border. They were somewhere below Toledo Bend Reservoir on the Sabine River when they reached Cooney Jones on the radio. "Porter, I thought I told you to stay on the ranch with Charlie and Bonnie, what are you doing traveling across no man's land coming to Louisiana?"

"I have been killing communists, sir."

Cooney paused for a moment and thought before asking, "How many communists have you killed thus far?"

"About 2 dozen so far."

"Put Sergeant Daniels on the radio."

"Daniels here."

"Is it true what I just heard?"

"Yes sir, he's the toughest little sunabitch I have ever been around. He asked if he could come along with us when we passed through Charlie Cross's ranch. We would all be dead if we hadn't allowed him to join up; he's now a corporal in the Constitution army."

Cooney stated, "I'll be damned. I'm a Captain in the Constitution army and I am placing you under my direct command. We are a gorilla outfit at this point. We will be defending a squadron of A10 Warthogs operating across the river at Natchez, MS. We should be able to defend and maintain the squadron at this time. The Chinese operating out of Alexandria, Louisiana, have been trying to get to Natchez; but, we have every major bridge blown with the exception of the bridge at Natchez and Vicksburg. All the bridges south of Natchez are sitting in the river. Even the bridges on the Pearl River and Hwy 90 are down. We can operate from the countryside because we know the area and have some local support."

Daniels asked, "What are your orders, sir?"

"I want you to help support us in Central Louisiana. I want you to make your way through central Louisiana, to join us in Catahoula Parish. If the Chinese get across the Black River at Jonesville they have a shot at getting to Natchez. They have a lot of helicopters, but they are short of transport aircraft for some reason. The A10s are hitting them but they are scattered out between Alexandria and Houston which limits what they can do."

"Why don't they just helicopter them in and drop them off on the Mississippi side?"

"The range is hurting them as well as the resistance from what's left of us. There is something else going on that we can't figure out. We are puzzled why they don't just start landing troops and equipment and just overwhelm us with sheer numbers. They could bring in 20,000,000 troops and they would never miss them. They're being born quicker than we can kill them."

"We should be there inside a week at the most; we're traveling cross country and avoiding the roads."

"Good idea, they have most of the roads patrolled in your area, in fact they have probably zeroed in on your radio transmission. Be careful, I don't want my grandson hurt, put him back on."

Porter answered, "Yes, sir?"

"You are under my direct command, you have to follow my orders, do you understand?"

Once again he answered, "Yes sir!"

"I want you guys to get here as soon as you can without exposing yourselves and getting killed. We are expecting a lot more trouble here and I am going to need every man, be careful, now get the hell out of there and hide until you can move."

CHAPTER 28

HOMEWORK

The sun was lighting the eastern sky as Dix went back down into the wine cellar. He opened a bottle of Tate's wine and drank heartily from the bottle as he slaked his thirst. He sat the half full bottle down and lay back on one of the mattresses he had brought down several days ago. Time and days were running together. He pulled one of the blankets on top of himself and drifted off. He slept until after lunch. He got up well rested for the first time in months. There were no nightmares he could remember. He raised the lid and climbed out of the cellar.

As usual he was wearing his shoulder holster and had Jake's AR15 slung around on his back. His hand was on the pistol grip of Jake's rifle. He went into Tate's garage and found a shovel. He pulled the patrol car out of the garage next door where he had parked it and pulled it up into Tate's driveway next to the back door. He opened the trunk and went inside. Tate's body or what was left of it was still wrapped up in the rug in the kitchen where Dix had placed it. Dix carried his friend out to the car and placed him in the trunk. He threw his pack in the back seat and headed down the street and out Cemetery Road. He drove around to a section where new graves were added, the old cemetery had been in use for several centuries or longer. He dug a grave and laid Tate to rest. He took a piece of treated 2X6 pine and carved Tate's name, year of birth and the year of death. If the time should ever come when he could get him a stone, he would. There were a lot of graves he would have to mark with gravestones one day.

He drove back down to the jail in the police cruiser. He flipped on the lights as he approached and drove real slow until Butch's men recognized him. Butch greeted him on the steps, "Looks like you've been hunting again."

"No, I've been sleeping. I had this one stashed from a few days ago."

"Our guys have been busy. They liberated the FEMA camp, the rest of the Mayor's people are dead and we strung the mayor's body up at the top of bridge hill. We want any of his loyal voters and supporters who are still around to see what happens to communists in our area."

"What's the word from Captain Miller?"

"The Chinese have been reinforced and are now moving north on Fort Polk. Evidently their run south was to secure a section of interstate within flight range of their carrier in the Gulf. They have landed some light armor and are bringing in troops and equipment in helicopters. They secured the spot that far south because it is at the farthest operational range of the helicopters without refueling them."

Dix thought about what Butch had said, "We need to be shooting down helicopters. Call your men and see if those Chinese left any munitions we can use. Have the A10's started coming in?"

"They're coming in tonight. We've got the generators running at the airport. And we have the landing lights up. We commandeered the fuel trucks from the bulk oil distributors and have enough diesel fuel under guard to run the generator for months. We also have 200,000 gallons of jet fuel at the airport and have another 100,000 gallons in railroad tank cars that were on a side track when the engineers and trainmen walked away from their trains."

"We lucked out with that," Dix said, "how's the gasoline looking?"

"The gas stations are pretty much empty, but the bulk oil distributors have a total of 135,000 gallons between them. Other than food, we have fuel to remain operational."

"What's the food situation?"

"We are fully operational until we start dying of starvation in three days."

Dix suggested, "Why don't you send some men to look in every car on those trains, some of those funny looking cars should hold bulk grain or soybeans. Also send some men to check every grain elevator within driving distance of here. Check every barge that they see; put a boat and motor behind their trucks, a lot of those barges were full of corn, rice and wheat."

"I'll get them on it."

Butch and Dix continued talking. It wasn't enough to just survive, they needed to live, to rebuild, not only for now but for the future.

Dix began thinking out loud, "One--We need to find a couple of old farmers still alive with tractors and equipment and get them some diesel. If we don't get some seed in the ground, no matter how much food we find, it will only postpone the inevitable. Two--try to start rounding up some livestock, buy them with corn and wheat, we've got to rebuild some herds. Try to get the old guys who want to fight, but can't, working on it. Three--there are bound to be some old Baptist Deacons running around that need something to do and see if there are any Mormon elders still alive, they can be a big help too. Do you remember Harris Communications over near the old tire plant, Butch?"

"Yea, I know it."

"Go by their shop, they used to have a working grain mill, I don't know if they survived, but either way the grain mill is probably still there, because nobody will know what it is. Find a couple of old guys to show you how it works, if there are any left, if not ya'll will just have to figure it out. I can show you if I haven't been killed by then."

"Butch, what direction does Captain Miller want us to go in now?"

"He wants us to hold Natchez and to keep the fuel coming to the A10's."

"Has anyone found those damned Chinese that left the airport?"

"We found an old man that was living back behind the airport on Rice Road. He said three twin rotor helicopters came in and left about an hour later. They came in from the west and left the same way."

Dix nodded at that information, "They evacuated them to join the battle. Unless you know someone who has a small plane we can use for reconnaissance, we have to assume they're gone. Let's put guys out around the airport with deer rifles and radios. Tell them to report first and shoot second, I'd say use four men and have them relieve each other every six hours day and night. I know they've all got climbing stands, get 'em up out of view where they can see. It wouldn't occur to the Chinese that there would be men in the trees. They don't have deer hunters where they're from. We can't assume that we don't have communists still running loose around the county, other than our missing Chinese."

Dix looked at Butch, "I'm heading back to the camp, when you get word on where the Chinese are heading, send somebody by to get me, or you come by and get some catfish. I'm taking that old patrol car; it's got enough gas to get me over there and back. Get word out it's me so I won't get shot."

Butch laughed and put out the word. Dix hopped in the cruiser and headed across the river on the old bridge. He was waved through the checkpoint and headed down the highway. He crossed the levee and pulled up at the camp. Beagle had a rifle on him until he recognized Dix getting out.

"Put that gun up old man, I'm ready for a mess of fish." Rachel looked out, "I'll make up some hushpuppies." Dix took a shower in the catamaran and changed clothes. Beagle had the wood fire under the Dutch oven heating the oil and the fish went in as soon as Dix sat down. Ben and Frank wanted to sit in his lap, but they were too big. Dix had spoiled them when they were little puppies and they couldn't understand why he didn't let them rest their heads on his shoulder. The night was cool but not cold, the mosquitoes would be out in a few weeks and it would be impossible to sit around outside unless there was a breeze.

Dix brought out another bottle of Tate's wine and everyone had a glass. They built a fire of drift wood and Dix told them what had happened. "Starting tonight a squadron of A10's will be operating out of Natchez. They're coming in tonight, over the next few days there will be support people flying in and they'll be conducting sorties from here.

We won't know for a couple of days what the Chinese will do. They have an aircraft carrier off shore and are deploying troops and light armor, if the fighting gets close we may have to move the boats up the lake or maybe even down the river. If I say go, we'll take the house boat down the lake and anchor it up, then you or we will take the catamaran pulling the fishing boat and head to shelter up or down the river depending on the flow of the fighting. They could very well bring transports up the river."

Rachel frowned, "Why would they bother us here?"

Dix gently told her, "At this point they realize that they are fighting everyone, not just the military, everyone is a soldier and a target. Do you think for a moment they want us here on their new land? We're fighting for our existence at this point. So how's our food supply holding up?"

Beagle did the math, "We can last about a month on what we've got, if I can keep catching fish we can last another four to six months or more. We're going to need to locate some more canned goods or something. I got down to nothing but catfish for about two weeks until you showed up. I'll be catching turtle now that the water is warming up. I've been catching some Buffalo and Spoon bills in the nets."

Dix suggested, "Try to swap the fish for whatever kind of food anyone will trade for. I don't care if its pecans or peanuts. We need to think about long term survival, if the Chinese don't hit us, we've got to eat. Try to locate some garden seeds in your trading, we can raise a garden up on the levee before it gets to steep. I wish I had brought more food when I left the coast, but at the time I only had to feed myself and I left some with my sister and her family. I left them so I wouldn't be an extra mouth at their camp. I don't think the die off is over yet, if the survivors don't get crops in the ground, all this fighting is for naught. The Chinese have food and that in itself is a good reason to kill them."

Rachel grinned, "What gives me the feeling that you are planning to get it?"

The next day Butch came over the levee early. He joined Dix and Rachel for biscuits and honey. Beagle was already running the nets.

Butch started talking before he could get his mouth full, "The A10's came in about 3:00am this morning. Their first sortie is after lunch. The air force has set up operations and we're ready to keep them supplied with fuel. We already found a barge full of wheat, another one of rice, a silo of corn, and a silo of soybeans; we are not going to starve. Chuck Harris is still alive, he's set up the grain mill, and will grind it in exchange for whatever we can swap him. He and his wife survived, but his parents didn't make it, they got sick and there wasn't any medical help."

"Tell him when you see him that I'll bring him some catfish," Dix replied. "What's the situation on the Chinese?"

"We expect them to try to take and hold the bridges here at Natchez. They may also try to take and hold the Natchez airport or make a bombing run to stop the A10's once the sorties start."

"Where are they now?"

"They are still dropping troops and equipment, one group has headed north, we think they're going to hit Fort Polk. But they could divert here to try and get across the river."

"I suggest you mine the bridges here, just in case."

Butch pointed to the map he drew of the area, "If they make a run this way, they'll have to cross the Red River at Marksville, or the Atchafalaya River at Simsport. I think it's more likely they'll try crossing the Atchafalaya; otherwise, they'll have to build a pontoon bridge at Jonesville. The other option they have is to transport them to a rendezvous point by helicopter. We can't control where they can deploy with helicopters, we can only try to respond, if they do that it will be close to the airport."

Dix studied the map, "I'd deploy as many people as I could around the airport. Not at the airport, but where we can intercept them prior to them hitting the airport. I'd cover all the approaches and the entire fuel route. Get Chuck Harris to monitor radio communications to see if they have any of the mayor's former supporters communicating with the bad guys."

"Five thousand trained and disciplined Chinese troops can chew us up and spit us out. You can't fight them in a conventional manner. We're short on men but heavy in sharp shooters, most of their guys never touched a gun until they were conscripted into the army. Our guys grew up in the woods. That gives us a leg up every time."

Butch nodded in agreement, "I follow you."

Dix continued, "If the Chinese come up the river road, we can slow or stop them using twenty men with deer rifles strung out over the 35 miles along the river. They would have a turkey shoot; particularly, if you barricaded the levee every four or five miles to slow them down, so our boys can have time to shoot. I would also put some guys in Catahoula Parish with radios."

Butch thought about what Dix had said, "That could work. What do you want to do?"

"I don't want to lead a squad again, I don't like being responsible for anyone other than me when I'm in the field. I'll go in wherever you think I can do the most damage."

"As soon as I get word, I'll let you know."

Rachel looked over at Dix, "You're the first General I've ever met who never gives orders."

"What do you mean? I'm just voicing my opinion."

"Maybe so, but you've led or orchestrated the battle from the moment I met you. Everyone looks to you for direction, what do you think they're going to do when you get yourself killed?"

"Look Rachel, I led my family and our friends and now they're all buried in the back yard. I'm not leading anyone but myself from now on." Dix was nearly shouting, "I can lead myself to the bad guys, I can kill the daylights out of 'em and I don't endanger anybody but me doing it." He turned his back to her.

"What about me, Beagle, Ben and Frank, we'd be dead right now if we didn't follow you."

Dix turned and pointed at her, "I never intended to make you dependant on me, as long as Beagle can catch catfish and teach you, you can trade for what you need. We confiscated that house boat for shelter. Rachel," he said gently, "You had better get used to the idea of me not coming back one day. My luck is going to run out, everyone thinks I'm this super warrior. I'm not superman. I've been shot at and hit several times. I am reckless and have been just plain stupid lucky. I am going to continue going on missions until my luck runs out or all the bad guys are dead."

Dix spent the day packing up his gear, once again he packed heavy. He was running short on MRE's so he took the fillets of about 30 catfish and smoked them into jerky over the driftwood fire. He put these into a pillow case along with some hardtack he made from some old flour. He had 12 thirty round magazines for Jake's AR15, his Browning 9mm with four extra magazines and the Beretta .22 in his back pocket. As usual, he carried his folding knife and the Kbar knife on his belt.

The A10's roared overhead when they came out of the Natchez airport. Dix knew that reports would come in from them as to the whereabouts of the Chinese. Butch showed up about an hour later as expected with a report for Dix. He hopped out of his truck grinning, "They caught them with their helicopters on the ground near Alexandria. The next sortie is on its way." They watched as three A10's roared overhead with three more about two minutes later. Dix looked back at Butch, "Where do you want me to deploy?"

"Do you mind heading back into Catahoula parish. If they come from that way, they'll have to come across next to the swamp south of Catahoula Lake on Hwy 28. We took out the bridges down on the Achafalaya and Red River. Their only chance to get equipment across is to build a pontoon bridge here on the Black River. We'll get you across the river with your four-wheeler and trailer and top off your gas tank. I've got you four five gallon cans of gas plus a couple of quarts of motor oil. How's your ammo holding up?"

"I'm good to go. All I've got to do is find a good camp. If I shoot up all the bullets I've got, I'll just have to find some more bad guys and get theirs."

Butch laughed, "I'm giving you a radio, oh, by-the-way, I'm Captain Erwin now, Colonel Miller told me to tell you that you are now officially conscripted into the Constitution Army at the rank of Major. You still have complete autonomy; but, we follow your orders when you bark."

Dix frowned, "I don't suppose any of this was your idea?"

"Look," Butch said, "We've been following your lead ever since you saved our butts, this just makes it official."

"Make sure that Beagle and Rachel get a barrel of ground wheat, a barrel of corn meal, rice and soybeans and take Chuck Harris a big mess of catfish in exchange."

Beagle came up about that time and Dix told him, "I just traded a big mess of your fish for several barrels of food, go get Captain Erwin a sack of fish."

He called Rachel out and told her and Beagle that he was heading back into Catahoula parish to do some scouting. "If the fighting comes here, take the boats down the lake and stay out of sight. Keep the fishing boat ready to run in the event you have to make a quick getaway."

Ben and Frank had finally given up trying to follow him every time he left, Dix thought to himself, "When all of this is over I need to try and take them with me more often." But he knew in his heart how it would probably all end.

Butch had a truck and trailer ready to load up the four-wheeler and its trailer. They headed into town and made a stop. Dix had found another four-wheeler with almost new tires and rims.

His guys swapped out the wheels on the four-wheelers, the tires on his old Yamaha Big Bear were almost worn down to nothing from all the road time. Dix was relieved that he had new tires, he had been afraid this would have been the Yamaha's last trip.

They had a ferry rigged up across the river with a barge and cables. The trip across went faster than it did when he and Butch had to float the four-wheeler across on its own tires.

Dix ran back along the gravel road on the river side of the levee until he came to the opening in the flood wall that protected a portion of Jonesville. He made a long run around the town and slowed when he passed the house his father was born in and where his grandmother and great grandfather died in 1930.

He ran the Yamaha in third gear because he was loaded and didn't want to tax the bike or take the chance of losing control. The Springfield was strapped on the gun rack and he was wearing Jake's AR15 on his back as usual. He ran out to an area known as French Fork that was located just east of Catahoula Lake. This was part of a huge drainage area in central Louisiana where the freshwater lake was a significant feature of the region.

He turned down a long straight gravel drive that made a dead end at the home of his grandfather's baby sister; she had died almost 20 years earlier. Dix had some cousins who had lived there now but hadn't seen them for years. He got down to the house and found that they had managed to survive with no casualties. They didn't recognize him but did recognize his name. They were self reliant people and had a working farm with gardens, crops, and livestock. Dix told them that the Chinese may come through there. His cousin Boyd explained, "We retreated back in the swamp with our food and animals when they came through the last time. We have animal pens already back there."

They gave him a dozen boiled eggs, a pone of corn bread and a jar of buttermilk. Dix thanked them and headed further into the zone where he would meet the enemy, if they made the run in this direction.

He camped down a dirt road in the edge of the swamp staying within ear shot of the road. Dix slept pretty good considering he was in the wilderness. At one time this area was full of wild hogs, deer and alligators. The alligators were probably still plentiful. This area's close proximity to Alexandria, LA, meant that it was one of the first places anyone who thought they could live off the land would come to; but by now, most of the big game and a lot of the small game were gone. Because much of this area was only accessible on foot or by boat, it would always have some dangerous game. The thought of a black bear or a big old razor back boar stayed in the back of Dix's mind, even as he tried to sleep.

The next morning he ate half his corn bread, drank his buttermilk and ate an egg. He topped off his gas tank and headed toward the intersection that anyone traveling from the east would have to cross. Dix determined that to set up here would be suicide, there was nowhere to retreat and the shooting would be no more than 100 yards distance. At that distance, a man with an AK47 could easily take him out. Dix didn't fear he would get killed, but that he would get killed before he had killed an appreciable number of the bad guys.

Dix ran back down the highway until he reached the intersection of Hwy 28 and Hwy 84. A local truck stop sat vacant about a quarter of a mile away. He went across the intersection and up and over the levee then hid the four-wheeler next to an old barn. He cleared out a narrow shooting lane so that he could lay on the back side of the levee and out of sight from down the highway. He had at least a one mile straight line of sight down the road. He could engage a target as far as he could see and shoot. He also had an escape route to the rear and could even cross the river if necessary.

Dix sat on the edge of the levee in the spring sun and waited. He finished the buttermilk and ate a couple of eggs. He wished he and his wife were heading up Back Bay in their fishing boat; but instead, he was man hunting again. He called Butch on the radio and told him he didn't have anything to report.

"Dix, you may get some action as the A10's have been running nonstop. The Chinese have to take the planes out, or they will be toast."

Dix had about decided that the Chinese weren't going to show. What he didn't realize, was how hard they had been hit by the A10's. When they came, they were rolling all out. Dix had expected scouts or something, not a flat out racing column of trucks and equipment.

He replaced the cartridges in the Springfield with five armor piercing bullets. He radioed Butch that the Chinese were five miles out of Jonesville and coming like a locomotive. Dix signed off and put the crosshairs on the driver of the lead vehicle. At 400 yards the 30 caliber armor piercing bullet passed through the bullet resistant glass, the driver's chest, the back of the seat and through five of the men in the back before passing though the back door. The personnel carrier careened off the highway and out into the field and sheared off a power pole. Dix didn't wait to see the results but concentrated on the truck behind it. This time, the armor piercing bullet passed through the windshield, the top ring of the steering wheel, the driver's arm at the elbow, and hit a rocket propelled grenade that exploded setting off a chain reaction among all of them in the box. The truck was blown into two pieces, one of which caused the truck behind it to careen off the road and turn upside down in the ditch.

Dix's third shot went through the windshield of the 4th truck missing the driver, but killing two men in the back before it passed through the radiator of the 5th truck. Dix cycled his action and with his fourth shot managed to hit the driver of the 4thth truck this time; the bullet continued on and wounded another man in the back. It continued through the back of truck and hit the 5th truck in the radiator and on to the engine block. It had lost enough momentum that it did not damage the engine block. Dix cycled the action again as the 4th truck came to a stop. The 5th truck with the radiator blowing steam pulled around it. Dix put the 5th and last armor piercing bullet through the front glass and it went through the fuel cans in the back. The truck swerved off the road, rolled over and burst into flames.

He thumbed four cartridges into the magazine. He fired again this time on the 6th personnel carrier in the line, it stopped instantly in the road. He had killed the driver and three of the men in the back. His next bullet went through the front window, on through the back killing two more and striking the 7th vehicle behind it. In the space of two minutes he had stopped seven vehicles, killed and wounded a number of men, and made several thousand more angry.

The levee seemed to come alive as all the AK47's in the hands of the dozens of men behind them opened up in his direction. He rolled off the back of the levee to head to the four-wheeler when all hell broke loose. Cannon fire turned the scenery in every direction to dust, fire and deafening sound. He lost all sense of space and time. The concussions took him off his feet. He was laying flat on his back with dirt and debris all around still in the air. He found his rifle and crawled on his elbows back on top of the levee. The A10's had made a run down the length of the Chinese column with the last few 40 mm cannon shells hitting the levee in front of Dix. The only reason he was alive was because he had turned to run. He topped off the magazine on his rifle and started looking for live targets. He quickly located them and made five shots. He reloaded and emptied his rifle again. He radioed to Butch that this column was destroyed and he was doing a little clean up. He kept firing until he could no longer see any targets within range. An A10 was making another run down the line so now was the time to make his escape.

It wasn't until he tried to return to the four-wheeler that he realized he had been hit. A hole in his lower back was matched by a corresponding hole on the right side of his abdomen. He was hurting all over from the concussions of the exploding shells; so, he didn't know if he had been hit by shrapnel or if he was hit by a rifle slug. He pulled up his shirt and examined the wound. It oozed a squirt of blood with every breath.

He strapped the Springfield on the back of his four-wheeler and headed down the river road until he could cross back onto the highway. A Chinese helicopter had landed in the highway in front of the bridge where it had been blown. He came under fire from men pouring out of the helicopter. Dix gunned the four-wheeler and turned south towards his dad's home place. He grunted as a bullet went through his leg high on his thigh and passed through the four wheeler seat. It was bleeding profusely when he stopped out of sight. He took a roll of duct tape out of his pack and wrapped the wound so that it would stop bleeding.

He pulled Jake's AR15 into position and limped back up the road until he could see the helicopter. He placed the yellow dot from the Trijicon sight on the men and started popping off rounds. He emptied the magazine and fell back, dropped the empty magazine and slapped in a fresh one. He paused long enough to turn and return fire. He emptied the magazine into the pilot and co-pilots positions. When the magazine was empty he turned to run and took another hit to his body. It felt like someone had hit him between the shoulder blades with a hammer. Somehow he got back on the four-wheeler and headed south. He would need to get to his bamboo camp at the old home place and lie up.

Dix ran the four-wheeler flat out and several times had to shake his head to clear the fog. He had lost a lot of blood. He stopped at Jones bayou to call Butch. "I'm heading back to my camp down on Grassy Lake; I've taken a couple of hits. There's a helicopter at the Jonesville Bridge, I shot it up pretty good, but had to retreat."

Butch said something but Dix couldn't understand, so he just rode on until he reached the old home place. He saw the old cypress tree down on the lake bank and stopped the four-wheeler in the road. Suddenly he felt a little better, he figured that the adrenalin was wearing off, so he took another sip of water and steered the four-wheeler down the hill towards the old tree. He lost control of it when his arms and legs went weak. The four-wheeler turned over in slow motion and he went flying.

He found himself lying on his back looking up through the branches and envisioned his father doing the same thing. He remembered looking up through those same branches when he was a little boy and marveling at how big they seemed. He dozed off and started to dream.

He woke to two big old ugly Catahoula Cur dogs licking his face. He pushed them off and looked up to see his Dad looking down at him, "You have a good nap?" Jake was there and so was his wife Maggie. His Dad said, "Dix, Mama Shelly's got lunch ready." They helped him up and he saw his mother waving from up the hill. The road was gone.

"I don't understand." He started to turn and look back; but his Dad put his arm around his shoulders, "There's no looking back, you're home, welcome home, son."

CHAPTER 29

THE DEVILS ARRIVE

D aniels Devils camped in an abandoned farm house west of Natchitoches, Louisiana. The next morning they spoke to some local farmers who told them where to attempt a crossing of the Red River. Up until this time they were able to cross the bridges on most of the creeks and rivers. Now they were trying to cross bridges controlled by the Chinese, so it was either fight for the bridge or swim the river with the horses. They didn't have enough men or equipment to challenge the bridges held by the Chinese.

Daniels asked the men, "Have any of you ever tried to cross a river or lake with horses?"

Hank, an older guy of about 50, told them, "It's best to get the first one started then all the others can follow. If they are heading in the right direction, just ease off the saddle and hang on to the saddle horn or their mane and let 'em pull you. If you are on top you tend to weigh them under."

"What about the packs weighing them down? We need to find a boat and transport all that we can across that way."

It took them about half a day to locate a local man who had an aluminum boat they could use. Luckily he had an electric trolling motor and batteries that were hot from a solar cell charger. They waited until dusk and were able to transport all the packs and equipment over in two trips. They repaid the favor with some salt and sugar from Porter's stash. None of the horses wanted to cross the river, so Porter brought Old Dollar and Ruth to the bank. Porter figured that Charlie and the boys had him cross the Pecos River in the past. Old Dollar did not hesitate but walked right on in and started across. As instructed Porter slid off on Old Dollar's left side and hung on the horn. They were across in no time with Ruth in tow. The other horses followed as they hoped. Their first crossing of a river went off without a hitch. They waved across the river to the local farmer who pulled his boat back up the bank and out of sight. They set up camp in the woods, cleaned their weapons and dried their clothes.

They were finally near Jonesville, Louisiana, in Catahoula Parish. They were surprised by a group of Chinese that seemed lost in the wilderness. Porter and his fellow troops were still in the hill country and had not gotten into the delta area around the rivers and lakes. Luckily, they spotted the Chinese first, so they just led their horses back up the logging road they were on and tied them off. They waited in ambush. Porter counted fourteen Chinese from where he crouched in the pine thicket.

Daniels whispered, "Don't fire until I do." they all nodded in agreement. As Charlie had taught him, Porter picked out his first 4 or five targets. He had come to realize that these guys had never really seen much combat; so, he knew he may have to carry the water for everyone. Porter had his gun up and resting against a small sapling next to him. The instant Daniels pulled the trigger, he opened up on the first then the second and so on. He never waited to see if his shot connected. After the fourth shot the targets were either down or scattered. He kept shooting until there were no targets moving.

He slapped a fresh magazine in the rifle and moved forward, a quick bullet through the head of one who was moving eliminated the threat. His fellow troops all rose and looked around. Porter took his time and popped all the other dead Chinese through their heads.

"Why did you do that, Porter?"

He unbuttoned his shirt and showed them the hole in his shoulder and side, "I woke up after taking two hits from one of these rifles and went on to kill a number of their comrades. I don't take chances, and I'm not taking prisoners after I've seen what they do. Unless you are planning on patching them up, I recommend you just send them on to their maker and get it over with. They're now buzzard bait." He gathered up a couple of full magazines from the Chinese packs and replaced the empty ones in his pack and gun. Daniels looked up, "Guys, I suggest you follow his lead, he hasn't been wrong about one thing since he joined us." He took his AK47 and also popped one in the head. They all gave Porter the thumbs up.

"These little cookies in the foil pouches are mighty tasty," Porter said holding one up. "I'd go through their packs and see what they have. I keep hoping I'll find some hand grenades."

Hank said, "Don't you think you are a little young to be playing with fireworks?" Everyone laughed including Porter. They had passed a milestone, although killing was serious business, killing communists now became sport.

They led the horses around the dead, they were afraid that the smell of blood would spook them. Porter led with Old Dollar and Ruth as they were the calmest animals. Spreading out about 100 yards apart each took a turn riding point. They traveled for several hours and set up camp within sight of a main highway intersection. They stayed put because there was a ditch full of rainwater and plenty of grass for the animals. They decided to let them eat and rest for a big part of the day. They set up their radio and were waiting for a response from Cooney before proceeding further towards Jonesville. A low rumble rose up from a column of trucks and equipment coming down the road. Porter set up his tripod and set his long gun across it. Under the highest power he could see that it was a Chinese column of trucks. A helicopter circled overhead and headed towards Jonesville.

Suddenly they heard a shot ring out in the distance. It was barely audible over the din of the trucks and heavy equipment. Trucks started leaving the road and there was a huge explosion in one. Porter was sitting about 400 yards east of the column. He looked back at Daniels with a questioning look, "Can I start shooting?"

"Hell yea!"

Porter started shooting men as they poured out of the trucks. A traffic jam had been created in the road. The Chinese were directing their fire at the levee straight in front of them. Porter yelled, "Grab my .308 ammo box off of my mule pack." The men came running up with the rest of his ammo and he reloaded his long gun and fired another volley. Suddenly, the column starting coming apart from the rear forward. Shells were literally turning the whole area into a horrible mess of men and machines. Debris and shrapnel fell all over the field with some landing almost on top of them. A deafening roar almost burst their ear drums as the A10 Warthog turned over their heads to line up for another pass down the column. Chinese troops were running for cover. Porter kept firing until he had exhausted his supply of ammunition. Another pass of the Warthog finished off the machines and anyone left alive in the column. Porter put away the empty long gun and went to the AK47.

Daniels called out, "Let 'em have it." They opened up from the woods on all they could see within 300 yards of them. They were out of targets, but not out of danger. There was still gunfire coming from the column and an occasional bullet zinged through the trees around them. They retreated back into the woods, saddled the animals, and reloaded the pack animals, keeping out a wary eye the entire time.

The radio crackled, it was Cooney, "Where are you guys located?"

Daniels answered, "We're involved in one hell of a battle just east of town, a Warthog just blew a Chinese column to hell and back, we've been killing the crap out of the survivors."

"Get across the levee, which is north of your position, and travel along it until you get into town. I'll meet you about a mile out. Is my grandson ok?"

"He's fine; he's the single biggest killing machine I've ever seen."

"Keep your eyes open, the biggest killing machine I know, Dix Jernigan, was also shooting at that column."

Daniels proclaimed, "We saw him in action, he stopped the whole damn thing, we never saw him, we just heard his gun and saw the results."

"Get started and look for him on your way, in case he was wounded."

They climbed on the horses and crossed the road, cut through a fence and were up and over the levee in short order. They swung east following the river. They didn't find any sign of Dix, other than a bloody spot in some matted down grass. There were a couple of 30-06 bullets lying there also, apparently they had been dropped.

They pushed the horses and mules hard in order to put some distance between them and the shot up column. They brought them to a stop and walked them after the three mile run. Cooney

Jones was set up under a tree with a radio operator. A rugged looking man with about a 3 week beard came driving up on a dirt bike. Cooney looked up and grinned when he saw Porter, "Dammit, you've turned into one fine man!" He grabbed Porter and gave him the biggest hug a man could give another man.

Butch Erwin who had just arrived on the motorcycle said," Don't I get a hug, I just finished off a helicopter and a pile of Chinese."

Cooney grinned, "Only if I can get a big old kiss too."

"I think I'd rather kiss that green lipped mule standing over there." They had a big laugh and then they got serious.

"Everyone this is Butch Erwin, he is Captain from Concordia Parish east. He wouldn't be over here unless it was important. What's the situation?" Butch cut straight to the chase, "Dix has been hit and was heading back to his camp down on Grassy Lake. He has quit answering the radio, so it can't be good."

Cooney shook his head, "We can't go after him now, and under the circumstances he wouldn't want us to. We have to finish cleaning up the Chinese around here while we have them on the run. You guys stow your gear in that barn and put the stock in the paddock. There's a water trough under the eave drip that's full. Report back to me. Butch draw me a detailed map of how to find Dix's camp, I'll send someone the instant I can."

The next three days involved a lot of sporadic fighting around the town and countryside. No more paratroopers showed up and no helicopters came in. The Chinese made a made run west out of the parish about four days later. They took a lot of fire when they headed out, but no one was anxious to get in their way. Everyone was now battle tested and exhausted. Butch rode up to where Porter was eating some hard tack and drinking water from his canteen. "Porter, Captain Jones ask me to give you this map to see if you can locate Dix Jernigan. He's probably dead or we would have heard from him by now. Look in all the ditches along the way, he was on an old four wheeler and probably ran off the road. Don't surprise him if you can help it, he may kill you before he thinks. Take a medical kit with you in case you have to patch him up some."

"I'll find him. If he is dead, what do you want me to do?"

"Just bury him and mark the spot, if he's hurt take care of him the best you can, and bring him back when he can travel."

CHAPTER 30

BACK TO PURGATORY

Dix suddenly woke up in a sitting position leaning against the ancient cypress tree on the lake bank. He sat there in a mental fog staring at a hole in his boot. The pain in his foot was coming and going in time with his beating heart. A fly was walking around the bloody hole in his boot and was soon joined by several more. He thought one was walking down the side of his face, but when he tried to swat it, realized that it was a trickle of blood. Running his tongue over his teeth he found one of his upper teeth loose. The lip was busted immediately in front of it. The vision in his right eye was blurry and it was almost swollen shut.

From where he sat he was hidden from the roadway above. The weeds and briars on the lake bank stood between him and the roadway. His four-wheeler lay on its side next to him. The dense shade from the old cypress tree created an area free of weeds and briars beneath it and the ground was covered in a dense layer of needles. The cypress tree is a relative of the California redwoods. It doesn't really have needles like a pine tree or even leaves like a regular tree. The leaves remind one of a delicate feather.

He had no idea what time it was. It was daylight, but his watch was missing. Every breath caused a spasm on his left side and it felt like there were broken ribs. His shirt was wet and sticky from blood on that side. His field of vision slowly narrowed to black and the pain disappeared.

The next thing he remembered was waking up still under the tree. It was cold and dark. He was still leaning against the tree and he was desperately thirsty. His right hand still functioned, so he rooted around in his shirt pockets and found a disposable lighter in the right pocket. He lit it and looked around. There was a canteen on his pack that was strapped on the back of the four-wheeler. He put the lighter back in his pocket and scooted on his rear over to it and retrieved the canteen. He slaked his thirst after drinking about half of its 1 quart capacity. He pulled open a side compartment on the pack and pulled out a small mag light and lit the area. By now his hands were shaking. Drift wood lay around him that had been deposited the last time the water from the lake had risen and fallen. From where he sat he was able to pull up a pile of the Cypress tree needles and covered these with small twigs. On top of this he added larger pieces and lit them with the lighter. The fire sprung to life and soon had the area bathed in light and warmth. He dozed by the fire leaning against the pack and only moved to tend the fire.

Dawn came on the lake. Dix could see cypress knees growing toward the sky from the shallow water. Fog hung over the water and the air was still. Drops of water would occasionally fall from limbs in small plops on the water as the fog condensed on them and formed into drops too heavy to stay where they formed. He drank from the canteen again and pulled up the remaining wood within arm's reach. It was evident that he would have to tend to his injuries. The busted ribs on his side made every move a nightmare. His right eye was swollen shut, only time would help it now. He dug around in the same compartment that held the flashlight and found a spare pair of glasses and put them on to see better. After unbuttoning his shirt he saw a long gash in the fabric that matched a slash across his ribs. He wasn't sure what caused the gash.

No matter how hard he tried he couldn't remember much. He recognized the four-wheeler and the pack but couldn't recall his name or where he was. He recognized the old tree but went blank after that. It was familiar, like meeting an old friend from years ago. He sucked on some hard candy from the pack and felt a little better once the sugar hit his blood stream. The smoke from the fire would occasionally blow over him providing momentary relief from the flies and mosquitoes.

As the day slowly progressed he started regaining some mobility. He pulled himself to a standing position and was able to urinate. He found a worthless Eisenhower dollar down in his pants pocket and his memory came flooding back. This was an old coin that his mother had squirreled away years ago, he carried it for luck. The years unfolded and things that were better left forgotten once again piled into his thoughts. All his dead family, friends, pets and companions flooded into his mind. He remembered everything and wished that he could forget the pain and horror that had enveloped him once again. The profound sadness that flooded over him tempted him to un-holster his pistol and end it all. He wanted to be with them, not remembering them.

The bullet wound through his leg was still oozing around the duct tape and the wound through his lower back and out his abdomen was still draining. The blood appeared old and there was a lot of clear liquid coming out with the clotting blood. It didn't feel as though his intestines were ruptured, but he had no way to know otherwise. This was the first time he had been gut shot. He figured it would get worse before it got better. It was low enough and close enough to the side that maybe he would avoid peritonitis this time. His ribs clicked with every breath. He still had a tremendous pain in the middle of his back. He did not know and couldn't know that a rifle bullet had ricochet and hit him between the shoulder blades. It had lost enough momentum that it did not penetrate his spine but knocked off one of the points of a vertebra and exited only leaving a massive bruise. The loss of blood from the leg wound had left him weak and led to him passing out and wrecking the four-wheeler.

He leaned on the four-wheeler in an attempt to push it back on its wheels. He only managed to get his leg wound pouring blood and he was soon collapsed next to it. His vision soon faded and the pain was gone once again.

Porter gathered up his gear, a medical kit along with a pack shovel, and climbed on Old Dollar. He took his time traveling down the road and kept an eye out down in the ditches as he went. No place did he see where a vehicle had left the road. It took him all morning to make the trip. There were abandoned farms and houses along the road. He saw one man tending a garden, he waved and the man waved back.

When Porter reached the camp he started to turn into the yard of the burned out house when out of the corner of his eye he spotted a Springfield bolt action rifle lying on top of a bunch of briar vines. The vines were crushed under the gun as it had pushed them to the ground but left the gun exposed on top. From his view from atop of Old Dollar he could see it. He climbed off the old mule and led him down the hill. There lying next to an overturned four wheeler lay a gray haired man flat on his back. Flies were crawling on his wounds; but, he was still breathing. Porter took his canteen and wet his handkerchief. He wiped the parched lips and the eyes slowly opened. Dix was looking into the face of a young man. The face looked to be about 14 years old with the beginnings of a mustache and a few whiskers. The face asked, "Are you Major Dix Jernigan?" Dix could barely nod before he passed out again. He pulled Dix to a sitting position and leaned him against the big tree they were under. He wet the handkerchief and pulled out Dix's bottom lip and dripped water behind it.

Porter spent the next two days nursing him. He sutured some of the wounds and removed his ruined little toe, before making a litter using a tarp and bamboo. He took all the gear and hid it in Dix's bamboo camp site. He couldn't crank the four wheeler, so using Old Dollar he pulled it up and into the bamboo camp where he could hide it with all of Dix's gear.

The next time Dix woke he was on a tarp between two bamboo poles being bounced and pulled behind a mule. Time meant nothing as he faded in and out of consciousness. He woke again next to a fire. The mule was hobbled nearby and the boy was cooking something on the fire in a skillet. His boots and pants were off and his leg was bandaged as well as his left foot and side. "Who are you?" Dix whispered.

The boy looked over at him, "I'm Corporal Porter Jones from California."

"How do you know me?"

"Captain Erwin sent me down here to check on you, he gave me directions to your camp. He thought I might find you dead."

"He may very well be right, I feel like I could die any minute."

"I tried to patch you up some; your leg kept bleeding so I sewed it closed with some thread while you were passed out. I used plenty of antibiotic salve. A medic may have to open it up to let it drain when we get back to town. I hope you don't mind, but

I had to cut the little toe off your left foot. It was just dangling by a piece of skin. The maggots were already in it. You took a bullet through your boot; I expect you will be limping for a while."

"What day is it?"

"It is Friday I think, April 27th."

Dix tried to remember, "I think I was shooting up that Chinese column last Saturday."

"Well," Porter said, "I've been with you since Wednesday, you've spent most of the time passed out or out of your head; but, I managed to get some food and water down you from time to time. This is the first time you have been talking in your right mind. I found your camp back in the bamboo and hid your four-wheeler. I couldn't get it cranked so me and Old Dollar pulled it out of sight. I loaded up your guns and backpack on Dollar and made a drag from some bamboo poles and your tarp. We are almost back to Jonesville."

"What about the Chinese?"

"They are retreating back to Houston, the Warthogs tore them a new one. They pulled out of the Parish so we are back in Jonesville. My Grandfather, Captain Cooney Jones, is commanding the force there. Captain Butch Erwin is heading up Natchez, Vidalia and Ferriday. I am a corporal, so we're all under your command."

Dix didn't want to argue the point about his being in command, so he simply said, "Take me to Captain Jones."

It took them another agonizing three hours to get back into town. The Constitution forces were set up in a nursing home in town. They occupied it two days after the A-10's knocked out the Chinese column. All the former nursing home residents were gone. Most were surely dead, a few maybe were back with family but that was highly unlikely. They had a makeshift hospital set up on one wing, barracks set up at the other.

Captain Jones came out on crutches. Dix knew the name having heard it from his father in years past. Cooney Jones had earned a reputation as a former Army Ranger who served in Viet Nam. His Dad and Dix's dad had served together in WWII in the Pacific theater of the war. Cooney Jones was wearing a .45 Colt 1911 in a shoulder holster.

Dix held out his hand to Captain Jones, "Sir, I'd like to introduce myself."

"There is no need for an introduction, I'm glad to meet you. I have heard about you my entire life and your reputation precedes you. You have accomplished more in the last 3 months than any of my best trained men could have done."

Embarrassed, Dix shrugged, "There is something you need to understand, I have not been doing this out of any noble purpose. All I wanted was to be left alone and to take care of my family. When my family was murdered, I got mad and mean. In fact, there are people who would say that I've gone insane, and I can't say that I disagree with them. Maybe I need to be locked up in an institution when all this is over. My plan was to kill the bad guys and to keep killing them until I was killed. Porter tells me that you are in charge. If you will let me lie around for a few days, I'll get out of your way and get back to my job."

Cooney grinned, "Your goals and my goals are one and the same, and we will probably share a room in that institution. You're the one in charge. You are the ranking officer here, what are your orders?"

Dix shook his head in disgust, "Crap! I'm sick and tired of being in charge. Since you won't listen, your orders are to maintain command of this sector as though I never showed up. I'm in no shape to fight or assume command. Nor do I have any desire to be in charge. This rank was thrust on me. I need to have my four-wheeler and gear brought up from my camp and if you have a medic, I need to get patched up. I would like to have my pistol in my hand and my rifles cleaned and the sights checked. In the meantime you are in command until I am back on my feet."

"I think we can accommodate you. Glad to have you back, I'll send word over to Butch."

Dix looked toward Porter thoughtfully, "Don't you think your grandson is a little young to be in the field?"

"Yes I do, but I would have a hard time stopping him. He has traveled from California, killed the men who killed our family and several more thugs. He also killed a pile of Chinese out in Texas and here. He even has two young women back in Texas that he refers to as his family."

"Hell in that case, promote him to Sergeant, he sounds like my kind of man."

Porter excused himself and took off to the radio hut. He was scheduled to get a call in to Charlie Cross in Texas. For the first time in weeks he heard Sandy and Ally's voices and he wished he were back on the ranch. It would still be some time before he could make the trip.

Dix spent the next two weeks in the hospital. Luckily he responded to veterinary antibiotics and was able to be transported across the river. His boot had the bullet hole hollowed out to take the pressure off his foot where he lost the little toe. Butch had his four-wheeler running and his remaining gear loaded on a trailer on the eastern side of Black River and was sitting on the fender of the trailer smoking a cigar when they helped Dix out of the boat.

"Where do you keep finding tobacco?"

Butch grinned, "I'm still smoking up the mayor's stash, of course it don't hurt being Captain and in charge."

"Hell I can't fault you for that, you earned it. By the way where are we in cleaning out the Chinese and communist Americans?"

"They are still fighting in California, Oregon and Washington. The big cities are in complete chaos with the communists and gangs fighting us and each other. We haven't been ordered to leave or do anything other than maintain order. Colonel Miller is now over in Alexandria and in charge of Louisiana, West Mississippi over to I-55 and as far into Texas as we can hold. Cooney is in command from Black River west, south to Hwy 90 and north to I-20. I'm in command from east of Black River, north to I-20, across I-55 and south to Hwy 90. I have officers and men scattered out across the country. We've had so many killed that we are spread really thin. I'm concentrating on my men acting like Texas rangers and keeping a handle on law and order. We took your advice and have as many people as possible farming and providing protection. Roaming bandits are becoming few and far between. We are still cleaning up stray Chinese soldiers from that convoy you and the A-10's took out. How many did you wind up killing?"

"I don't have any idea, all I know is I had more lead coming my direction than I can describe." They helped get Dix into the passenger seat of Butch's truck. The ride back to the catamaran was quiet.

CHAPTER 31

FINAL ASSAULT

The final assault came not from the Chinese but from a Saudi funded laboratory. The Islamists in Pakistan had developed a small pox virus that had a 90% mortality rate. It most areas it was 100% because there was no medical care available. It also had a prolonged infection period prior to the onset of symptoms serious enough to impair and kill the infected. The problem that the scientists didn't anticipate was the impatience of the Islamic clerics. The Ayatollah in charge felt that Allah would protect the worthy, so there would be no need to wait for a vaccine to be perfected.

Unbeknown to the world, an ignorant, religious zealot unleashed a plague that did not differentiate between the worthy or unworthy. It rapidly made its way across Asia and killed the wealthy Saudi prince who funded the lab about 3 months later. That was about the time that Dix was cleaning out Ferriday. The night that Dix shot the good mayor of Natchez, a Chinese Admiral arrived back at his fleet with an aide who had a fever.

In reality, Dix and all the other fighters could have just remained hidden in the countryside as nature took its course.

The virus was working its way from man to man. As each man became feverish a measles-like rash would appear. Within three weeks the rash would grow into pustules and each day the man would become more infectious until he died. The clothes, bedding and personal items remained tainted and infectious for weeks, as the virus was very resilient.

The Pakistani scientists were experts in their field and they thought of every contingency except the ignorant zealots they worked for. So they died along with their families, friends and everyone they ever knew, and along with them, the religion of peace and love.

Just as in the dark ages, the death followed the routes of travel and soon the tentacles of the plague were across the entire globe. As in the dark ages, the cities and armies were the first to go. In America the cities were cleaned out by the economic collapse. As it turned out, this was a godsend. The American population was reduced by at least 75% with the remaining population scattered across the rural countryside. There was limited contact between regions and populations. So the plague was slowed, but not stopped.

Butch and Dix received word on the trip back to the catamaran from Colonel Miller, "Captain Erwin, who is the senior officer in your sector?"

"Major Dix Jernigan is the senior officer and he is with me, sir."

Colonel Miller briefed them about the plague and what they knew.

Colonel Miller barked, "Jernigan, I haven't got time to argue about you being in command, just listen, this plague is almost out of control. You do whatever it takes to stop it from spreading in your sector."

Dix started to argue but simply said, "Yes sir."

For a moment Dix and Butch just looked at each other. Dix ordered, "Get Cooney Jones on the radio."

Cooney answered in short order, "Captain Jones here."

"Cooney, this is Dix Jernigan, are you aware of the situation concerning the plague?"

"I have been briefed, what are your orders?"

"I want any bridges still standing blown and the ferries and boat traffic stopped. I want all traffic stopped. No exceptions, order all your patrols to go to cover. Cease all offensive activity. I want our areas locked down.

If we are to survive, all contact, foraging and travel have to stop now. Effective sundown today everyone needs to be where they intend to stay for the next six weeks. No exchange of items or personal contact. Shoot anyone trying to cross the rivers or attempting to travel. Canvas your medics to determine who may be willing to deliver babies or set broken bones. Once they leave to render aid, they don't come back. If they do, shoot them. If someone shows up sick, shoot them along with whoever brought them and burn the bodies. All person to person contact with strangers or anyone who has been away from base or home has to end now. Do you understand?"

"Yes Sir."

Dix turned to Butch, "Take me to my catamaran and execute my orders. You are to report to me by radio and we will not get within breathing distance for at least six weeks."

It was at that moment Dix came to the realization that there was nothing he could have done to save his family. He didn't have the financial wherewithal to have moved his family to an isolated location in the western U.S. prior to the collapse. It was a miracle that he outlived them. They would all be dead and dying from the plague had they survived at their home.

Dix arrived at the boat camp to find Beagle, Rachel, and the pups busy with their chores. After telling Beagle and Rachel about the plague, Butch helped him onto the catamaran and helped Beagle move the catamaran and Rachel's house boat down the lake and away from the bank. Beagle dropped Butch off at the bank and they watched him disappear over the levee. Dix settled back in his bunk, took a couple of aspirin, and chased them down with a glass of bourbon.

Rachel looked at him, "What do we do now?"

Dix answered, "We live, we fight and we survive. Any questions?"